MIRACLE UNDER THE MISTLETOE

BY
JENNIFER TAYLOR

HIS CHRISTMAS BRIDE-TO-BE

BY
ABIGAIL GORDON

MILLS & BOON

Jennifer Taylor lives in the north-west of England, in a small village surrounded by some really beautiful countryside. She has written for several different Mills & Boon series in the past, but it wasn't until she read her first Medical Romance that she truly found her niche. When she's not writing, or doing research for her latest book, Jennifer's hobbies include reading, gardening, travel, and chatting to friends both on and offline. She is always delighted to hear from readers, so do visit her website at jennifertaylorauthor.wordpress.com.

Abigail Gordon loves to write about the fascinating combination of medicine and romance from her home in a Cheshire village. She is active in local affairs, and is even called upon to write the script for the annual village pantomime! Her eldest son is a hospital manager, and helps with all her medical research. As part of a close-knit family, she treasures having two of her sons living close by, and the third one not too far away. This also gives her the added pleasure of being able to watch her delightful grandchildren growing up.

MIRACLE UNDER THE MISTLETOE

BY
JENNIFER TAYLOR

MILLS
BOON

Published in Great Britain 2015
by Mills & Boon, an imprint of Harlequin (UK) Limited,
Eton House, 18-24 Paradise Road, Richmond, Surrey, TW9 1SR

© 2015 Jennifer Taylor

ISBN: 978-0-263-24751-0

Printed and bound in Spain
by CPI, Barcelona

Dear Reader,

Once again I have returned to Dalverston General Hospital and used it as the setting for this book. Although the town of Dalverston is purely a figment of my imagination, the area it is based on is one of my favourite parts of the world—the beautiful English Lake District. I always experience a little thrill of pleasure whenever I set a book there.

Molly is shocked when she discovers that Sean Fitzgerald is to be the new locum registrar, covering the busy Christmas and New Year period in Dalverston General's A&E department. When Sean worked there before they had an affair, and it has taken Molly a long time to get over it. To have Sean reappear in her life is the last thing she needs.

Sean knows that he hurt Molly and regrets it deeply— but he had no choice. He's made a solemn vow never to get involved with any woman and he has to keep it. However, seeing Molly again arouses all kinds of emotions and he struggles to remain detached. Can he break his vow and win Molly back, as he yearns to do? Or will he always regret it? Read on to find out!

If you would like to learn more about the background to my Dalverston series then do visit my blog at jennifertaylorauthor.wordpress.com.

Love,

Jennifer

CHAPTER ONE

'LEFT A BIT…a bit more. No, that's too far now.'

'For heaven's sake, Suzy, make up your mind. I'm starting to get vertigo from balancing on the top of this ladder!'

Molly Daniels rolled her eyes as she looked down at her friend, Suzy Walters. It was the start of her Friday night shift and from the amount of noise issuing from the waiting room things were already hotting up. With just three weeks to go until Christmas, the A&E unit at Dalverston General Hospital was coming under increasing pressure as people set about enjoying the festivities. She really needed to get down to some work so, tossing back her strawberry blonde curls, which as per usual had come loose from their clip, Molly held up the bunch of mistletoe once more.

'How about here? Maybe it's not the exact centre of the room but I doubt if anyone except you will notice that.'

'I suppose it will have to do,' Suzy conceded grudgingly. She grimaced as Molly pinned the rather wilted bunch of foliage to the ceiling above the coffee table. 'Although, according to custom, you are supposed to be standing *under* the mistletoe before anyone can kiss you and you can't do that with the table being there, can you?'

'Well, that's fine by me.' Molly made sure the drawing pin was securely anchored then climbed down from the ladder. 'I've had it with men calling the shots, so if anyone gets any idea about kissing me without my express permission they can forget it!'

'Oh, come on, Molly. You don't really mean that.'

Suzy followed Molly out of the staffroom, a frown furrowing her brow. They had met at university while they had been studying for their nursing degrees and had remained firm friends ever since. Molly knew that Suzy only wanted her to be happy; however, her friend's idea of happiness—i.e. finding the right man to settle down and have a family with, as Suzy herself had done—was no longer hers.

She had tried that and she had the scars to prove it too! Her dream had always been to find her ideal mate so that she could enjoy the kind of loving and supportive relationship her parents had. She had set out her stall accordingly, opting to date men who had possessed the right credentials. They had to be reliable and trustworthy, caring and kind. The problem was that although they had appeared to tick all the right boxes, they had turned out to be far from perfect. One was too bossy, another too needy, a third too *boring*—and so it had gone on.

The one and only time she had veered off course and dated someone who hadn't fitted her brief had been an even bigger disaster, though. She had had her heart well and truly crushed then and from now on she intended to take a very different approach when it came to relationships. There would be no more wondering if this or that man was Mr Right. And definitely no more sitting by the phone, waiting for him to call. The days of her being a lovelorn victim were well and truly over!

'I do.' Molly held up her hand when Suzy opened her mouth to protest. 'Save your breath, Suzy. I've heard it all before: one day I'll meet the man of my dreams and ride off into the sunset with him.' Molly snorted in disgust, her emerald-green eyes filled with cynicism. 'I may have believed in the fairy tale at one time, but I don't believe it now. The man doesn't exist who can make me change my mind about that, either!'

Molly spun round and headed to the nurses' station. Fond as she was of Suzy, she didn't intend to waste any more time debating the issue. She did the hand-over, listening closely while Joyce Summers, her opposite number on the day shift, updated her as to the status of the patients currently in the unit. As senior sister, Molly needed to know what stage they were up to in their treatment. She nodded when Joyce had finished.

'Not too bad, from the sound of it.'

'It's early days yet,' Joyce replied with all the weary wisdom gained from twenty-odd years spent working on the unit. She was due to retire after Christmas and was looking forward to it immensely.

'It is,' Molly agreed, laughing. 'So how are your plans coming on? Have you booked that cruise you were telling me about?'

'I have indeed. Three weeks in the Caribbean. I can't wait!' Joyce picked up her cardigan and started to leave then paused. 'Oh, I forgot to tell you that we've got a locum covering over Christmas and the New Year. He's starting tonight… Oh, talk of the devil—here he is! At least we know he's up to the job, unlike some I could mention.'

Molly glanced round to see who had come in through the main doors and felt her heart grind to a halt. It couldn't be him, she told herself sickly. Not now, after she had finally sorted out her life. It must be her imagination playing tricks, trying to test her newfound resolve after what she had told Suzy, but it wasn't going to work. Closing her eyes, Molly counted to ten, convinced that when she opened them again the apparition would have disappeared…

'Hello, Molly. Long time, no see, as the saying goes.'

Molly's eyes flew open as she stared at the man

standing in front of her. A wave of panic washed over her as she drank in all the familiar details, from the jet-black hair falling over his forehead to the deep blue eyes that were studying her with undisguised amusement. This man had been her one and only aberration. Even though she had known from the outset that he was far from being her ideal life partner, she had had an affair with him. He had possessed none of the qualities she had always deemed essential in a relationship. On the contrary, he wasn't reliable or trustworthy, and he definitely wasn't looking for commitment, but she had gone ahead anyway and slept with him. Now, as she saw the smile that curved his lips, Molly realised that any hopes she may have harboured about him being a figment of her imagination had been way off beam. Sean Fitzgerald wasn't some kind of hallucination. He wasn't even a memory dredged up from her past. He was completely and utterly real!

Sean managed to hold his smile but it wasn't easy. Although he had guessed that Molly might not be exactly overjoyed to see him again, he hadn't envisaged *this* reaction. As he took stock of the pallor of her skin, he was overcome by a feeling of shame he had never experienced before. It didn't matter that he had made his intentions perfectly clear from their very first date, or that he had frequently reiterated the fact that he didn't intend to commit himself to *anyone*. He had hurt her. Badly.

Sean's heart sank as that thought hit home. He had thought long and hard when the agency had phoned and offered him this post as locum senior registrar on Dalverston's A&E unit. He had been very aware that working with Molly could turn out to be challenging to say the least. His initial reaction had been to turn it down but in the end he had decided to accept it. He needed to work over the Christmas period, needed to be kept busy so that he wouldn't dwell on the past. He couldn't bear to leave it to chance that another post would come up, so he had set aside his qualms and accepted the offer. Now, however, he couldn't help wondering if it had been selfish to put his own needs first.

'I wasn't sure who would be working tonight,' he said lightly, struggling to behave as normally as possible. That was the key to handling this situation, he assured himself. After all, it wasn't the first time that he had found himself working with a woman he had dated and subsequently dumped and he had learned from experience that the best way to defuse matters was by acting normally. All he could do was hope that it would work this time too, although something warned him that he was being overly optimistic.

'No? You should have asked for a copy of the roster. Then you could have opted to work a different shift and avoided me, as I'm sure we both would have preferred.'

Molly's voice sounded harsh and so unlike the tone he remembered that Sean frowned. However, before he could say anything, she picked up a file from the desk and headed towards the waiting room. He watched her go, feeling a whole host of emotions hit him one after the other—slam, bang, wallop: regret, sadness, an unfamiliar sense of loss…

Sean blanked them all out, knowing how pointless it was to go down that route. He had done what he had had to do: ended their relationship when he had realised that Molly was getting far too attached to him. He had, in effect, done the honourable thing, he assured himself as he headed to the staffroom to deposit his coat. He had called a halt before things had gone too far—although how far was *too* far? he wondered suddenly as he keyed in the security code and unlocked the door. Should he have stopped after their first kiss? Or before they had slept together? And surely he should have called a halt before it had happened a second and a third time, even if making love with Molly had been the most wonderful experience of his life?

The door closed behind him with a noisy thud but he didn't even notice. Making love with Molly had been mind-blowing and there was no point denying it. He had felt things when they had made love that he had never felt before, not even with Claire, and the

thought was so painful that he winced. Was that why
he had been so brusque when he had ended his relationship with Molly? Because he had felt guilty? Had
it seemed like the ultimate betrayal of the woman
he had been going to marry to feel all those things
for Molly?

Sean knew it was true and it didn't make him
feel any better to admit it. For the past ten years
he had remained faithful to his dead fiancée. Oh,
admittedly, he had slept with many women during
that time but he had never become emotionally involved with any of them, and that was what counted.
However, it had been different with Molly. She had
touched him on so many levels; their affair hadn't
been purely physical, as he had wanted it to be.

It made him see that he would need to be very
careful while he was working at Dalverston. It would
be only too easy to break the vow he had made after
Claire had died.

It was a busy night, as Molly had predicted. By the
time she was due for her break, the unit was overflowing with people waiting to be seen. She shook
her head when Jason Roberts, the newest addition to
their staff, asked her if she was going to the canteen.

'I'll wait till things calm down a bit,' she explained then sighed as the doors opened to admit
another group of injured revellers. One of them was
bleeding copiously from a gash on his forehead. That

he was also extremely drunk as well was evident from the way he was staggering about. Molly beckoned to Jason to follow her as she headed straight over to him. In her experience it was better to get the drunks safely corralled so they couldn't upset the rest of their patients.

'Right, let's get you sat down for starters.' She guided the man to a chair and bent down to examine the cut on his head. Although there was a great deal of blood, it was only a superficial injury and would need just butterfly stitches to close it. 'Get him checked in at Reception, will you?' she told Jason. 'Then you can clean this up and apply a few butterfly stitches to hold it together.'

It was a simple enough task and one the young nurse was more than capable of performing; however, it appeared the patient had other ideas. Grabbing hold of Molly's arm, he pulled her back when she went to leave.

'I want you to do it, not him.' He looked at Jason and sneered. 'I don't want some young kid messing around with me.'

'Jason is a fully qualified nurse. He is more than capable of dealing with this,' Molly explained levelly. She tried to withdraw her arm from the man's grasp but he wouldn't let her go. His fingers tightened around her wrist, making her wince with pain.

'I said that I want you to do it.' He hauled her down so that their faces were mere inches apart and she had to stop herself gagging at the sour smell of alcohol coming off his breath. 'I pay my taxes, love, and if I say I want *you* to treat me then that's how it's going to be.'

'I'm afraid it doesn't work like that, sir. *We* decide who gets to treat you and *we* also decide who we won't treat, either. I have to say that you're number one on that list at this precise moment.'

Molly looked round when she recognised Sean's voice. Although he hadn't raised his voice, there was no disguising the anger on his face. It obviously had an effect on the drunk because he immediately let her go. Molly stepped back, her legs trembling a little as she hastily put some space between them. Although it wasn't the first time that she'd had to deal with an unpleasant situation, it was upsetting, nevertheless.

'Are you all right?'

Sean's voice was low, filled with something that brought an unexpected lump to her throat. He sounded genuinely concerned but that couldn't be right, not after the way he had ended their affair two years ago. He had been almost brutal as he had told her bluntly that he didn't want to see her any more. Although Molly had asked him why, *pleaded* with him to tell her what had made him reach such a decision, he had refused to explain. He had merely reminded her that he had made it clear right from the beginning that he wasn't looking for commitment, and that had been that. He had left Dalverston shortly afterwards to take up another post in a different part of the country and had never made any attempt to contact her since.

Sean had written her out of his life and it would be foolish to imagine that he cared, even more foolish to wish that he did. Even though Molly knew all that, she couldn't stop herself. Foolish or not, she wanted him to care about her and the thought was like the proverbial red rag. As Jason led the drunk away, she rounded on Sean, pain and anger warring inside her. The last thing she wanted was to feel anything for him ever again!

'I would appreciate it if you didn't interfere in future,' she told him furiously. 'I am more than capable of dealing with a situation like that.'

'I'm sorry,' he said quietly. 'I just thought maybe you needed some backup.'

'Well, you thought wrong,' Molly snapped. She glared at him. 'I don't need your help, Dr Fitzgerald, and I would prefer it if you didn't butt in.'

'Then all I can do is apologise and assure you that it won't happen again.'

He gave her a thin smile then walked away, leaving Molly fuming. She knew she had overreacted and it was frustrating to think that she had allowed Sean to get to her like that. The only way she would cope in the coming weeks while they had to work together was by remaining calm, indifferent even. Allowing her emotions to come to the fore, whether it was anger or anything else, certainly wouldn't help. No, she needed to remain detached, aloof, distant, and that way she would get through this. However, as she went to collect her next patient, Molly was bitterly aware that it wasn't going to be easy to be any of those things. Working with Sean was going to test her self-control to its absolute limit.

CHAPTER TWO

IT WAS A busy night, although not busy enough for Sean's liking. As one patient succeeded another, he found himself wishing for more—some kind of major incident that would mean he didn't have time to think about anything apart from the lives he was saving. It wasn't that he wanted people to get hurt—far from it. However, anything that would stop him thinking about Molly and the way he had reacted when that drunk had grabbed hold of her would be a relief.

'Lily should be fine, but don't hesitate to bring her back if you're at all concerned about her.' He dragged his thoughts back to the present and smiled at the anxious parents of seventeen-year-old Lily Morris. They had brought their daughter into the unit after she had woken during the night with an angry red rash all over her body. They had been worried that she had contracted meningitis but Sean had been able to allay their fears. It turned out that Lily had reacted adversely to some new shower gel she had bought off a market stall; she would be absolutely fine as long as she didn't use it again.

'Thank you so much, Doctor.' Mr Morris sighed as he shook Sean's hand. 'If it's not one thing, it's another when you have children. Lily gave us a right old scare when we saw the state of her, I can tell you.'

'I'm sure she did but, as I said, Lily should be fine so long as she sticks to her usual shower gel.'

Sean saw the family out then went to the desk and emailed the local Trading Standards office. The gel Lily had purchased had been purportedly a leading brand but he seriously doubted it was genuine. Hopefully, Trading Standards would be able to investigate and stop anyone else purchasing it and ending up in the same state as Lily.

Once that was done, he checked the whiteboard to make sure that nobody had been waiting longer than they should. Government guidelines stated that patients should be seen, treated and either transferred to a ward or sent home within a set number of hours. There was just one patient nearing that limit, so he made his way to Cubicles to check what was happening. The curtains were drawn and he pushed them aside, feeling his heart sink when he found Molly standing beside the bed.

Although they had spoken a couple of times since that incident involving the drunk, Sean had tried his best to stay out of Molly's way. Not only did he want to avoid another confrontation with her, but he wasn't comfortable with all the emotions she seemed to have stirred up inside him. He wanted to be indifferent to her but he knew deep down that it was beyond him. Maybe he had succeeded in dismissing all the other women he had dated from his mind but he couldn't rid himself of Molly, it seemed.

'How's it going in here, Sister?' he asked, falling back on professional courtesy seeing as everything else seemed way too difficult at the moment.

'Mr Forster was complaining of feeling sick,' she replied in the coolest possible tone.

Quite frankly, Sean wouldn't have thought her capable of sounding so frosty and blinked in surprise. Molly had always been known for her warmth, for her kindness, for her sheer *joie de vivre*. Her earlier anger had been upsetting enough but to hear her sounding so frigid was even worse. It sent a shiver straight through his heart. Had he done this to her? Had he turned her from the warm, loving woman he remembered to this…this chilly replica of herself? Even though he hated the idea, he couldn't dismiss it.

'I imagine it's the morphine,' he said evenly, clamping down on the guilt that threatened to swamp him as he lifted the patient's notes out of their holder. Frank Forster had been admitted after complaining of severe pain in his lower back. Apparently, he had been lifting a large Christmas tree off the roof of his car when it had happened. A subsequent scan had shown that one of the discs in his lumbar spine had prolapsed and was pressing on a nerve. The poor man was in a great deal of pain, which was why he had been given morphine while they waited for a bed to become vacant in the spinal unit. Now Sean frowned as he looked up.

'Why didn't Dr Collins prescribe an anti-emetic with the morphine?'

'I have no idea,' Molly replied coldly. She finished straightening the blanket and patted the middle-aged man's hand. 'I'll be back in a moment with something to stop you feeling so sick, Frank. Just hang in there.'

She treated the man to a warm smile and Sean felt some of his guilt ooze away. So the old Molly hadn't disappeared completely, as he had feared. It was just with him that she was so frosty; she was perfectly fine with everyone else. That thought might have set off another round of soul-searching if he had let it, only he refused to do so. As he followed her out of the cubicle, he ruthlessly shoved all those pesky feelings back into their box and slammed the lid. He had to focus on the fact that he had done what he had needed to do to protect her, and that he would do exactly the same thing all over again too if it became necessary...

Wouldn't he?

Sean felt his vision blur, the sterile white walls that surrounded him turning a fuzzy shade of grey. He would finish with Molly again if he had to—

of course he would! However, no matter how many times he told himself that, he didn't quite believe it. Maybe he was ninety-nine per cent certain but there was that one per cent of doubt lurking in his mind. One tiny but highly dangerous percentage of uncertainty that sent a chill rippling down his spine. Until he could erase it completely then he couldn't be sure exactly how he would react, so help him!

Molly made her way to the desk, trying to ignore the fact that Sean was following her. That was the best way to handle this situation, she reminded herself—she would ignore him and concentrate on doing her job. It shouldn't be that difficult. They were always so busy that there was little time to think about anything of a personal nature; however, she had to admit that several times she had found her thoughts wandering. Sean had had a major impact on her life and it wasn't easy to forget that when they had been thrust together again like this.

Molly's generous mouth tightened as she set about making the adjustment to Frank Forster's meds. Although she knew exactly what was needed to make the man comfortable, it required a doctor's signature on the prescription. She glanced round, hoping to catch sight of Steph Collins, their F1 student, but there was no sign of her. Although everything was calming down now, there were still a few patients in the unit. Undoubtedly, Steph was dealing with one of them.

'Here. I'll sign that.'

A large tanned hand reached over her shoulder and took the script from her and Molly jumped. She hadn't realised that Sean was standing quite so close to her and she couldn't stop herself reacting. There was a tiny pause and she held her breath as she willed him not to say anything. She didn't want him to suspect how nervous she felt around him, didn't want to admit it to herself even. She just wanted to be indifferent to his presence, as he was undoubtedly indifferent to hers.

The soft rustle of paper as he scrawled his name at the bottom of the script broke the spell. Molly nodded as he handed it back to her without comment, relieved that she had got off so lightly. She would be wary of that happening again, she thought as she took the keys to the drugs cupboard out of her pocket. The last thing she wanted was to appear vulnerable when Sean was around.

'Thanks. I'll get Mr Forster sorted out and then check if there's a bed available yet. He may have to be transferred to Men's Surgical if the Spinal Unit can't come up with anything soon.'

'Hardly ideal, is it, to shunt seriously injured patients about?' Sean observed.

'No. It isn't.' She shrugged, causing another wayward curl to spring out of its clip. 'However, needs must. We either move him to Men's Surgical or get a rocket off the powers-that-be for overrunning the time limit. I sometimes wish that they all had to do a stint down here. Then they might appreciate just how difficult it is to get a patient seen and treated within such a ridiculously short space of time.'

'Amen to that,' Sean murmured. Leaning forward, he carefully tucked the unruly curl behind her ear and nodded. 'There you go. All nice and tidy again.'

'I…erm… I'll get that anti-emetic.'

Molly turned and fled, uncaring what he thought as she hurried into the office. She could feel her heart pounding in her chest, rapid little flurries that sent the blood gushing through her veins in a red-hot torrent, and bit her lip. She didn't want to react this way, but she couldn't seem to help it. The moment Sean had touched her, it had been as though a fire had reignited inside her and the thought filled her with dismay.

She couldn't go through what she had been through two years ago all over again. Sean had meant the world to her back then; she had honestly thought that she had found her Mr Right, but she had been mistaken. Sean wasn't interested in making a commitment to her or to any woman.

'About what happened before, Molly, well, I'd hate to think that it might create a problem between us.'

Molly spun round so fast when she heard Sean's voice that the room started to whirl around her and she grabbed hold of the desk to steady herself. 'What happened before,' she repeated uncertainly.

Her heart suddenly leapt into her throat. Was Sean talking about their affair? Was he attempting to explain why he had ended it so abruptly? Even though it shouldn't have made a scrap of difference now, she found herself holding her breath.

'Yes. That incident with the drunk, I mean.' He grimaced. 'You were quite right to take me to task because I should never have interfered. I've always had the greatest respect for the way you handle even the most difficult patients and I should have left it to you to sort things out.'

'I…' Molly found herself floundering and desperately tried to collect herself. Of course Sean wasn't talking about their affair! That was over and done with so far as he was concerned. In fact, he probably hadn't given her another thought after he had left Dalverston. The idea was so painful that it cut through the muddle in her head as nothing else could have done.

'No, you shouldn't have intervened,' she said flatly, afraid that he would guess how hurt she felt. She drew herself up, forcing all the injured feelings to the deepest, darkest corner of her mind. Letting herself get upset at this stage was pointless. It wouldn't change what had happened; neither would she want it to. 'I was perfectly capable of handling it myself. However, there seems little point going on and on about it. It's all over and done with now.'

'Of course. I just wouldn't want it to cause any…

well, friction between us. I realise that working to-gether isn't exactly ideal but I'm hoping that we can call a truce. Do you think that's possible, Molly? Can we put what happened two years ago behind us?'

'It isn't an issue,' she said quickly and then flushed when she saw the scepticism in his eyes. 'Don't flatter yourself, Sean. Oh, I may have been upset at the time—I'll admit it. However, I soon got over it, I assure you.'

'Good. I'm pleased to hear it.' He grinned at her, apparently relieved to have got everything settled so successfully. 'Right, I'd better get back before we have a mutiny on our hands. The rest of the team will think we've gone AWOL!'

Molly filled in the sheet to say that she had taken the prescribed drugs after he had left then took a deep breath before she made her way back to the unit. From this point on she would follow Sean's example and treat him as nothing more than a col-league. It was only what he was, in all honesty, so it shouldn't be that difficult, especially after what he had said to her just now.

A tiny stab of pain speared through her heart but she steadfastly ignored it. Obviously, Sean didn't view her as anything more than someone he worked with and she was glad about that too!

CHAPTER THREE

IT WAS WELL after seven a.m. before Sean finally left the unit. Although he had been due to leave at six there had been a last-minute rush which had held everyone up, not that he minded. As he made his way to the staff car park, he deliberately set about erasing the night's events from his mind. There was no point dwelling on what Molly had said about how quickly she had got over him. And definitely no point wondering why he had felt so hurt when he had heard it. He had learned through experience that it was best not to examine his feelings in too much depth. No, they had called a truce and that was it. End of story.

Sean sighed as he unlocked his car and got in, all too aware how shallow it made him appear to take such a view. However, as he couldn't think of a better approach, he had to go along with it. There was a film of ice covering the windscreen and he switched on the engine to clear it. There were a lot of night staff leaving at the same time and he recognised several people from the last time he had worked at Dalverston.

He had enjoyed his stint here, he mused as he waited for the ice to melt. There was a strong community feel about the hospital, plus it was situated in such a glorious part of the country. He knew that they were desperately in need of a permanent registrar to fill the vacancy in A&E and was seriously tempted to apply for the post himself. He would enjoy living and working here full-time.

The thought shocked him, mainly because it was the first time that he had seriously considered taking a permanent post. After Claire had died so tragically in that road accident, he had found it impossible to settle. He had signed on with a leading medical agency and taken only short-term contracts ever since. Two months here, six months there; it had been exactly what he had wanted. To suddenly discover that his peripatetic lifestyle had started to pall was a shock and not a pleasant one either, especially when it was the thought of working here that had triggered it. It would be asking for trouble if he remained in Dalverston. Working with Molly, day in and day out, would be far too much for him to handle.

As though thinking about her had somehow conjured her up, Molly suddenly appeared. Sean felt his heart and what felt like the rest of his vital organs scrunch up inside him as he watched her walk over to her car. She had parked in the row behind him and he studied her reflection in his rear-view mirror. She looked weary, only to be expected after the

busy night they'd had, but was that the only reason
for the defeated slump to her shoulders? Or had it
anything to do with him? Had she found it a strain
to work with him after what had happened between
them in the past? Even though there was little he
could do about it, he hated to think that *he* was the
cause of her unhappiness. Out of all the women he
had dated since Claire had died, Molly was the only
one he had truly cared about.

Molly slid the key into the lock and opened the car
door. Picking up the can of de-icer, she squirted a
generous dollop onto the frosty windscreen. She
hated winter, hated the fact that she couldn't just
get in her car and drive away. There was no point
pretending—working with Sean had been an ordeal,
one she wished with every scrap of her being that
she wouldn't have to repeat, but there was no hope of
that, was there? He was covering the entire Christmas and New Year period which meant he would be
around for at least six weeks and probably longer if
the management team could persuade him to stay on.
Finding cover over the festive period was always difficult as most locums wanted to be with their families at this time of the year. There were very few
with Sean's skills and experience willing to relocate.

Molly tucked the can under the passenger seat,
trying not to think about the problems it could cause
if she had to see Sean on a daily basis. Slipping the

key into the ignition, she attempted to start the engine, only to be rewarded by a nasty grunting noise. She tried again with the same result. The battery, always dodgy, was completely flat. Brilliant! Now she would have to catch the bus, which was just what she needed after the night she'd had.

'Problems?'

Molly almost jumped out of her skin when her car door opened. She had no idea where Sean had appeared from and found it impossible to reply. He gave her a quick smile as leant into the car to try starting the engine himself.

'Sounds like a flat battery to me,' he declared when he received the same response. Resting his forearm against the roof of the car, he grinned down at her. 'They always go at the worst possible moment, don't they?'

It was the sort of comment anyone might have made in such circumstances, so Molly had no idea why she reacted as she did. 'Thank you, but I did manage to work that out for myself! Now, if you'll move aside…'

She gave the door a hefty push to fully open it, not even flinching when it caught him a glancing blow on his hip. It was his own fault for poking his nose in again where it wasn't wanted, she assured herself as she lifted her bag off the passenger seat. She didn't need his help. She didn't want anything to do with him. Quite frankly, if he disappeared in a puff of smoke it would make her day!

Slamming the car door, she started walking towards the gate, wondering how long it would be before a bus came along. She lived on the other side of the town and it took forever by bus, which was why she had saved up for a car.

She was just nearing the gate when she saw her bus coming along the road and started to run, but it was difficult to make much progress thanks to the frosty conditions underfoot. She groaned as she was forced to watch it drive away. She would have to wait at least half an hour before another came along.

'Hop in. I'll give you a lift.' Sean drew up beside her but Molly shook her head.

'No, thank you. I prefer to wait for the next bus,' she said snippily.

'Are you sure?' He shrugged, his broad shoulders moving lightly beneath his heavy quilted jacket, and Molly gulped. Sean had always possessed the most wonderful physique and it seemed little had changed in that respect. He had gone running when they had been seeing each other, setting off early each morning so he could fit in a run before work.

How many times had he come back from one of those runs and persuaded her to take a shower with him? she wondered suddenly. She had no idea but the memory of those times seemed to flood her mind. They had made love in the shower, their desire heightened by the sensuous feel of the hot water cascading over their naked bodies, and then followed it up by making love all over again in her bed. She had never realised that lovemaking could feel like that, had never experienced desire on such a level before. It was Sean who had taught her what it could be like. Only Sean who could make her feel that way again too.

The thought was too much. It made a mockery of all the plans she had made about how she intended to live her life in the future. What hope did she have of sticking to her decision to be in charge of her own destiny when one night working with Sean had had this effect? She had to rid herself of all these foolish memories, finally put an end to that episode in her life. Until she did so she would be always looking back, constantly comparing how she felt now to how she had felt then.

It was the way she should set about it that was the big question—how to totally and completely erase Sean Fitzgerald from her consciousness. Oh, she had tried her best over the past couple of years and thought she had succeeded too, but obviously not. He was still there in her head, a spectre from her past who refused to budge, and until she rid herself of him then she would never be free to move on. Maybe it had been a mistake to try to blot him out of her mind, to try and forget the heartache he had caused her. Maybe she needed to face up to it, to face up to *him*?

It was Sean who had called the shots in the past, Sean who had ended their affair too, but maybe she needed to take charge this time—instigate another affair with him and bring it to a conclusion when *she* decided the time was right. One of the worst things about the whole unhappy experience was the effect it had had on her self-confidence. She'd been left feeling used, feeling like a victim, and she wasn't prepared to put up with feeling that way any more. This time neither her life nor her heart would be left in tatters. This time she would make sure of that!

'So what's it to be then? Are you going to wait for the next bus—a long and undoubtedly chilly wait—or are you going to accept my offer of a lift? I mean we did agree to call a truce, so what's the problem?'

Sean dredged up a deliberately taunting smile although it wasn't easy, he had to admit. There was just something about the expression on Molly's face that had set all his internal alarm bells ringing. He had seen that kind of expression before on other women's faces and had learned to tread warily until he discovered its cause. Whilst he had no idea what Molly was planning, instinct warned him that he wasn't going to like it.

'There isn't a problem. Why not, if you're going my way?'

Molly walked round to the passenger's side and got in, leaving Sean suddenly wishing that he had never made the offer in the first place. The less time he spent with Molly, the better, quite frankly, but he could hardly renege on his offer now. He slid the car into gear and drove out of the gates, his mind racing this way and that. Was Molly plotting something, some sort of payback perhaps for the way he had treated her? It wouldn't be the first time it had happened, although fortunately he had managed to deflect the woman's ire before it had caused too much damage. However, if that was what Molly was planning then it might not be as easy to resolve the problem this time. The difference was that he *cared* about Molly and would hate to do anything that might hurt her even more.

They drove through the centre of the town in silence. Sean was so caught up in wondering what Molly might be planning to do that he found it impossible to make small-talk as he normally would have done. She lived in a tiny terraced cottage close to the river and he drew up outside with a feeling of relief. If she really was looking to pay him back then the best solution was to steer well clear of her. Fair enough, they would still have to work together, but outside of work he would make sure he kept his distance. It was only what he had intended to do after all—stay away from her—so it was surprising how much the idea stung.

'Right. Here you are. I bet you're looking forward to getting to bed. I know I am.'

It was meant to be an off-the-cuff remark, a throw-away comment free from any significance. However, the second the words were out of his mouth, Sean regretted them. Why in heaven's name had he mentioned *bed*? Stirring up those kinds of memories was the *last* thing he should be doing!

'Hmm. It's always good to snuggle down in a nice warm bed after working nights, isn't it?' Molly replied in a tone he had never heard her use before.

Sean felt the hair all over his body spring to attention and then salute. Felt other bits of him follow suit and almost groaned out loud in dismay. When had Molly perfected the art of sounding so…so *seductive*? Two years ago he would have described her as the girl-next-door: sweet, warm, loving and giving. Now she sounded more like a siren and, worst of all, he was responding to her call! Panic overwhelmed him at that point. It made no difference that he was highly experienced in the ways of women; it still took a massive effort of will to control his baser urges.

'It is.' He dredged up a smile, not wanting her to guess how he really felt in case it gave her an advantage. Quite frankly, it seemed to him that she was already holding all the aces. If he didn't want to end up with the losing hand, then he needed to be extremely careful how he played this game. 'Right, I'd better be off then. I hope you manage to get your car sorted out.'

'I hope so too.' She leant towards him as she unfastened her seat belt and he inwardly shuddered when he felt the warmth of her breath caress his cheek. 'Thanks for the lift, Sean. I really appreciate it. Can I tempt you to come in for a cup of coffee as a thank you, perhaps?'

Her green eyes stared straight into his and Sean felt his resolve start to crumble away when he saw the invitation they held. It was obvious that coffee wasn't the only thing on her mind.

'Thanks but I'd better get straight off home,' he mumbled, praying that he would manage to hold out long enough to make his excuses and leave, as the tabloid journalists were so fond of saying. 'There's a couple of things I need to do this afternoon, so the sooner I get to sleep the better.'

'Pity. Still, there's always another time.' She gave him a lingering smile then opened the car door.

Sean gripped tight hold of the steering wheel as she climbed out, knowing that if he let go he would regret it. He wouldn't follow her inside the house, he told himself sternly, not on any pretext. Not when he felt this way. He made himself sit there and wait while she unlocked the front door, even managed to wave before he drove away, but his heart was going nineteen to the dozen. He had a very good idea what Molly was plotting, what form her retribution would take. She was planning to seduce him and, once he was under her spell, then undoubtedly she would ditch him exactly as he had done to her. Quite frankly, he wasn't sure what shocked him most, the fact that sweet, *gentle* Molly should come up with such a plan, or how much the idea terrified him.

After all, now he knew what was afoot, he could take steps to prevent it happening, couldn't he? He could resist her overtures and stick to being a colleague and nothing more. It should be easy-peasy but he knew in his heart that it wouldn't be. The problem was that he wasn't sure if he could resist if Molly tried to lure him back into her bed. Even though he might know why she was doing it, would it be enough to put him off? Or would the thought of holding her in his arms and experiencing everything he had felt two years ago prove too much?

Sean groaned as he drew up at the traffic lights when they changed to red. Logically, the fact that Molly was simply trying to pay him back for what he had done to her should have been enough to guarantee that he would refuse to get involved with her again. However, it wasn't his head that was dictating his actions this time but his heart, and his heart was playing by its own rules. There was no guarantee that he could hold out if Molly was determined to get her own way. Absolutely no guarantee at all.

CHAPTER FOUR

MOLLY COULD SCARCELY believe what she had just done. As she made her way into the kitchen and flopped down onto a chair, she could feel her heart thumping. She had just—quite blatantly too—tried to seduce Sean!

She took a deep breath and made herself hold it for the count of ten, but it didn't help. Her nerves were fizzing, her heart racing, and other bits of her—well, she couldn't begin to describe what they were doing. Never in all of her twenty-seven years had she done such a thing. All right, so maybe she had decided to be more proactive in her approach to any future relationships, but it was one thing to think about it and another entirely to put it into practice. If Sean had come in for coffee then would she have gone through with it and invited him into her bed as well?

She shot to her feet, unable to deal with the thought or the one that followed it. Had Sean guessed what she was planning and was that why he had been so eager to leave? After all, it wasn't the first time he had rejected her, was it? Sean had made it perfectly clear two years ago that he wasn't interested in her and yet she had still gone ahead with her crazy scheme. He was probably laughing his head off at her pathetic attempt to seduce him!

Molly groaned out loud, feeling completely humiliated. How could she face him again after this? She would have to try to change her shifts and avoid working with him, although it wouldn't be easy to do so. The Christmas and New Year rosters had been prepared weeks ago and making changes at this late stage would create far too many problems. No, she couldn't see it happening, which meant she would just have to grit her teeth and get on with it. All she could do was pray that he wouldn't mention what had happened that morning. She honestly didn't think she could cope with being subjected to any of his teasing remarks or, worse still, becoming the object of his pity.

It was all very depressing. Molly's spirits were at an all-time low as she heated some milk in the microwave and made herself a cup of hot chocolate, hoping it would soothe her rattled nerves enough so that she could sleep. However, after an hour spent tossing and turning in her bed, she gave up. How could she sleep with all these thoughts milling around inside her head?

She went into the sitting room and curled up on the sofa, telling herself that it was silly to panic.

After all, nothing had happened, had it? Even if Sean had guessed what she had been planning to do, there was still time to change her mind. Quite honestly, it wasn't worth it if it caused this kind of upset; she would be stupid to go ahead… And yet there was still that niggling little thought at the back of her mind that she would never be entirely free of him until she had brought their relationship to a conclusion in her own time and in her own way too.

Molly closed her eyes, trying to imagine how she would feel afterwards. Elated, possibly? Relieved, hopefully? People continually trotted out that well-worn phrase about finding closure, so was that what would happen? Would it bring things to a nice tidy finale if she slept with Sean and subsequently dumped him?

She tried her best to imagine how she would feel but it was impossible to see into the future. She could only go by how she was feeling at this very moment—confused, embarrassed, scared. What if she followed through with her plan and it backfired on her? What if she slept with Sean only to find that she had fallen under his spell once again? That would only make matters even worse.

Her thoughts spun round and round in circles until she felt positively giddy. She knew that it was pointless going back to bed as she would never be able to sleep. She showered and dressed then left the house, hoping that a walk would help to calm her. She took the path leading to the river, carefully picking her way around the icy puddles. The river looked sluggish this morning, a skin of ice coating its surface. There were some ducks slipping and sliding their way across the ice and she stopped to watch them for a moment before the biting cold drove her on. When she came to the path leading up to the town centre, she hesitated, wondering if she should treat herself to coffee and a croissant before she went home. She hadn't had anything to eat since she'd got back from work and her stomach was rumbling.

Molly followed the path and soon arrived at the market square. The council had erected a huge Christmas tree in the centre of it and she stopped to admire it. There was a group of carol singers from one of the local churches gathered around it and she listened as they sang several well-known carols. It was all very festive and so very normal that she started to relax. There was no point getting het up. The choice was hers. She could either put her plan into action or forget about it.

'All very Christmassy, isn't it? I love hearing Christmas carols at this time of the year, don't you?'

Molly spun round, feeling her heart leap into her throat when she found Sean standing beside her. 'What are you doing here?' she snapped, unable to hide her dismay. That he should turn up just when she was starting to get her thoughts together was too much.

'Same as you, I imagine. Enjoying the singing.'

He gave her a quick smile then dug into his pocket and dropped a handful of change into the bucket when a child approached them, looking for donations, and the fact that he didn't even bother to check how much he had given struck a chord in Molly's memory. Sean had always been incredibly generous, the first to donate whenever anyone was raising money for a good cause. It was one of the things she had admired most about him, in fact, his unstinting generosity.

It was such a small thing yet it had a profound effect on her. Somewhere along the way, she had forgotten all the things she had liked about him. The pain of his leaving had negated everything else yet all of a sudden it all came rushing back: his generosity, his kindness, his compassion for those less fortunate than himself. Sean had possessed so many good qualities, so many things to commend him that she found herself wondering all of a sudden why he had behaved so out of character towards her. Sean cared about people, genuinely cared, so why had he been so cruel when he had ended their relationship?

'How about that cup of coffee you mentioned earlier?'

Molly jumped when he touched her lightly on the arm. She'd been so lost in her thoughts that she had no idea what he had said. 'Pardon?'

'Coffee.' He smiled down at her, his blue eyes

filled with laughter and another emotion that she had never expected to see again. Did he really care about her, or was he merely a highly accomplished actor? She had no idea and before she could attempt to work it out he slid his hand under her elbow. 'I fancy a coffee and a croissant so will you join me, Molly? I think we deserve a treat after the busy night we had, don't you?'

He briskly led her across the pavement to the café before she had a chance to reply, opening the café door with a flourish that set the brass bell jingling. Molly took a deep breath as she stepped inside, drinking in the scent of coffee and warm pastries. Her senses seemed to be ridiculously heightened all of a sudden so that the familiar aromas seemed richer and more enticing than ever. Even the colours of the checked tablecloths seemed brighter, the reds and blues and greens dazzling her eyes. It was as though she had stepped out of the gloom into full, glorious daylight and it was the strangest experience.

'Oh, look. That couple's leaving. Go and grab their table while I order our coffee.'

Sean gave her a little push towards the newly vacant table and Molly obediently headed in that direction. She sat down, automatically unwinding her scarf and removing her woolly hat. What was going on? Why did she feel this way, as though she had suddenly woken from a deep sleep?

'Here we go. They'll fetch our coffee over in a

moment. I ordered you a latte. I hope that was OK. It used to be your favourite, if I remember correctly.'

Sean had reappeared with a tray heaped with warm croissants and miniature pots of jam and Molly jumped. She could feel her pulse popping as she watched him unload everything onto the table, croissants and jam, napkins and knives. He was quick and deft, his hands soon setting everything to rights, but that was his way. Whatever Sean did, he did it well. From work to something as mundane as setting a table, he gave it his all. That was why it had been such a pleasure to be with him. Everything appeared more interesting, more *vibrant* when Sean was around.

Even her.

Molly took a croissant off the plate and bit into it, savouring its buttery richness. It had been ages since anything had tasted so good, two years in fact. Two long years, during which time she had lived her life in the shadows. Now Sean was back, everything had changed. Now she felt completely and fully alive. And it simply proved just how desperately she needed to break his hold over her.

'Thanks.'

Sean smiled as the waitress placed their coffees on the table. He saw the interest in the girl's eyes as she smiled back at him but he ignored it. At any other time he might have been tempted to follow up on it and ask her out on a date. It was something he had done more times than he could count over the years, but he wasn't even tempted. Not when he was with Molly. He simply wasn't interested in other women when he was with her. He never had been.

It was a sobering thought, doubly so when it was the first time he had admitted it. When he and Molly had been seeing one another, he hadn't looked at another woman. She had filled his thoughts to the exclusion of anyone else. Was that why he had ended their affair so abruptly? he wondered. Because he had realised on some inner level that he was getting far too involved with her? At the time he had told himself that he was doing it for her sake, that he was taking steps to protect her, but had his decision been less altruistic than he had thought? Had he been trying to protect himself as much as her?

It was an unsettling thought and one that Sean knew he was going to have to think about. He couldn't just brush it under the carpet as he normally would do—that wouldn't work. He needed to examine his feelings, face up to how he had felt two years ago, and take whatever action was necessary to ensure it didn't happen again. The problem was that he had put Molly on a bit of a pedestal, painted her in his mind as the ideal woman, and it was time he stopped doing that. Maybe Molly's plan wasn't so way off-beam as he had thought. If they resumed their affair, it could help *him* put things into perspective.

It was something else that Sean knew he needed to think about, but not right now. He helped himself to a croissant, murmuring appreciatively as he bit into it. 'This is delicious! No wonder the place is packed, although I don't remember the food being this good when I ate here before.'

'The café changed hands last year and, apparently, the new owner is French and only uses French milled flour for his croissants and pastries,' Molly informed him, wiping her buttery fingers on a paper napkin.

'Really? Well, good for him. It's obviously paying dividends.'

Sean grinned at her, thinking how pretty she looked that day. She was wearing a pale pink sweater and jeans and she looked so young and so fresh as she sat there, enjoying her breakfast, that it was little wonder that he had always loved being with her. And it was that thought which helped to unleash all sorts of memories he had thought he had buried.

'Remember those croissants we used to buy from the supermarket?' he said reminiscently. 'We used to heat them in the microwave so they were always slightly soggy yet we still ate them.'

'Yes, I remember,' Molly said quietly, wishing that he hadn't brought up the subject. It had become a sort of ritual for them—if their days off had coincided then Sean would make coffee for them while she warmed up the croissants and then they would take everything back to bed. More often than not the coffee would grow cold because once they were under the covers the inevitable would happen…

'We didn't always get to eat them, though, did we, Molly?'

His tone was brooding and she knew that he was remembering what had happened, how their desire for each other had overruled everything else. Sean had wanted her just as much as she had wanted him, which made his subsequent actions all the more difficult to understand. All of a sudden, Molly realised that she needed to know what had gone wrong, why he had ended their affair so abruptly and with so little warning.

'What happened, Sean? What went wrong?'

'I'm sorry?'

A frown furrowed his brow as he looked at her and Molly almost weakened. After all, what was the point of asking questions like that now? It wouldn't change what had happened—nothing would. And yet there was still this need to know why he had behaved the way he had. Even allowing for the fact that Sean had made it clear that he didn't do commitment, it was strange.

'Something must have happened to make you end our relationship so suddenly, so what was it? Was it something I did?'

'You didn't do anything. I just felt that it was the best thing to do,' he said flatly.

'Best for who?' She gave a brittle little laugh. 'Were you tired of me, Sean—was that it? Did you want someone more exciting in your life?'

'No. It wasn't that.' He reached across the table and touched her hand. 'I was never, ever bored when we were together, Molly. That's the truth. I swear.'

He withdrew his hand and she had a feeling that he was trying to decide what to say. She held her breath, wondering what he was going to tell her, but in the end he merely picked up his cup and drank some of his coffee.

Molly sipped her own coffee, wondering why she felt so deflated. There was no reason to believe that Sean had some secret he was hiding, yet she couldn't shake off the idea that something in his past had had a huge bearing on his actions. She sighed as she reached for another pastry. It was merely wishful thinking; she was looking for a complicated reason to explain why he had ended their affair when the truth was far simpler. He had tired of her and had wanted a change.

CHAPTER FIVE

SEAN COULDN'T BELIEVE how tempted he'd been to tell Molly all about Claire and the vow he had made. After all, what would it have achieved? It wouldn't have changed anything. On the contrary, it could have made matters worse. Molly might have thought he was aiming for the sympathy vote and he really couldn't bear that.

He reached for a second croissant then stopped when the café door was flung open and a woman came rushing in. Sean immediately leapt to his feet when he saw the panic on her face. He was already heading towards her even before she managed to speak.

'It's my husband! He's collapsed. Can someone help me? Please!'

'Where is he?' Sean took hold of her arm when she swayed. 'I'm a doctor so show me where he is and I'll see what I can do to help.'

'He's over there, by the Christmas tree. We were listening to the carol singers when he suddenly started acting really strange,' the woman explained as she led the way to where a crowd was starting to gather.

'In what way was he acting strange?' Sean asked, pushing his way through the onlookers. Someone had placed the man in the recovery position, so he knelt down beside him and checked his pulse then made sure he was breathing.

'I don't know…he couldn't seem to speak properly 'cos his mouth was drooping at one side and he couldn't move his left arm either.' The middle-aged woman bit back a sob. 'I tried to get him to tell me what was wrong but it was as though he couldn't hear me and then all of a sudden he just fell down onto the ground and didn't move.'

'I see,' Sean said quietly. It sounded very much like a stroke to him and the sooner the man was moved to hospital the better his chances would be. He looked up when Molly came to join them, nodding when she told him that she had phoned for an ambulance. 'Thanks. Can you get back onto Ambulance Control and tell them it looks like a stroke? That way, everyone will be prepared when he arrives at A&E.'

'Of course.' She swiftly made the call then knelt down beside him. 'How's his breathing?'

'So far, so good. Pulse is a bit erratic, but that's only to be expected.' He glanced up at the man's wife. 'Did he complain of a headache shortly before it happened?'

'No. He seemed perfectly fine. We were just going to listen to another couple of carols and then go and have a drink in the café before we went home,' the poor woman replied. 'Why did you ask that? Do you know what's wrong with him?'

'I'm afraid it looks very much like he's had a stroke,' Sean explained gently, knowing it would be a shock for her.

'A stroke,' she repeated. Tears rushed to her eyes. 'Is…is he going to die?'

Molly stood up and put her arm around her. 'Let's not assume the worst,' she told her quietly. 'The main thing now is to get your husband to hospital so he can receive treatment.'

'Can you treat him, though? My dad had a stroke when I was a teenager and there was nothing any-one could do…'

She broke off, too upset to continue, and Sean sighed. This was a part of his job he hated, trying to reassure relatives while not making any promises he might not be able to keep.

'We've made a lot of advances in the way we treat stroke patients in recent years. Your husband will be given anticoagulants to break down any clots that may have formed in his brain. It's a treatment that can have very positive results.'

'What if it's a burst blood vessel, though? That's what happened to my dad—a blood vessel burst and caused a massive bleed in his brain.'

'Your husband will have a CT scan at the hospital to rule that out. However, the fact that he didn't complain of a severe headache would point towards it being a clot rather than a bleed,' Sean explained.

He looked up when the wail of a siren announced the arrival of the ambulance. Molly was still talking to the woman, doing her best to reassure her, so Sean left her to it while he did the hand-over. It didn't take long as he hadn't administered any form of treatment so within minutes the ambulance was on its way. Molly sighed as she watched it drive off.

'Think he'll make it?'

'He stands a pretty good chance,' Sean replied quietly. 'Prompt treatment can make a huge difference in a case like this and that's what he will receive.'

'Yes, you're right. His poor wife, though. It must be a terrible shock when something like that happens to someone you love.'

'Your life changes in an instant,' Sean agreed, knowing only too well how that felt. Loving someone made you vulnerable and it was a timely reminder that he needed to get a grip on his emotions. He couldn't go through that kind of heartache a second time, which was why he needed to keep his distance from Molly.

It was a sobering thought. As Sean followed her back into the café, he realised that he needed to forget any ideas he had harboured about them resuming their affair. Although it might resolve certain issues, what if it created a whole lot more? Even though it wasn't easy to admit it, he had been far more involved with her than he had thought, and it was scary to wonder what might happen in the future if they grew close again.

'I'd better get off home. Thanks for the coffee.'

Molly pulled on her hat then wound her scarf around her neck in readiness to leave and Sean was suddenly struck by an inexplicable need to explain why he had ended their relationship two years ago. Would it help if he told her the real reason why he could never commit himself? he wondered. Once Molly understood then maybe they could both move on; she could put it all behind her and he could stop thinking about how he had felt when they had been together. The last thing he wanted was Molly going ahead with her plan to seduce him—that would be a complete and utter disaster!

'There's something I should have told you ages ago,' he said hurriedly.

'I really can't see the point of dragging up the past at this stage, Sean.' She looked up and her expression was so distant that he fell silent. She gave him a tight little smile as she picked up her gloves. 'If it was that important then you should have told me before now. It's really none of my business now, is it? We're not together any more.'

She was right; there was no point in baring his soul after all this time. He was only going to be in Dalverston for a few more weeks and after that he would make sure that he never came back here again.

No, the time for confessions was long gone and he would be foolish to imagine it would make any difference if he told her the truth.

'You're right. It's all water under the bridge, isn't it?' He treated her to a deliberately bright smile. 'I think I'll have another coffee before I head off home. I'll see you tonight, I expect.'

'I expect so.'

She matched his smile, wattage for wattage, then headed for the door. Sean went to the counter and ordered himself a double espresso, hoping that a serious shot of caffeine would help to get him back on track. He was allowing his emotions to get the better of him, something he never did, and he had to stop.

He sighed as he took his coffee back to the table and sat down. It was being around Molly that was causing him to behave so out of character. It had been exactly the same two years ago—he had known that he and Molly could never have a long-term relationship, yet he had put off breaking up with her until it had been almost too late. She had the strangest effect on him, made him long for things he knew he could never have, but he was going to stand firm, no matter what.

He took a sip of coffee, shuddering as the caffeine hit his central nervous system. It might be tempting but being back in Molly's arms was something he intended to avoid at all costs.

CHAPTER SIX

MOLLY FELT EXHAUSTED when she arrived at work that night. The lack of sleep combined with everything else that had happened recently had taken their toll and her energy levels were at an all-time low. It was all she could do to dredge up a smile when she found Suzy in the staffroom.

'You look absolutely shattered!' Suzy exclaimed. She put her hands on her hips and glared at Molly. 'I hope it hasn't anything to do with Sean Fitzgerald. You had a bit of thing for him the last time he worked here, didn't you?'

'All water under the bridge,' Molly declared, groaning when she unwittingly repeated the phrase Sean had used only that morning. It shouldn't have been a surprise. After all, she had spent most of the day thinking about him. Had he been going to share some sort of a confidence with her? she wondered for the umpteenth time, and sighed. Even if he had, he had soon thought better of it. No, Sean wasn't about to share any confidences with *her*. She wasn't that important to him.

She brushed aside that depressing thought. 'You know what they say, Suzy. You have to kiss a lot of frogs before you find a real live prince.'

'And that's honestly how you view him, is it?' Suzy retorted. 'As just another frog?'

'Well, he certainly hasn't turned into a prince,' Molly stated.

She swept out of the door before Suzy could reply, knowing that she wasn't up to having a discussion about this particular frog prince. Although Suzy knew that she had dated Sean when he had last worked there, her friend had no idea how Molly had really felt about him. After all, everyone in the hospital knew that Sean didn't do commitment so there was no reason why Suzy should have guessed that she had fallen so heavily for him and that was how she wanted it to remain. It was bad enough knowing what a fool she had been without everyone else knowing it too.

Molly did the handover then took her first patient to Cubicles. Abbey Jones was suffering from severe stomach cramps which she thought were the result of a curry she had eaten that lunchtime. Her boyfriend had brought her into hospital but Molly asked him to remain in the waiting room while she got Abbey settled. She needed to ask Abbey some questions and she preferred to do so in private as it didn't sound to her as though Abbey was suffering from food poisoning.

'Have you been sick?' Molly asked once she had made Abbey comfortable on the bed.

'No. It's just these pains in my stomach.' Abbey drew up her legs and moaned. 'It really hurts!'

'The doctor will be here to see you in a minute,' Molly said soothingly. 'Let's get these leggings off you for starters.' She helped the girl remove her boots and leggings, trying to hide her dismay when she discovered that Abbey was bleeding from the vagina. 'Did you know that you were bleeding?'

'No! I knew I felt a bit damp down there but I slipped over in the car park on my way in and landed in a puddle so I thought it must be that. What's happening to me, Sister?'

'Is it possible that you might be pregnant?' Molly said carefully.

'Pregnant,' Abbey repeated, looking stunned.

'Yes. Can you remember when you last had a period?' Molly persisted.

'I'm not sure… I've always been very irregular, you see. Sometimes I can go five or six weeks between periods so it's difficult to say for certain.' Abbey gulped. 'If I am pregnant then why am I bleeding like this? Am I having a miscarriage or something?'

'It's possible.' Molly patted her hand, knowing what a shock it must be for her. Not to have realised that she was pregnant and then have this happen would be a lot for any woman to deal with. After she had split from Sean, she'd had a worrying few days herself when her period had been late, even though they had been meticulous about using protection. Thankfully, everything had resolved itself although she couldn't help wondering what she would have done if she had been pregnant. Would she have contacted Sean and told him about the baby? She wasn't sure. After all, he had made it abundantly clear that he hadn't wanted anything more to do with her, hadn't he?

Molly pushed aside that thought as she focused on finding out if Abbey was indeed pregnant. She fetched a pregnancy testing kit from the cupboard and helped her to the bathroom. When Abbey reappeared a few minutes later, she was shaking.

'It's positive,' she whispered. 'I had no idea I was pregnant and now it looks as though I'm going to lose the baby.'

'I'm so sorry,' Molly said gently as she helped her back onto the bed. 'It must be a terrible shock for you, but the main thing now is to get you sorted out. Do you want me to tell your boyfriend or would you rather do it yourself? It's entirely up to you.'

'I don't know!' Tears began to pour down Abbey's cheeks. 'We've only been going out for a couple of months and we've never even spoken about having kids. I really don't know what I should do for the best.'

'You don't have to decide right this very minute,' Molly assured her, understanding only too well what a dilemma it must be for the girl. She and Sean had never discussed having children either, for obvious reasons, i.e. he'd had no intention of committing himself for the long-term. A child would have caused an unwelcome disruption to his plans, and the thought hurt even though she knew how stupid it was to let it affect her.

'I'll just tell him that you're being transferred to a ward for further tests,' Molly said hurriedly, not wanting to go any further down that route.

'Yes. Thank you.' Abbey wiped her eyes. 'It's such a lot to take in.'

'It must be.'

Molly treated her to a smile then went to the desk and phoned the maternity unit. Sean appeared as she was ending the call and she quickly explained what was happening.

'Sounds as though you've sorted everything out.' He frowned. 'Who brought her in?'

'Her boyfriend.' Molly nodded towards the waiting room. 'He's over there. I had a feeling that it wasn't food poisoning and asked him to remain out here while I examined Abbey.'

'It will be a shock for him too, I imagine,' Sean observed.

'If she chooses to tell him.' Molly smiled tightly, conscious of the dilemma she would have been in if the same thing had happened to her. 'They've only been seeing one another for a few months and she isn't sure if she wants him to know or not.'

'Really?' Sean's tone was grim. Molly frowned because it wasn't how she would have expected him to react. If anything, she would have thought that he would be all in favour of Abbey keeping the news to herself if it meant there would be less pressure put on her boyfriend.

'Yes.' She shrugged. 'Maybe it's a good idea if they're not in a committed relationship.'

'I disagree. Keeping something like this a secret only creates problems, in my opinion. But if it's what the patient wants then we have to go along with it.'

He didn't say anything else as he made his way to Cubicles to see Abbey. Molly wasn't sure what to make of it all as his reaction had been the complete opposite to what she would have expected. Did Sean have personal experience of this kind of situation? she wondered suddenly as she went to speak to Abbey's boyfriend. And was that why he had taken such a hard stance just now? Her mind raced off at a tangent and she gasped. Did it also explain why he avoided commitment? Because he had been so badly hurt at some point in his life that he refused to run the risk of being hurt ever again?

It was an intriguing thought, but Molly knew that she mustn't make the mistake of reading too much into it. To allow herself to believe that it was the true explanation for the way he had treated her two years ago would be asking for trouble. No, the truth was probably much simpler: Sean had grown tired of her and ended their relationship.

By the time everything was sorted out quite a large queue had formed in Reception. Suzy was doing triage that night—making sure the most seriously injured were seen first. Ambulance control had rung as well to say there was a young man who'd been involved in an RTA on his way. He had a suspected fractured pelvis so Molly told the paramedics to take him straight to Resus when he arrived and buzzed for Sean. As the senior doctor on duty, he was the one who would need to deal with this casualty and she would assist him.

'Right, so what's happened here?' Sean hurried into Resus and came straight over to the bed. Molly moved aside to give him some room as he bent over the bed. He was wearing light blue scrubs that night and she found herself thinking all of a sudden just how much the colour suited him, emphasising the intense sapphire-blue of his eyes. Sean was an extremely handsome man, with that jet-black hair and those clean-cut features, and it was impossible to ignore the fact too. It took every scrap of willpower she could muster to concentrate as the lead paramedic did the handover.

'This is David Gregory, aged twenty-two. He

came off his motorbike after hitting a pothole in
the road and slammed into a stone wall,' the paramedic explained. 'There appears to be some instabil-
ity around his pelvis which is why we fitted a belt.
He's had ten mgs of morphine for the pain plus eight
mgs of metoclopramide to counteract any sickness.'
The crew finished off with an update of the patient's
BP and Sats before they left.

'Hello, David. I'm Dr Fitzgerald. I know you must
be in a great deal of pain but I need to check what
damage you've done to yourself. OK?'

Sean set about his examination when David nodded. He was quick but thorough, his hands moving
as gently as possible over the young man's hips and
pelvis. He glanced at Molly and she could see the
concern in his eyes. 'Can you organise an X-ray,
please, Sister? There's quite a bit of movement here
and I'd like to check if we're dealing with more than
one fracture.'

'Of course.' Molly hurried to the phone and summoned the radiographer. She arrived just moments
later and quickly set about taking the X-rays they
needed. Resus was equipped with an overhead X-ray
machine so there was no need to move the patient.
They all stepped aside while the films were taken
and in a very short time the results were up on the
screen. As Sean had suspected, David Gregory had
fractured his pelvis in not one but two places, which
made the situation even more complicated.

'He needs to go to Theatre ASAP,' Sean said after studying the films. 'If I'm not mistaken, there's some damage to the bladder and that needs sorting out immediately. Who's the surgeon on duty tonight—do you know?'

'I think it's Adam Humphreys,' Molly informed him. 'Do you want me to phone him and tell him we have a patient for him?'

'If you wouldn't mind.' Sean smiled at her. 'Thanks, Molly. It will save me a job.'

'No problem.' Molly gave a little shrug before she hurried over to the phone but she couldn't ignore the fact that her heart had lifted when Sean had smiled at her. Was she right about him being hurt in the past? she wondered once again and then sighed. She had to stop trying to find excuses for him and simply accept that he had finished with her because he hadn't wanted to be with her any longer.

Molly deliberately turned her mind to tracking down Adam Humphreys, not an easy task, as it turned out, as he wasn't in the surgeons' lounge or in Theatre, and he wasn't responding to his pager either. She finally traced him to Women's Surgical, where he was checking on a patient he had seen earlier in the evening. He was full of apologies when she politely pointed out that his pager appeared to be switched off. He promised to come straight there and, true to his word, he arrived a couple of minutes later.

Molly knew him quite well and had always found

him a pleasant if not very exciting kind of a man. He had asked her out a couple of times, but she had always made an excuse and refused. However, when he repeated his invitation after he had finished examining the X-rays, she found herself accepting. Maybe she should go out with Adam and forget about Sean. Having Sean turn up out of the blue like that had had a highly detrimental effect and she hated the fact that she couldn't seem to get him out of her head. Why, just look at the way she had seriously considered instigating another affair with him! It had been madness, pure, unadulterated madness, to come up with such a crazy plan. Going out with someone as uncomplicated as Adam Humphreys would help to put her back on track. And who knew what might happen in the future? It could turn out that Adam Humphreys was her Mr Right, the frog who finally turned into her very own prince.

Sean had to bite his tongue when he heard Humphreys asking Molly out on a date. It had nothing to do with him who she dated, he told himself sternly. She was a free agent and he had given up any claim on her two years ago. It was no less than the truth but it was hard to take such a balanced and rational view. For some reason he didn't intend to examine too closely, he couldn't bear the thought of Molly seeing the other man.

The night wore on, the usual mix of the mundane

and high drama. Several of the people he saw should have been seen by their GPs rather than turning up at the A&E unit. Sean politely explained that if something of a similar nature occurred again they should contact their local surgery, but he knew that most wouldn't take his advice. Why wait for an appointment when they could be seen immediately? was their view. The fact that it simply added to the pressure the A&E staff were under was of little concern to them.

It was all very depressing and, added to his previous thoughts about Molly and this date she was planning, it had a marked effect. Sean's spirits were at an all-time low when he left the hospital and it didn't help when he saw Molly getting into Adam Humphreys' car. He knew from what he had overheard her saying that her car still wasn't fixed and he couldn't blame her for accepting a lift rather than waiting for the bus, but it made no difference. He didn't want the other man driving her home, certainly didn't want to think about her inviting Humphreys in for coffee! Maybe he didn't have any right to dictate what she did and who she did it with, but it didn't matter. Deep in his heart, tucked away in the very darkest corner, lay the truth: he wanted Molly to belong to him and only him.

Thankfully, Molly managed to get some sleep and awoke feeling a lot better than she had done. She showered and dressed, taking extra care as she blow-dried her hair so that it fell in soft red-gold waves around her face. Adam had asked her if she fancied having lunch with him that day at one of Dalverston's newest and most expensive restaurants and she had accepted. It had seemed propitious to put her plan to forget about Sean into action as soon as possible.

The restaurant was beautiful if a tad formal for Molly's taste. She was glad that she had chosen to wear a smart lilac dress for the lunch date rather than something more casual. The clientele was somewhat older than her and Adam, although she had to admit that he seemed very comfortable with the surroundings. He was obviously well known to the staff too because they were immediately seated at one of the best tables overlooking the river. Molly had to hide her amusement as Adam and the sommelier had a long and intense discussion about the best wine to accompany their lunch. It all seemed slightly over the top to her but she knew that Adam would be very hurt if she let him see how she felt.

Lunches out with Sean had been very different affairs, she found herself thinking as she listened to the two men discussing the merits of Sauvignon Blanc compared to Chablis. One day it had been a picnic of bread and some deliciously crumbly cheese produced by one of the local farms, all washed down with a bottle of beer, while on another occasion they had stopped at a mobile burger bar on the bypass and consumed huge and highly calorific egg and bacon sandwiches. A smile twitched at the corners of her mouth as she remembered how Sean had laughed when the egg had oozed out of her sandwich and dribbled down her chin. Bending forward, he had delicately licked the bright yellow eggy goo away, not something she could imagine Adam doing…

'Excellent! We'll have a bottle of the Chablis, Pierre. I'm sure you will appreciate it, Molly. It has the most exquisite bouquet.'

'I… I'm sure I shall,' Molly replied, hurriedly driving that disturbing thought from her mind as Adam turned to her. She had come here today specifically to stop herself thinking about Sean and she refused to allow her thoughts to get hijacked this early in the date!

She listened attentively as Adam continued with his theme, explaining in great detail the qualities of the various wines. He was obviously something of an expert but Molly could drum up very little enthusiasm for the subject. In her view, wine was wine and you either liked it or you didn't. Spending time discussing it wasn't something she and Sean had ever done—they'd had much better ways to occupy their time!

Once again her thoughts rushed off along their own path and she swallowed her groan of dismay. She didn't want to think about the hours she and Sean had spent lying in each other's arms, certainly didn't want to remember how wonderful it had felt to make love with him. It wasn't fair to Adam to think about another man when he had invited her for this very expensive lunch. No, she wouldn't give Sean Fitzgerald another thought, even if it killed her!

'So which is your very favourite wine, Adam?' she asked, leaning forward and adopting an expression of what she hoped would appear to be deep and undivided interest. Out of the corner of her eye, she saw the head waiter escorting someone to a nearby table. However, it wasn't until the waiter moved away to fetch a menu that Molly realised who it was. All of a sudden her blood began to boil, growing hotter and hotter until it felt as though she would explode. What on earth was Sean doing here?

CHAPTER SEVEN

WHAT IN HEAVEN'S name was he doing here?

Sean could hear the question drumming inside his head as it had been doing for the best part of an hour, yet he still hadn't come up with an answer to it. Or not a truthful one, anyhow. Oh, he had listed at least half a dozen reasons to explain why he'd felt a sudden need to dine in the lap of luxury but he knew in his heart that not one of them was valid. He didn't *really* feel that he deserved a treat after working so hard. Neither did he *honestly* believe it was essential he tried out the restaurant in case he decided to invite someone here for dinner. He had come here today for one reason and one reason only—because Molly would be lunching here with Humphreys. *Hell!*

The waiter returned to take his order and Sean pointed to the first thing on the extensive menu. He had no idea what he'd ordered after the man left and didn't care. He wasn't here for the food. He was here because he couldn't bear the thought of Molly schmoozing with the other man. OK, so he was behaving like the proverbial dog-in-the-manger but so what? Humphreys wasn't right for Molly. Maybe he didn't know much about the other man, granted, but he could tell that just by looking at him. Humphreys was too staid, too solid, too damned reliable—everything *he* wasn't.

Molly needed someone with more pizzazz, someone who would treasure her, appreciate her beauty and her kindness as well as her generosity of spirit. He had appreciated all of those things, even though he had had to let her go. But Humphreys? No way was he right for her and she was making a big mistake if she thought he was!

His lunch arrived and Sean picked up his knife and fork even though the thought of actually eating the food that had been set before him was making his stomach churn. Molly was leaning across the table now, laughing at some comment her companion had made. Sean glowered, hating to hear the sound of her laughter and not be the cause of it. He had enjoyed making her laugh; it had made him feel incredibly happy—happier than he had felt for such a long time. He couldn't bear the thought that some other guy was basking in the same happy glow.

He applied himself to his lunch, wanting to get it over and done with as quickly as possible so he could leave. Coming here had been a huge mistake. Although Molly hadn't acknowledged him in any way, he knew that she had seen him. The thought of having to dredge up one of those pitifully lame excuses if she demanded an explanation for his presence was more than he could handle. To heck with the food; he was leaving this very minute!

Sean pushed back his chair then stopped when he became aware that someone was standing beside his table. He looked up, carefully smoothing his features into a non-committal expression. 'Molly! What a surprise. Are you having lunch here as well?'

'Yes, I am.' She smiled back at him, her green eyes filled with a disturbing mixture of emotions. There was definitely anger there, Sean decided, plus indignation, but as for the rest—well, he couldn't quite work them all out. And before he attempted to do so she rounded on him.

'How dare you, Sean? I've no idea what you think you're doing—'

'Having lunch. Why—what else would I be doing in a place like this?'

'So it's just coincidence that brought you here today?' She gave an unladylike snort of disbelief. 'It hadn't anything to do with the fact that you knew Adam was bringing me here?'

'Of course not. Why should it?'

Sean fixed a smile to his own mouth, desperately trying to play the part of the injured innocent. Admitting that she had hit the nail squarely on its head was out of the question. If he did that then he would have to explain why he had followed her here and that was something he couldn't do. How could he explain this strange compulsion he felt to keep her for himself when he didn't fully understand it himself?

'Someone mentioned that this was *the* place to eat so I thought I would check it out for future reference.'

He gave a small shrug, thinking how beautiful she looked as she stood there glaring down at him. It wasn't often that Molly's temper was roused; she was far too kind and loving to kick up a scene. The only time he had seen her this angry, in fact, was when he had told her that he no longer wanted to see her. He had been far too upset at the time to appreciate the change in her but now he couldn't help noticing how glorious she looked with her green eyes blazing and her wonderful red-gold hair shimmering in a fiery halo around her head. Molly was not only kind, loving and giving—she was a highly passionate woman as well.

'Oh, I see. So what have you decided? Does it meet your requirements or not?'

'Requirements,' Sean echoed, trying to get a grip on his libido, which seemed to think that this was the right moment to make itself known.

'The perfect place to seduce your latest victim, of course.' She glanced around the beautifully appointed dining room and there was both hurt and scorn in her eyes when she turned to him again. 'She must be rather special if you're thinking of shelling out for dinner here. I mean, the prices are a lot steeper than they are at your usual venues but there again you must think she's worth it. Not every woman you go out with is a cheap date, I imagine.'

She spun round on her heel, leaving Sean wondering what he should do. Oh, he knew what she had meant by that last scathing comment—it had been painfully obvious! However, she was wrong—very, very wrong—if she believed he had taken her out to places which hadn't cost the earth because he had thought she wasn't worth anything better. Those picnics and that trip to the burger van had been red-letter occasions for him. Not even the *fanciest* dinners at the *most* upmarket restaurants could compare to them. He had not only enjoyed the food but he'd enjoyed it because of Molly's company and that had raised those occasions to a whole different level. Why, even a meal of bread and water would have tasted like manna from heaven if they had eaten it together!

Sean stood up, determined that he was going to set matters straight. No way was he letting Molly get away with accusing him of such despicable meanness. However, before he could go over to have it out with her, he saw Humphreys return to the table. He gritted his teeth as he watched the other man bend down and whisper something in her ear. Molly laughed as she rose to her feet, smiling up at her companion as he slid his hand under her elbow and led her to the conservatory, where coffee was being served.

Sean felt his insides start to churn. The whole

thing smacked of an intimacy that he resented. Bitterly. He wanted nothing more than to follow them and thump Humphreys on the nose but he knew it was out of the question. Humphreys hadn't done anything wrong. If Molly hadn't wanted him to be so familiar then she would have stopped him. How could *he* follow them and make a scene when it was obviously the last thing Molly wanted?

Sean took a deep breath before he summoned the waiter so he could pay his bill, murmuring something suitably appropriate when the man asked him if he had enjoyed his lunch. Enjoyment wasn't the word he would have used, although Molly probably had a very different opinion. Maybe she hadn't been pleased to see him there but he doubted if it had spoiled the date for her. No, this was just the first of many such occasions for her and Humphreys: exquisite dinners at top-flight restaurants, high-brow concerts, trips to the theatre and the ballet—that was undoubtedly Humphreys' style. Who could blame her if she was seduced by such lavish treatment? The best he'd done was to buy her an egg and bacon roll from a mobile burger van. That really must have impressed her!

Molly wasn't looking forward to seeing Sean that night when she went into work. She was still smarting from what had happened at lunchtime. She simply couldn't believe that he had, quite coincidentally, turned up at that particular restaurant. And yet, on the other hand, what reason did he have for following her there? It wasn't as though he was interested in her, was it? Maybe he *had* been sussing out the place for a future occasion and that thought stung more than all the others. Sean was only doing what he did best—dating a variety of women. So why on earth should it matter to her?

It was a relief when she discovered that he was tied up in Resus as it gave her a breathing space before she had to speak to him. She collected her first patient and took him into the treatment room. Bert Feathers was eighty years old but still very active. He had been taking his dog for a walk when he had slipped on some ice and cut his arm on a broken bottle lying on the footpath. His neighbour had brought him into hospital after he had knocked on her door and asked to borrow a sticking plaster.

'This might sting a bit,' Molly warned him as she cleaned the cut with antiseptic solution. The gash was several inches long, quite deep and needed stitching. She wanted to make sure that it didn't become infected. 'Sorry.'

'Don't you worry, lass. It's fine.' Bert gave her a toothless grin. 'I've had worse than this, believe me.'

'Have you indeed?' Molly picked up a fresh piece of cotton wool with her tweezers and swabbed his arm once more. 'So you're an old hand at being patched up, are you?'

'Aye. I was a hill farmer, you see. We lived too far out of town so we were used to fending for ourselves. Me and my brother, Cedric, were pretty handy with a needle if needs be.' He held out his right arm. 'See that scar? Cut my arm real bad while I was mending the tractor one day. Cedric stitched it up for me and it never gave me a bit of trouble afterwards.'

'He did a good job,' Molly agreed, thinking what a tough life the old man must have led. She could only imagine how painful it must have been to have such a large cut stitched without any form of anaesthetic. 'Do you still have your farm?' she asked as she broke open the seal on a fresh pack of sutures.

'No. I had to give it up after Cedric died. It was too much for me on my own so I sold up and moved into town. I got one of them sheltered housing bungalows in the centre of town. Moving there was the best thing I ever done, as it happens.' Bert nodded at the elderly lady sitting beside him. 'I met Doris there, you see. She lives next door and we're right fond of each other. Never had a lady friend when I was younger—never had time, what with the farm and everything. I've made up for it since, though!'

'Good for you!' Molly laughed in delight. 'You're never too old to fall in love, are you?'

'Definitely not. When the lightning strikes, there's nothing you can do about it.' Bert laughed. 'Me and Doris are getting married next week. We've got the church all booked and we're having a bit of a do afterwards at the Green Man. Thought it was time we put things on a regular footing, you understand. You must come along, Sister. We'd love to have you there to help us celebrate, wouldn't we, Doris? And you too, Doctor. The more the merrier, as they say, and you'll be very welcome.'

Molly glanced round, suddenly realising that someone had come into the room. Her heart lifted and then just as quickly sank again when she saw Sean. All of a sudden she felt her resolve start to crumble. Although her lunch with Adam had been pleasant enough, it wasn't Adam who had occupied her thoughts for the rest of the day. It made her wonder if she would ever erase Sean from her life. They had spoken for—what?—five minutes, possibly. But she had then spent the next five *hours* thinking about him.

It was as though Sean was imprinted in her consciousness and nothing could remove him, not even spending time with another man…especially not spending time with another man, she corrected herself, remembering how often she had found herself comparing Adam Humphreys to Sean during their lunch date and finding the former decidedly lacking. It had been the same ever since Sean had ended their affair too; she had never met anyone who matched up to him and she wasn't sure if she would. Sean might have broken her heart but he still had a hold over her and it was distressing to admit it. It was an effort to hide how she felt as Sean turned to the elderly couple and smiled.

'I missed the start of the conversation. What are you celebrating?' he asked, leaning his shoulder against the wall.

'I was just telling Sister here that me and Doris are getting married next week,' Bert explained. 'Friday, at St Marie's church in the town centre. We're having a party afterwards at the Green Man and we'd be delighted if you two young folk came along and helped us celebrate.'

'I'm not sure if it will be possible,' Molly began, hurriedly searching for an excuse to refuse the invitation. Panic swept over her. The last thing she needed was to spend any more time with Sean.

'If you're worried about what shift we're working, there's no need.' Sean turned to her and Molly's heart sank even further when she saw the expression in his eyes. Sean knew exactly what she was thinking and, from the look of it, he had no intention of letting her wriggle out of the invitation. 'I've seen the roster and we're both off next Friday, so we would love to come along. Wouldn't we, Molly?'

Molly had no idea what to say. Short of upsetting Bert and Doris by refusing, there was little she could do except agree. Gritting her teeth, she nodded. Sean grinned at her, obviously enjoying the fact that he had got his own way.

'Great! It will be something to look forward

to, won't it, Molly? A lovely lead-up to the Christmas festivities.'

'Yes.' It was difficult to get any words out through her clenched teeth but she would hate him to know how annoyed she felt. 'Did you want me for something?'

'Ah, yes.' There was a note in his voice, a hint of some emotion that made her blood heat as he excused himself and drew her to one side, but Molly refused to speculate on the reason for it. They were discussing a work-related issue, she reminded herself sternly. Anything else was inconsequential. It appeared she'd been right too because there was no trace of anything untoward when he continued.

'The patient in Resus has asked if we can contact his family in India. Apparently, he's a student at the local college and he doesn't have any family living here. There isn't a telephone number where we can reach them so we may need to go through the Embassy. I was hoping that you would be able to sort it out.'

'Of course,' Molly said formally. 'I'll get straight onto the Embassy once I've finished in here.'

'Thanks.' He half turned to leave then paused. 'Did you enjoy your lunch and coffee, by the way? You never gave me the chance to ask what you thought of the restaurant.'

'The food was excellent,' she said shortly, refusing to let him goad her into saying something she would regret. If he'd had an ulterior motive for being there then she didn't want to know what it was. She treated him to a deliberately bright smile. 'Adam and I had a great time, I have to say. In fact, I'm sure we shall go back there again in the future.'

'Good. I'm glad you didn't find it too stuffy.'

He sketched her a wave and headed back to Resus before she could ask him what he meant by that comment. Had Sean found the place rather too formal, as she had done? she wondered as she started suturing Bert's arm. Although the food had been delicious, the restaurant had lacked atmosphere, although maybe that had been down to her companion, she mused. Although Adam was extremely attentive, he lacked any real charisma. Adam certainly wouldn't have been able to make lunching at a burger van feel like a Michelin star experience!

Molly's mouth tightened. Once again she was comparing Adam to Sean and she had to stop. She finished suturing Bert's arm and saw him and Doris out then collected her next patient. She had no intention of wondering who Sean was planning to invite out for an expensive dinner. He could date every single woman in the hospital if he wanted and she wouldn't lose a wink of sleep worrying about it! However, despite such stalwart claims, she couldn't deny that the thought of Sean seeing some other woman hurt. It brought it home to her once more how vital it was that she erased him from her life for good.

CHAPTER EIGHT

SEAN HAD THE next two days off and had decided to spend them looking for a place to live. As it had been a last-minute decision to accept the post in Dalverston he had booked himself into a bed and breakfast, but if he was to spend the next six weeks working here he desperately needed his own space.

He set off early to visit the local estate agent's office and came away with a list of four properties, all available on a short-term lease. However, he quickly discovered that the agency's glowing descriptions fell far short of the reality. By the time he arrived at the last property he was starting to feel very despondent. *Cosy* probably meant tiny and *full of character* undoubtedly meant it was riddled with damp or overrun with mice or both. He almost gave up but the thought of having to put up with living in one room for the next few weeks spurred him on. He would go crazy if he had to stare at the same four walls much longer!

Sean got out of the car. The cottage was tucked away down a narrow lane close to the river and he stood for a moment, drinking in the peace and quiet. He frowned because the area seemed strangely familiar for some reason. Looking around, he realised with a start that it was very close to where Molly lived. Why, he could remember running along this very lane one morning after he had stayed the night at her house! He sighed. It put him in a bit of a quandary. Molly had made it abundantly clear on more than one occasion that she wanted nothing to do with him outside of work, hadn't she? On the other hand, he was pretty much out of options by now, he reasoned, and it wasn't as if he and Molly would be next door neighbours. The thought helped him make up his mind and he went and knocked on the front door. It opened a crack and a wizened face peered out at him.

'Yes?'

'Mrs Bradshaw? I believe you're renting out your cottage. The estate agent gave me the details.' He showed the old lady the letter the agency had given him and smiled at her. 'They said they would ring and let you know I was coming.'

'That's right, dear. Come in, come in.' She opened the door wider and ushered him inside. 'I'm off to New Zealand, you see, to stay with my son and his wife over Christmas. They've asked me umpteen times if I'd go and stay with them but I've always refused in the past because I didn't want to leave

Henry.' She sighed. 'He's no longer with us, I'm afraid, so I've no excuse not to go now.'

'I'm so sorry,' Sean said quietly, thinking how sad it must be to lose one's partner after what must have been a lengthy relationship. 'Were you married a long time?'

'Married?' The old lady laughed. 'Oh, no. Henry wasn't my husband, dear. He died many years ago. Henry was my dog and a bad-tempered old thing too, but I still loved him. He finally went to doggy heaven a month ago so I decided to book my flight. The problem is that I don't like the thought of leaving the cottage standing empty while I'm away. One of my neighbours, who lives just round the corner, did offer to pop in and check everything was all right, but I thought it was too much for her when she's so busy working, which is why I decided to rent it out.'

'I see.' Sean laughed at his mistake then looked around the living room. It was small, admittedly, but it felt wonderfully cosy and inviting. 'This is lovely,' he said truthfully. 'It feels so...well, homely, is the best way to describe it.'

'I'm glad you like it, dear. I've lived here for over forty years and I love the place. Why don't you look round and see if it's suitable for you?' the old lady suggested. 'I'll put the kettle on and make us a cup of tea.'

Sean did as he was told, checking out the small but functional kitchen, the bedroom with its old-fashioned dark wood furniture and the surprisingly large and well-equipped bathroom. He had already decided to take it by the time he returned to the living room and he told Mrs Bradshaw that he would get straight onto the agency.

'That is good news, dear.' Mrs Bradshaw beamed as she handed him a delicate china cup and saucer. 'I'm so pleased. Not only will I know the place is being well looked after but it means that Molly won't have to bother about it.'

'Molly,' Sean repeated, his hand shaking ever so slightly so that the cup started to rattle in its saucer. He hurriedly set it safely down on the end table, telling himself that he was being silly. It wouldn't be his Molly; that would be too much of a coincidence. No, Mrs Bradshaw's Molly was most likely a kindly older lady like herself. 'Is she a friend of yours?'

'Yes. Molly's a real sweetheart. I'm sure you'll like her. She's been like a daughter to me—pops to the shop for bread and milk if I run out; fetches my Sunday paper if she's not working at the weekend.' Mrs Bradshaw sighed. 'She's a nurse in the A&E department at the hospital and she works the most terrible hours but she still finds the time to visit me. You can understand why I don't want to burden her with having to look after my cottage while I'm away, can't you?'

'I…erm…yes. Of course,' Sean replied, his heart sinking as he realised that he couldn't in all conscience take the cottage now he knew that there was a very real risk of him bumping into Molly.

'Mrs Bradshaw,' he began, knowing that he had no choice in the circumstances other than to tell the old lady that he had changed his mind. Maybe he did love the cottage but it wasn't worth taking it if it meant upsetting Molly.

'It's such a weight off my mind!' the old lady declared, cutting him off mid-flow. She patted his hand. 'Now I shall be able to go off and enjoy my holiday without having to worry. I just know that you will take very good care of everything here, dear.'

'Of course,' Sean murmured because he really couldn't find it in his heart to disappoint her after hearing that.

Maybe there was no need to do so either, he thought as he picked up his cup and drank his tea. He would just have to be extra careful to stay out of Molly's way. After all, with him there, taking care of the cottage, there would be no need for Molly to pop in, would there? By the time he left, he had more or less convinced himself that there was nothing to worry about. After all, he needed somewhere to live and the cottage was perfect for his needs. The downside of living the way he did was that he had never had a real home and all of a sudden he found himself longing for a place of his own.

It was such an unprecedented thought that it threw him completely. Leaving his car parked in the lane, he made his way to the river. It was bitterly cold down there but he didn't notice the chill. Having a home of his own had been all tied up with the plans he and Claire had made for their future together. He had never considered the idea since she had died but there was no point denying how tempting it was and the realisation made him feel overwhelmed with guilt, as though he was betraying Claire by even considering it.

Closing his eyes, he tried to conjure up Claire's image but it just wouldn't come. Her face was hazy, her features too indistinct to see her clearly. Slowly but surely, Claire was slipping away from him and it was painful to know that he was incapable of keeping her safe in his heart where she deserved to be. He had planned to spend his life with her, so what kind of a man must he be if he had allowed her memory to fade?

Unbidden, another image began to form in his mind's eye and Sean felt his breath catch when he recognised the familiar features: those deep green eyes; the long black lashes; that tumble of red-gold curls...

He opened his eyes and stared across the river in despair. He might not be able to recall Claire's face but he had no difficulty at all conjuring up Molly's.

Molly had been planning to go into town to do some much-needed food shopping. However, on a sudden whim, she decided to take the less direct route along by the river. It was a beautiful day, even if it was bitterly cold, and the fresh air would do her good after three days of working nights. She walked to the top of the path and came to a sudden halt when she spotted Sean standing on the riverbank. He was staring across the river and there was an expression of such intense pain on his face that her heart seemed to scrunch up inside her. Even though she knew it wasn't any of her business what was troubling him, she simply couldn't walk on by and leave him like this.

'Hello, Sean,' she said softly as she made her way towards him. He glanced round and she could see the effort it cost him to pull himself together.

'Hello, Molly. What are you doing here? Out for a walk?'

'Hmm. I needed to get some shopping so I thought I'd kill two birds with one stone and get some fresh air at the same time.' She pushed her hands deep into her pockets, afraid that she would do something really stupid like touching him. Maybe he *was* hurting but there was no reason to think that he would welcome her concern.

'So what brings you here?' she asked brightly, not wanting to dwell on that thought. 'Are you out for a walk as well?'

'No, actually, I was viewing a house that I'm hoping to rent.' He turned and pointed back up the path.

'It's just up there, Lilac Cottage—the last cottage in the row.'

'You don't mean Mrs Bradshaw's cottage!' she exclaimed and he grimaced.

'Yes. I had a feeling that you wouldn't be too pleased if you found out I was living so close to you. Not to worry. I shall tell the letting agents that I've changed my mind.' He turned to walk back up the path but Molly shook her head.

'There's no reason why you should do that. I really don't care where you live, Sean. Plus I know for a fact that Mrs Bradshaw has been very worried about finding someone suitable to rent the cottage while she's away.' She gave a careless little shrug, determined not to let him know how disturbing she found the idea of him living so close to her. It wasn't only in work that she would have to take steps to avoid him, it seemed. 'If you think the cottage is right for you then you should take it.'

'Are you sure?' he asked and her skin prickled when she heard the doubt in his voice. It was obvious that he didn't think she could cope with them living in such close proximity and she needed to squash that idea right away.

'Of course I'm sure! It's you who's making such a big deal of it, not me.' Molly deliberately shifted the conversation along a different path, not wanting to have to keep on reassuring him when, in truth, she felt so ambivalent about the idea. 'Why are you so eager to move in the first place? I wouldn't have thought it was worth it when you're only going to be in Dalverston for such a short time.'

'You're right, and normally I wouldn't dream of swapping and changing. However, it was a last-minute decision to accept this job and the only accommodation I could find was a room in a B&B close to the bypass.' He shrugged. 'It's all right but I'm starting to get cabin fever from staring at the same four walls all the time. At least I'll have a bit more space in the cottage.'

'It must be odd to keep moving around all the time,' Molly observed thoughtfully. 'Have you never wanted a place of your own?'

'No. Well, not until recently, anyway.' His voice was low but laced with so much anguish that it immediately made her set aside any qualms she had. Reaching out, she touched his hand.

'Why, what's happened to make you change your mind recently?'

'I'm not sure. Maybe it's being here—who knows?' He turned his hand over and captured hers. 'I don't want to feel this way, believe me, but I can't seem to stop. And it makes me feel so damned guilty!'

'Guilty? I don't understand. Why should you feel guilty about wanting a home of your own?' It was impossible to keep the surprise out of her voice and she heard him sigh.

'It doesn't matter. Take no notice of me. It's probably a case of the midwinter blues.' He gave her a tight smile as he let go of her hand and started to walk back up the path, but if he thought he could fob her off like that he could think again.

'Of course it matters!' Molly declared fiercely. She stepped directly in his path so that he was forced to stop. 'It's obvious that something's troubling you, Sean, so what is it? Surely it can't be whether or not to buy yourself a house. I mean, that would be crazy!'

'Maybe it seems crazy to you, but the situation is far more complicated than it appears.'

He gently eased her aside but there was such pain on his face that Molly knew she couldn't let him leave. Catching hold of his arm, she held him fast. Maybe it didn't have anything to do with her but Sean was hurting and she wanted to help him any way she could.

'Then tell me about it.' She stared into his eyes, willing him to trust her, wondering if he would. 'I know things haven't been exactly easy between us, Sean, but I want to help you. Really I do.'

Sean leant forward in the chair, warming his hands in the heat coming from the fire. He felt cold to the core, as though his very flesh and bones had turned to ice. The rational part of his brain knew that he'd been mad to let Molly persuade him to come home with her but the other part didn't care. He couldn't bear it if he had to spend the rest of his days eaten up by guilt for the part he had played in Claire's death. For ten long years he had kept it to himself; even his family didn't know the full story. But maybe it was time that he brought it all out into the open and faced the criticism that would undoubtedly follow. It had to be better than living like this—knowing he was to blame and constantly trying to avoid thinking about it.

'Here we go. Hot chocolate to warm us up. I don't know about you but I'm absolutely frozen!'

Molly came back with a tray bearing two steaming mugs of chocolate. Sean nodded his thanks as she placed one of the mugs on the table next to his chair. Going over to the sofa, she sat down, curling her legs under her, and the very normality of the scene helped to ease a little of the tension that gripped him. Reaching for his own mug, he cradled it between his hands, relishing the heat that flowed through his icy fingertips. He had no idea what Molly would think once he told her the whole sorry tale; he would just have to deal with it whichever way he could.

'So, are you going to tell me what's wrong?'

Her voice was gentle. Sean knew that if he changed his mind she wouldn't push him. It was up to him if he confessed what he had done—how his actions had resulted in the death of the woman he had been planning to marry. Just for a moment, he wavered, unsure if he could face the condemnation that would surely follow. However, the thought of continually feeling this way was more than he could bear. Even facing Molly's revulsion couldn't be any worse than this.

'It's all to do with Claire and what happened to her.' He placed the mug on the table when he felt his hands start to tremble. The only way he would get through this was by keeping a tight rein on his emotions. Once he lost control of them then all the remorse and guilt that had consumed him these past years would come spilling out and he couldn't bear to think that Molly would witness it.

'Who was she? Your girlfriend, I assume.' Molly's voice was just as gentle and undemanding and Sean felt a little more tension seep out of him.

'Yes. Well, she was my fiancée, actually. We were childhood sweethearts; I suppose that's how people would describe us. Our parents were friends so we grew up together. We were both only children, you see, and it was great to have a sort of surrogate sister to play with.'

'I see. I can understand how close you must have been,' she said softly.

'We were, very close, right through school and on into university. Claire studied law at Liverpool while I went to Cambridge and did medicine so we didn't see much of one another, but it didn't make any difference. We just picked up where we'd left off whenever we met up.' He shrugged. 'It seemed only natural that we should get engaged once we had qualified. Both our families were thrilled, as you might expect, and set about planning our wedding.'

He tailed off, not sure how to tell her the rest. What would Molly think once he told her the truth? Would she blame him, as he blamed himself? Even though it shouldn't have mattered what she thought, he knew deep in his heart that it did.

'We were both working incredibly hard, trying to establish our careers,' he continued before his courage deserted him. 'Claire had been accepted for pupillage at a leading firm of barristers in London and I was working as a junior registrar at a London hospital in A&E. Although we shared a flat, we actually saw very little of one another.'

'It's difficult to find time for a relationship when you're starting out on your career,' Molly agreed, and he sighed.

'That's what I told myself, especially when we fell out, as we seemed to do with increasing frequency. I told myself that we just needed to get through the next few months and it would get easier once we were married, but the situation grew worse, if anything. It got so bad that I avoided going home some nights, just to get a break from all the arguing. And then one night Claire phoned me at work and told me that she needed to speak to me urgently. I wasn't off duty until eight p.m. so I arranged to meet her at a bar we sometimes went to.

'It was one of those nights you learn to dread, as it turned out. Dozens of patients, all with major complications. There was no chance of my being able to leave on time so I phoned Claire and explained that I couldn't make it. She was already there, waiting for me, and I could tell she was upset when I cancelled, but there was nothing I could do about it.'

He broke off, steeling himself to tell Molly the rest of the story. He had reached the real crux of his tale, the part that he found it the most difficult to voice. He took a steadying breath before he continued in a voice that was devoid of any emotion.

'That was the last time I ever spoke to her. She left the bar a short time later and was hit by a taxi while she was crossing the road. She died instantly. One of the bar staff said at the inquest that she had been crying when she had left—and that was all down to me, Molly. If I hadn't been so curt with her then she would never have stepped in front of that cab.'

CHAPTER NINE

MOLLY HAD NO idea what to say. She was so stunned by what Sean had told her that her thoughts were in a complete turmoil. And then, slowly, one thought rose through all the confusion in her head: Sean wasn't to blame. It had been an accident, a tragic and terrible accident.

'It wasn't your fault!' She got up from the sofa and went to kneel beside his chair. 'It was an accident, Sean, awful, I know, but you can't blame yourself for what happened.'

'No? So why does it feel like it's my fault?' He shook his head. 'No, if I hadn't been so offhand with her then Claire would never have got so upset. She'd told me that she needed to speak to me urgently and I should have realised that it had to be something really important.'

'Do you have any idea what she wanted to tell you?' Molly asked hesitantly then immediately wished that she hadn't when she saw how tormented he looked.

'Oh, yes. It came out at the inquest.' He took a deep breath but she could hear the torment in his voice. 'Claire was pregnant when she was killed—roughly eight weeks, according to the coroner. I had no idea but it makes no difference, does it? I'm not only responsible for Claire's death but for the death of our baby as well.'

Molly couldn't think of anything to say. The sheer horror of what he must have been through was simply too much to take in. And it was obvious that Sean had misinterpreted her silence. He laughed harshly as he stood up.

'I can tell by your expression what you think, Molly, and I don't blame you. I mean, what kind of a man doesn't even suspect his fiancée is pregnant, especially when she's sending out all the right signals?'

'Wh…what sort of signals?' she murmured, getting to her feet as well.

'All the rows, of course. Claire was never the sort of person to start an argument—she was far too quiet. I should have realised that something was going on and made her tell me what it was, but I was too preoccupied with my job and with making a good impression.'

'But that's ridiculous! You had no way of knowing that she was pregnant unless she chose to tell you. I mean, why did she wait so long? Surely it would have been far more in character for her to tell you the moment she suspected that she might be having a baby?'

'She probably would have done if I hadn't been so completely wrapped up in my work.' He gave her a grim smile. 'I was far too busy to find the time to sit down and talk to her.'

'She must have been busy too,' Molly pointed out. 'You said that you were both trying to make a go of your careers.'

'Yes. But it doesn't negate what I did or, rather, what I didn't do. I wasn't there when Claire needed me and because of that she and the baby died.' His voice broke. 'And I will have to live with that every day of my life.'

Molly acted instinctively then. Perhaps if she had been thinking clearly she wouldn't have done what she did but every instinct she possessed was urging her to comfort him. Reaching out, she drew him into her arms and held him, simply held him, hoping that he might take comfort from the closeness of another human being. She had never suspected that Sean—live-for-the-moment Sean—was carrying such a burden around with him, but somehow she had to make him understand that he wasn't to blame for what had happened.

If she could.

The thought that he might live out the rest of his days blaming himself for the tragedy brought a rush of tears to her eyes. Molly tried to hold them back but more kept on coming, pouring down her face in a relentless torrent. She realised all of a sudden that

she wasn't crying only for him but for herself as well.
Sean must have loved Claire so very much, far more
than he could ever have loved her, and it was almost
too painful to bear to know that she could never have
matched the other woman in his affections.

'Molly?' She felt him go still before he slowly
set her away from him. Bending, he looked into her
face. 'You're crying.'

'Take no notice.' She sniffed loudly, hunting in
her pocket for a tissue and typically not finding one.
She couldn't bear it if he guessed just how devastated she felt, couldn't add to his burden in any way.
It wasn't Sean's fault that his heart belonged to another woman.

'Here.' Sean plucked a tissue from the box on
the coffee table but, instead of handing it to her, he
tipped up her face and gently wiped away her tears.
Tossing the soggy tissue into the waste bin, he smiled
at her. 'Better now?'

'Yes. Thank you.' She went to move away but his
hands fastened lightly around the top of her arms
and held her fast.

'I'm sorry, Molly. I never meant to upset you like
this.'

'I know. It's just that I can't bear to think of you
blaming yourself when there's no need,' she said,
deliberately blanking out any thoughts about how
she felt. It was Sean who needed consoling, not her.

'Isn't there?' He sighed as he drew her into his

arms and held her against him. 'I wish I could believe that.'

'Then you must try harder,' she said fiercely. She pulled back and glared at him, determined to make him see sense. 'It was an accident, Sean. A tragic accident, but you weren't to blame!'

'Oh, Molly, I want to believe you. Really I do.'

He drew her to him once more, planting a gentle kiss on her cheek. It was meant to be no more than a token, a simple expression of gratitude for her support, and it might have remained that way too if she hadn't chosen that precise moment to turn her head. Molly froze when she felt his lips glide from her cheek and come to rest at the corner of her mouth. She knew that she should do something to stop what was happening, but it was as though her body was suddenly refusing to obey her. When his lips started to move again, but deliberately this time, she could only stand there, motionless.

His mouth found hers and she heard him sigh, felt the warm expulsion of his breath on her lips, and it was that which broke the spell. However, if she'd hoped that it would bring her to her senses she was mistaken. Her lips seemed to possess a will of their own as they clung to his, eagerly inviting him to continue. And he did.

Molly moaned when she felt the tip of his tongue start to explore the contours of her mouth. She could taste the richness of the chocolate he had drunk on his tongue and it merely heightened her desire for him. Opening her mouth, she allowed him all the licence he needed to deepen the kiss and he wasn't slow to take advantage. They were both breathing heavily when they broke apart, both shaken by the speed and the depth of their need for one another. They might not have planned on kissing but Molly knew that neither of them could deny that it had had a profound effect on them both.

'I didn't mean for this to happen, Molly.'

'I know.' She gave a little shrug then stilled when she felt desire scud through her once more as his hands slid from her shoulders and down her arms. It had always been this way, she thought sadly. Sean had only needed to touch her and her blood had raced. And the most terrifying realisation of all was that nothing had changed.

'I never planned it either,' she said huskily, trying to damp down the fear that engulfed her. She didn't want to feel how she had felt two years ago, definitely didn't want to risk having her heart broken once more. Now, more than ever, she needed to be sensible—now that she knew about Claire. She had to nip these feelings in the bud before they could grow into something even bigger and far more dangerous.

'I suppose we should put it down to the heat of the moment. Everything got a bit tense just now, didn't it?' His hands skimmed back up her arms and came to rest against her collarbone. Molly could feel the coolness of his fingers seeping into her heated flesh through the thickness of her woollen sweater and shivered.

'It did.' She dredged up a smile. 'My crying like that probably didn't help either. Sorry.'

'Don't apologise. I was touched that you felt that way.' He returned her smile. 'You always did have a tender heart, Molly.'

'In other words, I was a soft touch,' she retorted, deliberately whipping up her anger in the hope that it would help set her back on track. 'It's a good job I've decided to make some changes to how I behave. There will be no more wearing my heart on my sleeve in future, believe me!'

'So today was a one-off, was it? You'll be hard-hearted Molly from now on?'

'Yes!' Molly declared roundly when she heard the teasing note in his voice and realised that he didn't believe her. The last thing she wanted was for Sean to think she was a pushover. 'I'm going to concentrate on what *I* want for a change.'

'Then I'm glad that we had this conversation today.' He brushed his knuckles down her cheek. 'I feel a lot better than I did, Molly, and it's all thanks to you.'

'I'm glad,' she said huskily, so touched by the admission that her anger immediately melted away. 'So does that mean you'll think about what I said, about you not being to blame? It was an accident, Sean, and it wasn't your fault.'

'I'll try.'

Although he agreed readily enough, Molly had a feeling that it would never actually happen. Sean was determined to blame himself for the tragedy and it hurt to know that his life would be blighted for ever by it. Reaching up, she cupped his face between her hands.

'Then you must try really hard!' Her voice caught. 'I can't bear to think of you ruining your life this way.'

'Oh, Molly!'

Turning, he pressed his mouth against her palm and she shuddered when she felt desire spike through her once more. When she felt the tip of his tongue start to stroke her skin, she moaned softly. It was almost too much to feel the light moist pressure of his tongue caressing her flesh. Closing her eyes, she gave herself up to the moment, blanking out any thoughts about the wisdom of what she was doing. She didn't want to think—she just wanted to feel.

The tip of his tongue moved from her palm to her wrist, lavishing it with the same attention. Molly had never realised before that her wrist could be an erogenous zone and closed her eyes, savouring the moment. Kisses were fine but this was different. This gentle act of seduction implied an intimacy that she had never expected. Maybe she was mistaken but she couldn't imagine that Sean had done this with many women.

The thought filled her with a sudden sense of peace. One of the hardest things to deal with had been the thought that she had been just one of many women in Sean's life. However, the gentle pressure of his tongue as it moved over the delicate inner skin of her wrist put paid to that; it made her feel special. Wanted. Cherished.

He raised his head and his eyes were so dark that they appeared almost black as he looked at her. 'I know I shouldn't be doing this but I can't help myself,' he said hoarsely. 'Tell me to stop, Molly, if it isn't what you want.'

Molly bit her lip, unsure of what she wanted. Oh, she didn't want him to stop—that was a given. But was it wise to let this go any further, to risk falling under his spell all over again? He had hurt her so badly and she didn't think that she could go back to that dark place again. But if she called a halt then would she regret it, always wish that she had taken the risk in the hope that it might bring her closure?

'I don't know what I want, Sean. Part of me is terrified at the thought of feeling like I did two years ago. I can't go back there. I don't think I could bear it.'

'Oh, sweetheart, don't! Please don't upset yourself because I behaved like such a crass idiot.' He tipped up her chin and kissed her lightly on the mouth. 'I regret it more than I can ever tell you, Molly.'

'Do you?' she whispered, her blood humming inside her veins at the feel of his lips on hers.

'Yes. I hurt you and I never meant to do that. It's just that I found it so hard to do what was right.' He brushed her mouth with another sensual kiss. 'I knew I should end our relationship but I kept putting it off, and there's no excuse for that.'

'Why did you keep putting it off?' she asked, her breath coming in rapid little spurts so that it sounded as though she was having difficulty breathing, which she was. Being held in Sean's arms like this, having him kiss her, was making her feel breathless… *As well as a lot of other things*.

Sean knew that he shouldn't answer that question. Admitting that he had delayed ending their relationship because he couldn't bear to part with her wouldn't help either of them. It was all in the past and it should remain in the past too. And yet some tiny part of his brain was insisting that he told Molly the truth, that he should hold up his hands and confess why he'd had such problems letting her go. Surely he owed her that much at the very least?

'Because I hated the thought of being without you.' He rested his forehead against hers, not wanting to look into her eyes in case he weakened. 'That time we spent together was one of the happiest times of my life and I wanted it to continue, even though I knew it couldn't.'

'Because of Claire?'

He heard the catch in her voice and hated to think that he might be causing her yet more pain. But it was two years since they'd parted: she'd had two years to get over him. The thought helped to steady him even if it didn't come as the relief it should have been.

'Yes. I made a vow after Claire died that I would remain true to her memory and I can't break it, Molly, not for any reason or anyone.'

'I understand, Sean. Really I do.'

She stepped back, deliberately setting some distance between them, and Sean had to stop himself hauling her back into his arms and telling her that he had changed his mind. He felt bereft without her in his arms, empty, incomplete. It took every atom of willpower he could muster not to say too much but he mustn't mislead her. After the heat of the moment had passed then he would regret breaking his vow...

Wouldn't he?

'Thank you.' His voice grated and he cleared his throat, unable to deal with all the conflicting emotions rioting around inside him. Did he really want to let Claire go and look to the future? Could he bear to do so when he might be consumed by guilt for ever? He had to be sure because he couldn't play with Molly's emotions, couldn't lead her to believe that they had a future together when in all likelihood it wouldn't amount to anything.

'There's nothing to thank me for.' She gave a little shrug and he almost weakened when he realised how brave she was being. However, it would be wrong to allow this to go any further, so very wrong to risk hurting her all over again.

Sean's heart was heavy as he said goodbye and made his way to the door. Molly saw him out although she didn't wait to wave him off, not that he could blame her. She was probably glad to see the back of him after what he had told her. He stood in the road for a moment, sucking in great gulps of the frosty air. It should have been a relief to tell her about Claire and explain his reasons for breaking up with her but it wasn't relief he felt. Not right now anyway. Maybe relief would come later but at the moment all he felt was a deep sense of sadness for what he could have had if things had been different.

If he hadn't made that vow then he could have had Molly in his life. For ever and always.

CHAPTER TEN

SURPRISINGLY, SEAN DISCOVERED that he did feel better after his talk with Molly. He wasn't sure why when it had thrown up so many other issues but it felt as though some of the weight had been lifted off his shoulders. There was a definite spring to his step when he went into work two days later but, sadly, it didn't last very long. One glimpse of Molly chatting to Adam Humphreys soon put paid to it. Even though he knew it was wrong, he hated to see her with another man.

Fortunately, the department was as busy as ever so he had no time to brood. There'd been a car crash on the bypass which resulted in several casualties being brought in at more or less the same time. Molly was doing triage that day and she quickly dispensed with the less seriously injured, leaving him to deal with the rest. However, it was only when the paramedics rushed the trolley into Resus that Sean discovered one of the casualties was Joyce Summers, the most senior Sister on the unit.

'Let's get her on the bed.' Sean did the count as they quickly moved Joyce off the trolley. She was receiving oxygen as her Sats were worryingly low. She was unconscious and had been since the paramedics had arrived at the scene. She had suffered a serious head injury and Sean's heart sank as he ordered a CT scan because he knew it would be touch and go whether she pulled through. Molly had followed the ambulance crew into Resus and she asked if she could accompany Joyce to Radiography.

'Of course,' Sean agreed immediately. He sighed as he watched her help the porters wheel the bed out of Resus. If Joyce didn't make it then he knew that Molly would be terribly upset and he hated to think of her suffering that way.

He forced his mind back to the job as he set about dealing with the second casualty, a young man called Sam Prentice who, thankfully, wasn't as seriously injured. He had several broken ribs which were causing him some problems breathing. Sean suspected—rightly so—that Sam had a haemothorax and set about sorting it out with the help of Steph Collins, their F1 student. It was the first time that Steph had performed the procedure so Sean guided her through it, showing her how to insert the needle through the tough intercostal muscles between the patient's ribs while they drew off the blood that had collected in the pleural cavity and was compromising Sam's breathing. By the time they had done that,

Joyce was back so Sean left Steph to keep an eye on their patient while he went to check the results of the CT scan. It was immediately apparent that it wasn't good news.

'Heavy bleeding on the left side of the brain,' Sean observed, pointing to the area in question. 'The blow to the right side of her head must have carried enough force to knock the brain sideways and cause it to collide with her skull. She's going to need immediate surgery.'

'What are her chances?' Molly asked and his heart ached when he heard the catch in her voice.

'Not good, I'm afraid.' He sighed. 'The bleed is extensive and even if the surgeon manages to stop it then there's probably going to be extensive brain damage.'

'It's so unfair. Joyce is due to retire this Christmas and she and her husband have a whole list of things they are planning to do, including her dream holiday, cruising around the Caribbean.'

'You're right. It isn't fair,' Sean said quietly. He dredged up a smile, wishing there was more he could say by way of comfort. However, he understood better than most how one's plans could alter in mere seconds. 'All we can do is hope that things aren't as bad as they appear.'

Molly didn't say anything. Sean suspected that she didn't believe it any more than he did. He went to the phone and asked for one of the neurosurgical team to attend, aware that his efforts to reassure Molly had failed dismally. He sighed. There was very little else he could have said as it wouldn't have been fair to raise her hopes but it didn't stop him feeling bad about it.

He frowned as that thought sank into his consciousness. If only he had thought harder about being fair when they had been seeing one another then maybe he wouldn't have ended up making such a hash of things. He had known for weeks that he should end their affair but he had kept putting it off because he hadn't wanted to let her go. He had behaved with the utmost selfishness and he would always regret it.

Molly deserved someone better than him, someone without all his attendant baggage. Someone like Adam Humphreys, for instance—steady, reliable, ready and eager to make a commitment. Quite frankly, he should be glad that she had met someone like Humphreys but as he went back to his patient Sean knew that it wasn't happiness he felt, not by a long chalk. Right or wrong, but he couldn't bear the thought of Molly falling in love with the other man.

Sean tried to put that thought out of his mind but, typically, it seemed that Humphreys was never out of the department. Every time he turned round, he spotted Molly and Humphreys chatting to one another. Fair enough, most of their conversation was related to their patients but Sean could feel his irritation rising each time he came across them. Surely the guy could tell that he needed to give Molly some breathing space rather than…than bombard her this way! He did his best to ignore them but when he happened to overhear Humphreys inviting her out for dinner that coming Friday, he finally flipped. No way was Molly spending the evening with Humphreys. Not while there was any breath left in his body!

'I hate to butt in, guys, but you already have plans for Friday, Molly.' He smiled as Molly turned to him in surprise. 'It's Bert and Doris's wedding reception—remember?'

'I'm sure they aren't really expecting us to go,' Molly said shortly, glaring at him. 'They probably only asked us for politeness' sake.'

'Not at all.' Sean held his smile although the way Molly was glowering at him would have made a less determined man waver. 'In fact, Bert assured me that they're both looking forward to seeing us there.'

It was only the smallest distortion of the truth but Sean crossed his fingers anyway. Bert had said that he and Doris would be delighted to see them when he had issued the invitation but he had no intention of explaining that to Molly.

'When did you speak to him?' Molly demanded.

'Oh, I'm not sure—a few days ago,' Sean replied, crossing the fingers on his other hand as well. 'It doesn't really matter, does it? I mean I'd hate to disappoint them, wouldn't you?' He turned to Humphreys and grimaced. 'Sorry to scupper your plans, and all that. But it's important to keep a promise, don't you agree?'

'I…erm… Yes, of course.' Adam Humphreys both looked and sounded decidedly put out but Sean didn't care.

Sean turned to Molly, smiling winningly at her.

'We'll sort out the time nearer to the day. At least I won't have to drive very far to pick you up.' He laughed. 'I'm moving into the cottage this week so we'll be living just around the corner from each other very soon.'

He didn't say anything else as he went to fetch his next patient; however, he could tell that Molly was seething about the way he had railroaded her into falling in with his plans. Tough luck, he thought, as he headed to Reception. Although Humphreys might appear perfect on paper, he wasn't right for Molly. He was convinced about that—

'What the hell do you think you're doing?'

Sean stopped dead when Molly came hurrying after him. That she was furiously angry was obvious and he experienced a momentary qualm. Maybe he shouldn't have interfered like that but the thought of her and Humphreys getting cosy was more than he could swallow. He adopted an expression of bewilderment as he turned to face her.

'I'm sorry…?'

'Don't give me that!' She put her hands on her hips

and glared at him. 'You know exactly what you've done. You, quite deliberately too, came up with that to stop me going out with Adam, didn't you?'

'I merely reminded you that you had a previous engagement,' Sean replied in his most ingenuous tone. He shrugged. 'I'm sure you don't want to disappoint Bert and Doris, do you?'

'No. But that's not the point, is it?'

'Isn't it? So why do you imagine I butted in to your conversation like that?' he said evenly although his heart was thumping. Did he really want Molly to guess just how much he hated the thought of her dating Humphreys when it would give rise to so many awkward questions?

'I have no idea,' she began and then stopped abruptly when a middle-aged man came hurrying in through the main doors. 'Oh, that's Joyce's husband—Ted. He's going to be devastated when he finds out what's happened to her.'

'Take him into the relatives' room and we'll talk to him in there,' Sean said quickly, hating himself for feeling so relieved at the interruption. 'Once we've explained what's happened then maybe you can take him up to Recovery. Joyce should be finished in Theatre soon and I'm sure he will want to see her.'

'What if she didn't make it?' Molly said with a catch in her voice.

'Then we would have heard by now.' He reached

over and squeezed her hand. 'I left a message with the theatre sister to phone us if anything happened.'

'Oh, right. Well, I suppose that's a good sign,' she said quietly.

Sean let her go, watching as she hurried over to Joyce's husband and led him towards the relatives' room. He went to the phone and called Recovery to get an update on Joyce's condition. She had come through the operation successfully but she was being kept sedated as it was hoped that it would help her brain to heal. Although the person he spoke to didn't say as much, he knew that it was still touch and go. Now he had to try and explain all of that to Joyce's husband the least stressful way he could.

Molly sat quietly as she listened to Sean explaining the extent of Joyce's injuries to Ted Summers. He didn't try to paint a brighter picture but carefully and methodically outlined the difficulties Joyce faced. Molly's heart ached when she heard the compassion in his voice. Sean had always been marvellous with grieving relatives and now she understood why he was able to empathise with them to such an extent. He had been on the receiving end of devastating news like this when Claire had died and he had first-hand knowledge of how it felt to have your hopes and dreams ripped apart.

It made her anger over the way he had butted into her conversation with Adam seem very trivial. Maybe she didn't understand his reasons for doing so but it obviously wasn't jealousy at the thought of her and Adam going out together, not when she could hear the underlying grief in his voice. Sean was re-membering Claire, recalling how devastated he had felt when he had lost her; how devastated he still felt, in fact. Molly found herself suddenly wishing with every fibre of her being that one day he would be able to move on, even if she wouldn't be around to help him.

'I'm sorry the news isn't better, Ted. All I can say is that Joyce has come this far and that's a positive sign.' Sean stood up, bringing an end to the meet-ing. 'I'm sure you must want to see her so Molly is going to take you to Recovery. Joyce will be moved from there to ICU very shortly.'

'Thank you.' Ted Summers rose shakily to his feet. He looked completely poleaxed by what he had heard and Molly hurriedly got up and put a guiding hand under his elbow to lead him to the door.

'There's no need to rush back, Molly. It's not that busy in here so take as long as you need.'

'Right. Thank you.' Molly glanced back, feeling her heart scrunch up inside her. It was only Sean who could make the decision to put the past behind him; no one else could make it for him. And the thought that he might never get over losing Claire was so painful that it was hard to hide how much it upset her.

'Are you all right?' he said softly and she knew

that he had noticed she was upset but had assumed it was because of Joyce.

'Yes. I'm fine.'

She turned away, not wanting to burden him with her feelings. Sean had enough to contend with and it would be wrong to encumber him with anything else. She had to deal with her own emotions and come to terms with the situation as it was. The sooner she did that too, the better.

The rest of the week passed and Friday rolled around. Molly had seen very little of Sean, as it happened. He had agreed to swap shifts with his opposite number, who needed time off that coming weekend to visit an ailing relative. While she was glad of the respite, she had to admit that she missed him. Sean was fun to have around, always bright and cheerful and ready to lend a hand. In fact, the department didn't seem the same without him, although maybe it was a good thing that he wasn't there if it gave her a chance to get used to being without him. She must never forget that Sean's time in Dalverston was strictly limited.

By the time she left work on Friday evening, Sean still hadn't contacted her to arrange when he would pick her up to attend Bert and Doris's wedding reception. Molly made her way home, assuring herself that she was relieved that he had apparently changed his mind. An evening watching the box was far preferable to one spent agonising over matters she couldn't change.

She changed into a comfy old tracksuit and settled down in front of the television with her supper on a tray. When the doorbell rang she was engrossed in the latest episode of her favourite soap opera and reluctantly got up to answer it. She'd had several visits from local children out carol singing so she fetched her purse before opening the door then gasped in surprise when she found Sean standing on her step.

'What are you doing here?'

'Collecting you so we can go to Bert and Doris's do.' He frowned as he took stock of what she was wearing. 'I'm sorry. Am I too early?'

'Seeing as we never agreed on a time, then no, you aren't,' Molly replied testily, overwhelmingly aware of how awful she looked in the ratty old tracksuit.

'Oh, no! I never phoned you, did I?' He slapped his forehead with the palm of his hand. 'I've been so busy moving my stuff into the cottage that it went straight out of my mind. Sorry!'

'It's OK.' Molly shrugged, not wanting it to appear as though it mattered an iota. Nevertheless, the thought that she was so easily forgettable didn't exactly cheer her up. She pushed that foolish thought aside. 'As you can see, I'm not ready so it's probably best if you go without me...'

'Not at all,' Sean said quickly. 'There's plenty of time for you to get changed.' He held up his hand when she started to speak. 'I know for a fact that Bert and Doris will be very disappointed if you don't go tonight, Molly.' His voice dropped, sounding so deep and seductive that a shiver ran through her. 'Me too. I've been looking forward to this evening all week.'

Molly knew that she should stand firm but the note of longing in his voice was her undoing. Stepping back, she ushered him into the sitting room, telling herself that it was ridiculous to imagine that Sean was so desperate for her company. It was probably one of his many ruses, she told herself as she hurried upstairs. A trick he had used umpteen times before to get his own way. However, despite all that, she simply couldn't find it in her heart to refuse to go with him and she sighed as she went into the bathroom and turned on the shower. Where Sean was concerned, she was like putty in his hands—pliable, malleable and far too easily led astray!

CHAPTER ELEVEN

THE GREEN MAN was crowded when they arrived. It appeared that Bert and Doris had invited every single person they knew to help them celebrate their marriage. Sean grabbed hold of Molly's hand as they made their way through the fray to where their hosts were seated, not wanting them to become separated. It had been pure good luck that he had managed to persuade her to come tonight after that mistake he had made and he didn't intend to waste a single precious second of her company.

He glanced at her, feeling his heart lift as once again he found himself thinking how lovely she looked. She had chosen a slim-fitting deep green dress for the occasion. If he'd been better versed in fashion-speak he would have been able to describe it in detail but all he knew was that the soft velvety fabric clung to every delectable curve. She was wearing high-heeled shoes and her legs looked fabulous—long and shapely—as she led the way through a gap in the crowd.

Sean swallowed a sigh as he forced his gaze away from the enticing curve of her calves. She looked gorgeous and, what was more, she *was* gorgeous inside and out. No wonder he was having the devil of a job behaving sensibly. One of the reasons why he had agreed to swap shifts was the fact that it would give him a breathing space. Taking some time out away from Molly had seemed propitious and it had worked too. Or it had done until she had opened the door tonight and he had found himself right back where he had started; right back where he had left off two years ago, if he was honest. It couldn't carry on this way—he couldn't cope! At some point he would have to make some decisions about what he intended to do, but not tonight. Tonight he was just going to enjoy being with her.

'So you made it. That's grand, that is. We did wonder if you'd come as we know how busy you both must be, what with your work and everything.' Bert Feathers beamed in delight as he stood up to greet them and Sean hastily returned his thoughts to the reason why they were there. Bending, he kissed Doris's cheek.

'We've been really looking forward to tonight, haven't we, Molly?' Sean said as he straightened up.

'I…um… Yes, of course.' Molly bent and kissed Doris then gave Bert a kiss as well. 'Congratulations to you both. I'm sure you'll be very happy together.'

'Oh, there's no doubt about that!' Bert laughed as

he sat down and squeezed Doris's hand. 'We plan to make the most of whatever time we have left, don't we, love, starting tomorrow with our honeymoon.'

'Where are you going?' Sean asked, trying to hide his chagrin at the way Molly had hesitated. He knew that he had railroaded her into coming with him so it shouldn't have been a surprise if she appeared less than thrilled about spending the evening with him; however, the thought that she would have preferred Humphreys' company to his didn't sit easily with him.

'The Canary Islands. We're flying to Tenerife in the morning and spending Christmas and New Year there,' Bert informed them happily. 'I've never been on a plane before, never even had a holiday, in fact, unless you count a day trip to Scarborough when I was a lad, so this will be a first for me. I'm right looking forward to it, too. So's Doris.'

'How wonderful!' Sean exclaimed, genuinely delighted for them. Another couple of guests came over to speak to them at that moment so he and Molly moved aside. People were milling about, chatting to friends or sampling the buffet which had been arranged on long trestle tables at the far side of the room. Sean grimaced when his stomach rolled at the thought of the delicious-looking spread and he saw Molly look at him.

'I never got chance to eat anything today. I was

too busy putting things away into cupboards and drawers and forgot all about lunch.'

'Why don't you get something now?' she suggested, leading the way to the buffet tables. Picking up a plate and some napkin-wrapped cutlery, she handed them to him, snatching her hand away when their fingers accidentally touched. 'It all looks delicious,' she declared but Sean could hear the quaver in her voice and didn't know whether to be pleased or sorry. Obviously, Molly wasn't as indifferent to him as she was making out.

'Aren't you having anything?' he asked, trying to batten down the rush of emotions that hit him at that idea. Did he want her to feel something for him or not? Quite frankly, he couldn't decide or, rather, he chose not to arrive at a conclusion. It was too risky to do that, to examine his feelings and come up with an answer that might only complicate matters even further.

'How about some of this smoked salmon?' he suggested, spearing a morsel on the end of his fork. He offered it to her and smiled, praying that she couldn't tell how ambivalent he felt, how confused. He wanted her so much but he couldn't have her unless he broke his vow to Claire. And the thought tore him in two. 'You always loved smoked salmon, didn't you?' he added inanely because he needed to keep talking, otherwise he might do something really stupid. He couldn't promise Molly the earth when it wasn't his to give.

'Yes, I did.' She looked back at him and Sean could see a host of memories in her eyes, recollections of all the other times when they had eaten together, laughed together, got to know one another's likes and dislikes. When she leant forward and delicately closed her lips around the morsel of food Sean felt the blood surge through his veins. There in a room filled with people laughing and enjoying themselves, he and Molly stood alone, set apart from everyone else by their memories. He knew then that he would always remember this moment because it was when he realised that he wouldn't have changed what had happened between them even if he could have done. That time he had spent with Molly was far too precious; he needed the memory of it far too much. It was the one bright and shining period to come out of all these long years of darkness and despair.

Molly could taste the savoury tang of the salmon on her tongue and shuddered. She wasn't sure why she had done that—leant forward and accepted the treat Sean had offered her. The action smacked of an intimacy that she knew she shouldn't encourage and yet she had still done it, hadn't she? Why? Did she want to experience their former closeness once more when it would mean risking getting hurt all over again? Surely she wasn't so foolish as to imagine that this time it would be different, that this time

Sean would want her to remain in his life for good? After what she had learned about Claire, the possibility of that happening was zero.

Picking up a plate, Molly started to fill it with delicacies even though the thought of actually eating any of it made her feel sick. However, it was something to do, something normal and stress-free, and that was what she needed desperately. Sean had loaded his plate with a selection of goodies and was looking round for somewhere to sit down; he nodded towards a couple of vacant chairs in the corner near the window.

'Let's go over there while we eat this little lot,' he suggested, leading the way.

Molly followed him in silence, half afraid that all the thoughts whizzing around inside her head would somehow pop out into the open. It wasn't Sean's fault if he could never love her like he had loved Claire and it would be wrong to make him feel guilty about it. Sitting down, she spread the paper napkin over her lap then balanced her plate on her knees, hoping that she would manage to eat some of the food she had collected.

'Mmm, this is delicious. Did you pick up one of these?'

Sean showed her a tiny pastry tart filled with cream cheese and prawns and Molly shook her head then swallowed as a wave of nausea suddenly struck her.

'No? Then have this one. I picked up two, greedy guts that I am, so it's only fair that I share them with you.' He went to pop the tartlet on her plate but Molly pushed his hand away.

'No! I… I don't like prawns,' she muttered, using the first excuse she could come up with to explain why she'd been so abrupt.

'Really?' Sean frowned, his dark brows drawing together as he stared at her in surprise. 'Since when? You used to love prawns. Why, they were your favourite sandwich filling. Whenever I asked you what you wanted from the canteen, it was always a prawn mayonnaise sandwich.'

'I probably ate so many that I sickened myself of them,' Molly said snappily, wishing that he didn't have such excellent recall. Was he going to dredge up every itty-bitty scrap of information about her? she thought sourly, then realised how contrary she was being. The fact that Sean remembered which sandwiches she had liked should have been a boost to her ego. It proved that he hadn't simply dismissed her from his mind the minute he had left Dalverston, as she had imagined.

The thought was unsettling, far too unsettling to explore at that moment. Molly concentrated on her supper and managed to eat at least some of the food on her plate. Sean was tucking in with gusto and sighed with contentment when the last morsel had disappeared.

'That was delicious. Best food I've eaten in days. I love living in the cottage but I haven't quite got to grips with the Aga yet.' He groaned. 'I didn't think it was possible to burn water but I managed it. Or rather I burnt the potatoes that were supposed to be boiling in it!'

Molly laughed as well, thinking how handsome he looked as he sat there, his deep blue eyes filled with self-mocking laughter. Sean had never taken himself too seriously. He had such an easy manner about him that both staff and patients alike were always comfortable when he was around. He was very different in that respect from Adam Humphreys. Adam tended to stand very much on ceremony—he was the doctor and he wanted everyone to remember it too. She couldn't imagine Adam laughing at himself like that and it was the last thought she needed when, every time she compared the two men, Sean came out on top.

'You need some lessons,' she said, hurriedly steering her thoughts down a less dangerous track.

'If that's an offer, then yes, please. Both me and my poor stomach would be eternally grateful if you could give me a few tips on how to master the wretched thing.'

'Oh, I…um…' Molly floundered, caught completely off-guard by the suggestion.

'How about tomorrow morning? You're off this

weekend and I'm on a late on Saturday so it would
be perfect.'

He looked so hopeful that Molly found the refusal dying on her lips. After all, what harm could
there be in giving him some pointers about the art
of Aga cooking?

'All right. Around ten, shall we say?'

'Brilliant!' He rolled his eyes lasciviously. 'Oh, I
can't wait to cook myself a meal that doesn't taste—
or smell—as though it's been cremated!'

Molly laughed. Even though he was hamming it
up for all he was worth, it was good to know that
she could help him at least with regard to his cooking skills. As for the rest, well, there was very little
she could do about that.

Thankfully, there was no time to dwell on that
thought as the best man called for silence just then
and asked everyone to raise their glasses to toast
the happy couple. Once that was done, music began
to play and Bert and Doris took to the floor in a
stately and surprisingly accomplished waltz. Other
people started to join in and Molly jumped when
Sean touched her lightly on the arm.

'Fancy a go?' He grinned at her. 'I can't promise
not to tread on your toes but I'll give it my best shot.'

'Why not?' she said because it seemed churl-
ish to refuse when everyone else was dancing. She
followed him onto the dance floor, steeling herself
when he took her in his arms. Even though he was

holding her at arm's length, it wasn't easy to ignore the powerful attraction of his body. They completed a full circuit of the floor, their steps fitting so perfectly that there was no danger of him trampling on her toes. Tossing back her hair, Molly treated him to a mock-fierce stare.

'I think you were spinning me a line, Sean Fitzgerald. You're an excellent dancer so what was that rubbish about not treading on my toes all about?'

'Because on the few occasions when I've attempted to dance like this before, I've left my partner with multiple bruises.' He twirled her round, bending her backwards over his arm and leering comically down at her like some fifth-rate gigolo. 'You, my lovely, have inspired me!'

Molly laughed as he pulled her back up. It was such a load of nonsense and yet she couldn't help enjoying the way he made everything seem like such fun. When the music changed to a much faster rhythm this time, they remained on the floor, simply enjoying the chance to be together in such an undemanding fashion. They were having fun: it was as simple as that. And if she was having more fun because she was with Sean then Molly refused to think about it. It was easier this way. Less complicated. Less painful.

Sean collected Molly's coat from the cloakroom, wishing that the evening didn't have to end. It had been a wonderful night and he wanted it to carry on but everything had to come to an end at some point. Just for a second he found himself refuting that idea. It didn't need to end if he didn't choose to let it. To-night could be the start of a whole lot more wonder-ful nights. All he had to do was make the decision and the future could be his. He could move on with Molly at his side…

If he left Claire behind.

The thought sent a stab of guilt through his guts. It was hard to hide how upset he felt as he went back to find Molly and helped her on with her coat. Bert and Doris were standing by the door, seeing their guests out, and he and Molly kissed them both and wished them well before they left. It was freezing cold out-side, their breath clouding like cartoon speech bub-bles as they hurried to his car. Sean zapped the locks then turned to help Molly into the seat, cursing softly when the car keys slipped out of his numb fingers.

'I'll get them.' Molly bent down to retrieve the keys at the same moment as he did and their heads collided. 'Ouch!' she exclaimed, straightening up.

'I am so sorry!' Sean declared. He turned her so that she was facing the light from a nearby streetlamp and grimaced. 'Oh, dear. It looks as though you're going to end up with a lump on your forehead.'

'Not to worry.' She ran a tentative finger over her forehead and groaned. 'Ooh, that hurts!'

'We'll put some ice on it as soon as we get you

home.' Sean helped her into the car then climbed behind the wheel, feeling dreadful about what had happened. It only took ten minutes to reach her house and he was out of the car and standing beside her door before she could protest. 'No. I am not letting you go without at least trying to make amends for my clumsiness.' He gave her a severe look. 'I mean, what kind of a doctor would I be if I left some poor injured soul to her own devices?'

'It's just a bump, Sean.' She rolled her eyes as she slid out of the car. 'It's not as though my head is in any danger of dropping off!'

'You can't be too careful with head injuries,' he said, adopting his firmest tone. He locked the car and followed her up the path to the front door. 'Are there any ice cubes in your freezer?' he asked once they were inside.

'No. The best I can offer you is a bag of frozen peas.' Molly led the way into her tiny kitchen and opened the freezer door. She handed him a bag of peas. 'Do these meet with your requirements, Dr Fitzgerald?' she asked a shade sarcastically.

'They'll do.' Sean whipped a tea towel off the rack and wrapped the bag of peas in it then told her to sit down, ignoring her huff of annoyance. Maybe he was going over the top but he intended to make up for having injured her even if she didn't appreciate it. Taking care of Molly was just something he needed to do.

The thought that he wouldn't be able to look after her once he left Dalverston whizzed through his brain but he blanked it out. He pressed the make-shift ice pack against her temple and felt her flinch. 'Sorry, did that hurt?' he asked, bending to look at her.

'No. It's just that it's so cold it made me jump.'

Her voice sounded husky and Sean felt a ripple of awareness spread throughout his body. Was it the coldness or his nearness that was making her sound so on edge? he wondered as he continued to hold the ice pack against her temple. The thought that it might be the latter made him shudder too and he strove to get a grip on himself, not an easy thing to do in the circumstances. Standing this close to her, he could smell the delicate floral fragrance of her perfume and his heart ran wild. All of a sudden it wasn't enough to minister to her this way. He wanted to touch her far more intimately, to run his hands over her and let them relearn the luscious curves, the dips and hollows, to lose himself in the wonder of her delectable body. But should he? Could he? Or would he simply be storing up a whole load of heartache for both him and Molly? How could he take what she could give him when he had nothing to offer her in return?

Molly could feel the tension swirling around them and swallowed the sudden knot in her throat. She knew what was happening and had a very good idea what Sean was thinking too. Would he act upon these feelings that filled the air? Would he take her in his arms and make love to her, because that was where this was leading? But was it what she wanted, *really* wanted, when she knew in her heart that it could only end in yet more heartache? At the end of the day, it wouldn't change anything. He would still be in love with Claire, no matter what they did tonight.

The thought brought her back down to earth with a bump. Pushing his hand away, she stood up. It was hard to control her emotions but she refused to make a fool of herself again. Maybe she did want him to make love to her but she couldn't bear the thought of how she would feel afterwards. When he left Dalverston and left her.

'I think it's time you went, don't you?' she said, hearing the strain in her voice but unable to do anything about it.

'Yes.' He put the makeshift compress on the table and took a deep breath. 'I'm sorry, Molly—'

'Don't!' Molly gave a sharp downward thrust of her hand, unable to deal with the thought of him apologising for what had so nearly happened. It would take very little to change her mind and that was something she mustn't do. Until Sean was free of the past then he wouldn't be free to love her or any other woman.

He didn't say anything more as he turned and walked down the hall. Molly followed him out, pausing when he stopped and turned to face her. There was such sadness in his eyes that her heart ached but she couldn't afford to weaken. What it came down to was one simple fact: Sean could never love her while he was in love with someone else.

'I think it's probably best if we forget about tomorrow.' He gave her a quick grin but it was for show rather than a true expression of his feelings. That he was as upset as she was wasn't in any doubt and Molly's aching heart ached all the more. 'I shall muddle through and master that wretched cooker somehow.'

'You will. It's not exactly rocket science, is it?' Molly did her best to play her part in the proceedings; however, the catch in her voice somewhat spoiled her efforts.

'It isn't.' He gave a small shrug then started to open the door before he suddenly swung back to face her. 'I wish things could be different, Molly. Really I do!'

Molly had no time to react when he pulled her into his arms and kissed her. Maybe she should have pushed him away, remonstrated with him, done *something* to show it wasn't what she wanted, but she was incapable of doing anything at that moment. His lips clung to hers, demanding a response she was powerless to refuse. The kiss might have lasted seconds or hours—she had no idea which it was—but she was trembling when Sean let her go. He didn't say a word as he opened the front door, didn't look back as he got into his car and drove away, but she understood. If he had spoken to her or looked at her then he couldn't have left. He would have had to stay.

Molly was trembling as she closed the door and went and sat down on the stairs. She could tell herself until the moon turned blue that she was glad she hadn't let him make love to her tonight but it would be a lie. She knew that and, what was more, Sean knew it too.

CHAPTER TWELVE

THE NEXT COUPLE of weeks passed in a blur. Sean offered to work extra shifts whenever they were short-staffed and managed to fill up his time to the exclusion of everything else. He did fit in some Christmas shopping on a rare day off, buying presents for his parents as well as some chocolates for the rest of the team in A&E, but that was the full extent of his preparations. Christmas and New Year were always difficult times; they brought it home to him how different his life might have been if Claire hadn't died, although, strangely, he found it less painful this year. The thought that he was moving on, and that it had a lot to do with how he felt about Molly, filled him with guilt.

Although he saw Molly most days in work, he had the distinct impression that she was going out of her way to avoid him. Although they lived only a short distance apart, he never ever bumped into her in the street. He hadn't even seen her driving into work, which struck him as very odd, seeing as they must have driven along the same route. When the thought occurred to him that she might be spending more time with Adam Humphreys, possibly even sleeping at Humphreys' house, it didn't exactly fill Sean with cheer. The sooner his stint at Dalverston was over, the better!

Molly had managed to cram some much-needed Christmas shopping in after work and had parcelled up the presents she intended to send home to her parents and younger sister. She was rostered to work all over the Christmas period so she wouldn't be able to give them their presents in person this year.

She had been due to have New Year off but Joyce's accident had caused problems with the time sheets and she ended up volunteering to work then as well. Although Joyce was still in ICU, she was making some progress and the neurosurgical team were cautiously optimistic. Molly popped in most days to check on her and have a word with Ted, who was constantly at her bedside. His devotion was touching and Molly was sure that if the power of love could affect the outcome then her friend had a very good chance of recovering.

The thought naturally reminded her of Sean but then again he was rarely out of her mind. He was the first thought that popped into her head when she woke each morning and his was the last face she saw before she fell asleep. She had taken to avoiding him, even going to the extent of taking a circuitous route when she drove into work. What had almost happened that night after Bert and Doris's wedding reception had come as a timely warning about how vulnerable she was. Whenever Adam asked her out, she always accepted even though she found him extremely dull company. The fact that their relationship had never moved beyond a courteous peck on the cheek was another indication that there was no spark there, at least on her part. No, Adam definitely didn't ring any bells. Not like Sean had done. And still did.

In an effort to distract herself, Molly packed as much as possible into each and every day. When she wasn't working, she was either cooking or cleaning. Her house sparkled from top to bottom while the fridge and freezer were crammed to overflowing with goodies. Why, if an entire army had descended on her this Christmas, she could have fed them! By the time Christmas Eve arrived there wasn't space for another morsel of food in the house.

She was rostered to work that night but arrived early as she had volunteered to sing in the staff choir. They had decided to dress up in the uniforms that had been worn by nurses during the First World War and there was much hilarity as they donned the floor-length dresses and heavy woollen capes. The caps were the most difficult to master; it took Molly half a dozen attempts before she managed to anchor the starched folds of cotton to her hair and even then she wasn't confident that it would stay on her head. The men had opted to wear soldiers' uniforms and a cheer went up when they marched into the canteen, resplendent in their khaki kit. Molly hadn't realised until that moment that Sean would be with them and her heart leapt when she spotted his tall, muscular figure standing at the back of the group. She couldn't help thinking how impressive he looked in his uniform.

They set off around the hospital, stopping at each ward to sing a selection of well-known carols. The staff dimmed the lights so that they sang in the glow given off by the lanterns they were carrying. It was very atmospheric and Molly noticed several people wiping away a tear or two. By the time they finished doing the rounds, it was declared a resounding success. Molly changed back into her usual attire and made her way to A&E. Sean was already there and he smiled when she went over to the desk.

'Back to normal, I see. Although I have to admit that your previous outfit was very fetching, especially that cap. It was a miracle of engineering!'

'I…erm…thank you.' Molly felt the blush start at her throat and work its way upwards. Reaching over the desk, she snagged the daily report sheet and bent over it, hoping to hide her embarrassment. Just because Sean had paid her a compliment, it wasn't an excuse to start behaving like a giddy teenager.

'Mind you, fetching though the dresses were, I

don't know how the women coped with those long skirts. It must have been a nightmare trying to keep them clean.'

'It must.'

Molly gave him a quick smile then went to check what everyone was doing. There were three nurses working that night, including herself, plus Sean and a locum doctor. Once she was sure that everyone knew what they were doing she went back to the desk, relieved to find that Sean had disappeared. So long as they stuck to work then everything would fine, she assured herself. It was when they got onto more personal issues that the problems started.

The night started off slowly enough and it looked as though it was going to stay that way too. Molly took her break at eleven o'clock and was in the staffroom making herself a cup of coffee when she heard the emergency telephone start to ring. Abandoning her drink, she hurried back to the unit to see what was going on. Sean had taken the call and her heart sank when she saw how grim he looked as he hung up.

'What's happened?' she asked, going straight over to him.

'A private plane has crashed onto the old brewery in the town centre. Apparently, it was heading to Barton airport near Manchester but the pilot reported that they were experiencing engine problems.'

'Oh, no! They renovated the brewery a couple

of years ago and turned it into luxury apartments. Heaven only knows how many people are living there now.'

'Incident control is liaising with the police to try and establish that. It's not going to be easy, mind you. At this time of the year a lot of folk could have gone away to visit relatives or even be on holiday.'

'It's going to be a major task,' Molly agreed. 'So what's the plan? Are you declaring it a major incident and calling in extra staff to deal with the casualties?'

'I don't think I have a choice.' Sean grimaced. 'On Christmas Eve too. I really will be popular.'

Molly left him to speak to the switchboard, who would phone everyone on the list of staff who were down to attend when something like this happened. She called the rest of the team into the office and quickly explained what had happened. By the time that was done, Sean had finished and came to find her.

'Incident control has asked us to send a team to the site. You and I will go, obviously, but we could do with another nurse plus a doctor to make up our numbers. Who do you suggest? I know Steph is on her way in but I can't take her. Apart from the fact that she hasn't done the necessary training, it will leave us short in here.'

'Jayne will be the best person to accompany us,' Molly replied, referring to Jayne Leonard, one of their most experienced staff nurses. She frowned.

'I'm not sure about another doctor— Oh, how about Mac—James MacIntyre, remember him? He used to work here. He's not only done the necessary training but he dealt with all sorts of incidents when he was working overseas for that aid agency. The experience he's gained from that could be very useful.'

'Great! I remember Mac from when I last worked here. He was a first rate doctor too.' Sean frowned. 'How come he doesn't work here any longer?'

'He's moved to the new paediatric A&E unit. He's senior registrar and, rumour has it, he's tipped to be their next consultant when their current boss retires next year,' Molly explained, leading the way to the store room.

'Really?' Sean unhooked a waterproof suit off its peg and started to pull on the trousers. 'I didn't think that Mac was the sort to settle down in one place for very long.'

'He's changed a lot since he and Bella got married,' Molly told him and laughed. 'They have a little girl now—she must be almost a year old, in fact. And, according to Bella, Mac is a doting father!'

'Well, that's great,' Sean said, trying to ignore the pang of regret that pierced his heart. He had ruled out the idea of having children after what had happened with Claire, yet all of a sudden he found himself envying the other man. How wonderful it must be to have a wife and a child to love and cherish.

He drove the thought from his mind as he gath-

ered together everything they might need. An incident like this could create all sorts of problems and
he wanted to be as prepared as it was possible to be.
Once he had made arrangements with the switchboard to contact Mac, he led the way out to the front
where a rapid response car was waiting to ferry them
to the old brewery. Ambulances had already been
dispatched although more could be called in from
neighbouring health authorities if they were needed.

It took them less than ten minutes to reach the
brewery and Sean's heart sank when he saw the state
of the place. The plane had struck the roof of the
building, causing it, along with several floors beneath, to collapse. The fire department was pump-
ing foam onto the burning jet fuel but the right hand
side of the building was ablaze. There were groups
of people dotted about, some standing and others
lying on the ground. The place looked like a war
zone and he realised that his most pressing task was
to get everyone organised.

'Right, guys, gather round.' He waited until everyone had assembled at the side of the car park. 'I
doubt if we'll be allowed inside the building until
they have got that fire under control so we'll deal
with the people out here first.' He turned to Molly.
'If you and Jayne can sort out the most seriously injured that would be a huge help. I'll check with the
incident commander to see if they've managed to

find somewhere to house the casualties. Then we can round them up and get them away from here.'

'Will do.'

Molly picked up her backpack before she and Jayne hurried away. Sean watched her go and sighed as he found his mind skipping back to what he had been thinking earlier. There was no doubt at all that Molly would make the most wonderful mother but they definitely wouldn't be his children that she gave birth to.

It was an effort to force the thought from his mind but he knew that he couldn't afford to waste any time in getting everything organised. Once he was sure that everyone knew what they were doing, he went to find the incident commander. Fortunately, she had already arranged for a local church hall to be opened up and used as a temporary field hospital so within a very short time the first casualties were being taken in there. Molly was kneeling beside a young woman when Sean arrived. She shook her head when he asked her if she needed anything.

'No, we're fine. Just a few cuts and bruises, I'm pleased to say.'

She squeezed the girl's hand and Sean felt his throat close up when he saw the compassion on her face. Whether it was the fact that his mind had been skittering this way and that, he had no idea, but he couldn't help feeling touched. Molly really cared about the people they treated—it wasn't just an act.

She was such a genuinely kind and generous person yet he had treated her appallingly. If he achieved nothing else while he was in Dalverston then at the very least he had to make his peace with her. The thought of her thinking badly of him for the rest of her days was more than he could bear.

Molly finished patching up the young woman and left her in the care of her boyfriend. Sean was attending to a man who had been struck by some falling masonry when the roof had caved in. He had suffered multiple rib fractures which had resulted in a flail chest—a condition whereby the damaged section of the chest wall was sucked in when the patient breathed in and moved out when he exhaled. This type of injury could lead to respiratory failure and Sean was in the process of strapping the patient's chest to support the damaged section before the paramedics rushed him off to hospital. He shook his head as he watched the crew wheel the trolley out of the hall.

'He's going to need artificial ventilation until those ribs heal. I've seen a couple of flail chests before but none as bad as that.'

'Thankfully, he doesn't have far to go to reach the hospital,' Molly said quietly.

Sean nodded. 'You're right. He's lucky in that respect, although I doubt if he feels very lucky. Apparently, he only moved into the building last week.

His apartment is one of those in the section that's burning so he's lost everything.'

'At least he wasn't in the apartment,' Molly said firmly. 'Things can be replaced but people can't.'

'True.'

He gave her a quick smile before he turned away but she had seen the sadness in his eyes. Was he thinking about Claire and how he would never be able to replace her? Although he hadn't come out and actually said so, it was obvious that he was still very much in love with Claire.

It was a painful thought. Molly had great difficulty setting it aside as she attended to several more casualties. Mac had arrived now and he and Sean were busy dealing with a woman who had suffered a severe abdominal injury when one of the fire crew appeared and hurried over to them. Molly frowned as she watched them confer. It was obvious that something had happened.

Sean came over to her as soon as the fireman had left. 'I need your help, Molly, but I have to warn you that it could be risky, so you must say if you feel that you don't want to do it.'

'Why? What's happened?' she asked.

'The search and rescue team have located a woman trapped in one of the first floor apartments. The problem is that they have only managed to clear a very small area to get to her—more like a tunnel is how the fireman described it. It's not wide enough for any of their men to get through and they daren't risk enlarging it in case the floor above caves in. It's just possible that you might be able to get up there if you're willing to give it a shot.'

'Of course,' she said immediately. 'Have they spoken to the woman and do they know if she's been injured?'

'Yes.' He grimaced. 'Her name is Karen Archer and, although she isn't injured, she is pregnant. The baby was due at the end of January but she thinks she might be having labour pains.'

'Oh, dear. That doesn't sound good, does it? The sooner I take a look at her the better.'

Molly hurried to the door, pausing only long enough to tell Jayne what was happening. Sean led her over to the officer in charge of the search and rescue team and explained that she was willing to try to reach the woman. Molly nodded when the man explained the situation once more, emphasising how difficult it was going to be to get to the apartment.

'I understand,' she said, her heart thumping. 'I'd still like to give it a shot, though.'

'Are you sure, Molly?' Sean asked softly as the officer went off to speak to one of his team. He took hold of her hand and gently squeezed it. 'Nobody will blame you if you decide not to go ahead.'

'We can't leave that poor woman on her own if the baby's coming.' She dredged up a rather wobbly smile. 'I'll be fine, Sean. Don't worry about me.'

'I can't help it. I couldn't bear to think of anything happening to you, Molly.'

He gave her fingers another quick squeeze then let her go when the officer came back. Molly forced herself to concentrate as he ran through a list of instructions aimed at keeping her safe. She knew it was important that she listened to what he was saying but it wasn't easy to remain focused. *Sean cared about her, really cared about her.* It had been clear from the tone of his voice that he had been telling her the truth just now and she wasn't sure what to make of it. All she knew was that it changed things, gave her a reason to hope, although she wasn't ready to admit exactly what she was hoping for. That was a step too far. Or, at least, it was at the moment.

CHAPTER THIRTEEN

THE SITUATION WAS even worse than Sean had expected. Once they were inside the building, it soon became clear just how much structural damage had occurred. The stairs leading to the upper floors had collapsed, leaving behind a pile of rubble in their place. The fire crew had managed to clear a narrow passageway which Molly would have to scramble through to reach the first floor. Although sturdy metal props had been erected to help support the upper section of the building, he was very aware that it could collapse at any second. The thought of Molly risking her life was more than he could bear and he drew her aside.

'I can't allow you to go up there, Molly. It's far too risky.'

'I have to go. We can't leave that poor woman on her own while her baby is born.' She shrugged. 'I'll be fine, Sean. After all, they wouldn't allow me to try it if they thought I'd be putting myself in danger, would they?'

Sean knew she was right, although it wasn't much comfort. He shook his head. 'I still don't like the idea. If anyone's going up there then it has to be me.'

'How? You're too big to get through that gap, Sean. Why, even I'm going to have difficulty so you definitely won't make it.'

'I suppose so.' Sean sighed as he was forced to concede defeat. 'All right, but you're to promise me that you will turn back if you encounter any problems.'

'Cross my heart.' She drew an imaginary cross over her heart with her fingertip and he laughed.

'You do realise that I'm going to hold you to that, Sister Daniels?'

'Of course!'

She treated him to a smile before one of the crew came over to ask if she was ready. Sean sucked in a tiny breath of air, feeling ripples of heat running through him. Molly had smiled at him the way she had used to do and it felt wonderful to be on the receiving end of all that warmth again.

There was no time to dwell on the thought, however. One of the search and rescue team was attaching Molly to a safety harness. Once he was sure that she understood how it worked, he handed her a two-way radio receiver and led her to the bottom of the gap, showing her where to place her foot to begin her ascent. Sean's hands clenched as he watched her start to scramble up over the rubble. The surface was very unstable but somehow she managed to find the necessary hand and footholds. Within seconds she disappeared from sight, leaving him feeling more anxious than ever. She was on her own now and he didn't like that idea, not when he wanted to be there to protect her.

Sean froze as the full impact of that thought hit him squarely in the chest. He wanted to protect Molly from harm and not just for now either. He wanted to be there for her for ever and ever more.

Molly was out of breath by the time she made it to the top of the passageway. It had been a difficult climb but, thankfully, the first floor appeared to be relatively undamaged. She unfastened the safety harness then picked her way around the chunks of plaster that had fallen from the ceiling until she came to the apartment. The door was wide open and she hurried inside, her heart sinking when she found the woman slumped on the living room floor.

'Hi! It's Karen, isn't it? I'm Molly and I'm a nurse. So how are you doing?' she said, kneeling beside her. She was somewhat older than Molly had expected, probably in her early forties, and it was obvious how scared she was.

'I think I'm in labour.' She looked up and there were tears in her eyes. 'Please don't let my baby die. We've waited such a long time to have a child of our own and I couldn't bear it if anything happened to it now.'

'Nothing is going to happen to you or your baby,' Molly said firmly, knowing this wasn't the time to worry about the ethics of making such a statement. Karen needed all the reassurance she could give her if she was to get through this ordeal. 'Let's make you more comfortable for starters. Can you stand up if I help you?'

'I'll try.'

'Great.' Molly put her arm around her and managed to get her to her feet and onto the sofa. 'I need to examine you to see if you are actually in labour, if that's all right.'

Karen nodded, her face scrunching up with pain. Molly suspected it was labour pains but she still needed to check that it wasn't a false alarm first. She quickly removed Karen's underclothes, hiding her dismay when she discovered that the woman was fully dilated. There was little doubt that the baby was going to make his or her appearance very shortly.

'You're definitely in labour,' she told her. 'I've brought everything we need with me so I'll just get ready. Have you been to any antenatal classes?'

'Oh, yes. Mike—that's my husband—and I have done them all. Breathing and relaxation techniques, what happens during the delivery and afterwards.' Karen gave a slightly hysterical laugh. 'We thought we were completely prepared for the birth, but the one thing we didn't foresee was that this would happen!'

'No wonder.' Molly laughed. 'Where is your husband, by the way?'

'He went to fill up the car with petrol to make sure he wouldn't run out over Christmas,' Karen explained. 'I wish he was here. I'd feel a lot happier if he was around to talk me through all those breathing techniques we learned.'

'I'm sure you would but we'll manage fine.' Molly squeezed Karen's hand. 'The fact that you've done the classes will be a big help.'

'But the baby is still going to be born early,' Karen said anxiously.

'Yes, but only by a few weeks so the lungs should be fully developed,' Molly assured her. 'Right, I'm just going to fetch what I need and then listen to your baby's heartbeat.'

Opening her bag, she took out the emergency birthing pack that was part of their standard equipment. Fortunately, she'd done a refresher course earlier in the year on delivering a baby so she had few qualms in that respect. However, delivering a child in the confines of the A&E department was very different from what was happening here. Just for a moment, she found herself wishing that Sean was there with her before she sighed. Sean wasn't here and she would have to get through this on her own. It would be good practice for the future because, once Sean completed his contract, he would leave Dalverston and she doubted if he would ever come back again.

The time seemed to pass with excruciating slowness. Sean found himself continually checking his watch, unable to believe that mere minutes had passed when it felt like hours since Molly had disappeared into the upper reaches of the building. What was happening up there? Had Molly found the woman? Or had she encountered some sort of a problem? His mind raced over a dozen different possibilities, each worse than the one before, and he groaned. He would drive himself crazy if he carried on this way!

The crackle of the radio receiver cut through his thoughts. Sean's heart lifted when he heard Molly's voice issuing from the speaker as she asked to speak to him. He took the receiver with a nod of thanks, overcome by relief.

'How's it going?' he asked, trying not to let her know how worried he had been. 'Have you found the woman?'

'Yes, and she's definitely in labour. She's fully dilated so it shouldn't be long before the baby arrives. I've checked its heart rate and everything seems to be fine but can you arrange for an ambulance to be standing by just in case anything happens at the last moment?'

'Of course.' He paused but the words had to be said, no matter what repercussions they might cause.

'Be careful, won't you, Molly? I don't want you putting yourself at risk. You're too important to me.'

'Am I?' she said so softly that he had to strain to hear her.

'Yes.' He took a deep breath but it was time he admitted the truth to himself as much as to her. 'You always were.'

There was no time to say anything else as there were too many other issues to deal with. Sean handed over the radio while one of the crew ran through the emergency evacuation procedure with Molly. He listened while the other man explained what would happen once the baby was delivered but it was difficult to concentrate when his thoughts were in such turmoil. Maybe he had been wrong to tell Molly that he cared but he needed to set matters straight once and for all. If it weren't for that vow he had made then he knew that he would never have let her go.

Sean knew it was the wrong time to think about such matters. Forcing his mind back to the current crisis, he headed outside to arrange for an ambulance to be standing by. He had just reached the door when a shout went up and the next moment the ceiling started to collapse. Huge chunks of debris rained down on them as he and the crew scrambled to safety. He came to a halt in the car park, bending double as he tried to clear the dust from his lungs. The air was thick with it so that it took a while before he could see what had happened and his heart seized

up at the sight that met him. The entire front of the
building had collapsed, leaving what remained of the
upper floors suspended in mid-air. And, somewhere
inside that wreckage, Molly was trapped.

Molly had no time to do anything when the building
started to shake. She simply knelt down beside the
sofa and gripped tight hold of Karen's hand. There
was a tremendous roar, like an express train rushing
through a tunnel, and then silence. Clouds of dust
were swirling around them, making it impossible
to see across the room, and she waited until it had
settled before she stood up.

'Where are you going? Don't leave me!' Karen
grabbed hold of her hand in panic and Molly paused.

'I'm just going to see what's happened. I'll only
be a second.'

She eased her hand free and picked her way
around the chunks of masonry that littered the living room floor. The apartment was a mess but it
was only when she reached the bedroom that she
discovered the full extent of the damage. There was
a gaping hole now where the front wall should have
been. She didn't dare go any closer because the floor
was tilted at an angle but, from what she could tell,
it appeared that the entire front section of the building had collapsed.

Molly's heart was racing as she made her way
back to the living room to find the radio receiver,

hoping that someone would be able to tell her how long it would take before they got her and Karen out. However, one glance at the shattered remains of the handset soon put paid to that idea. All she could do now was pray that help would arrive before the rest of the building collapsed as well.

'Some bits of the front wall have collapsed,' she explained as she crouched down beside the sofa. She dredged up a smile, deciding that it would be better to play down the true extent of the damage. The last thing she wanted was to cause Karen any more stress. 'I'm sure they'll sort it out so let's concentrate on you and this baby, shall we? Have you decided on a name yet?'

'Mike and I decided that we didn't want to know what sex it was—we preferred to wait and see when it was born. So it's Holly if it's a girl and Nicholas if it's a boy,' Karen replied and then groaned. 'Oh! Here we go again.'

Molly checked the time but there was no doubt that Karen's contractions were coming closer together, a sure sign that the birth was imminent. She held Karen's hand until the pain eased and nodded. 'You're doing really well. It shouldn't be long before your baby is born so what I need now is something to wrap him or her in. Do you have a blanket handy?'

'Everything's packed in that green case near the window in our bedroom.' Karen's face screwed up as she focused on getting through the next contraction.

Molly bit back a sigh because the case, along with everything else at that side of the bedroom, was now in the car park.

'I'm afraid I can't get at it at the moment so we'll have to use something else, like a towel, for instance. That would be fine.'

'Oh. Well, there's clean towels in the bathroom cupboard.'

'Great.' Molly hurriedly fetched a couple of towels and placed them on a nearby chair. She checked Karen once more. 'The baby's head is crowning, so you're nearly there.'

She carefully supported the baby's head as it emerged, checking that the umbilical cord wasn't wrapped around its neck, which could prevent it breathing. Then first one shoulder and then the other were delivered. The rest of the body slid out in a rush as the child began to cry lustily.

Molly laughed in relief. 'Congratulations! You have a beautiful little boy who, from the sound of it, has a fine pair of lungs.' She cleaned the baby, tied and cut his umbilical cord, then wrapped him in a towel and handed him to Karen. 'Well done. You were absolutely marvellous, especially as you didn't have the benefit of any pain relief.'

'It doesn't matter,' Karen murmured, staring at her baby son in awe. 'It was worth all the pain to be able to hold my own child in my arms at last.'

Molly left them to get to know one another while

she tidied up. Once the afterbirth had been expelled, she left the apartment and gingerly made her way towards where she had entered the building. There was no sign of the passageway that the crew had cleared for her, only a heap of rubble. It looked as though they were trapped up here until help arrived. Once again she found herself wishing that Sean was there with her before she drove the thought from her mind. It would be stupid to allow herself to become dependent on him.

Sean had never pulled rank before but he had no qualms about doing so now. The rescue crew had set up a long ladder with a cage on the top and were proposing to enter the building to search for Molly and Karen by using that. He shook his head when the officer in charge explained once more that his men were all trained in the use of first aid.

'No, it's not enough,' he said shortly, determined that if anyone was going into the building, it was going to be him. The thought of having to stand here and wait any longer for news was more than he could handle. He needed to find Molly and make sure that she was all right. He would never forgive himself if anything had happened to her.

It was hard to deal with that thought but he needed to convince the other man it was essential that he was included as part of the team. 'There's a woman up there who is about to give birth under the most difficult circumstances. Add to that the fact that the baby is premature and you can see why it's vital that I go with your men.'

The officer obviously saw the logic of what he was saying. Sean sighed in relief when he was briskly told to get kitted up. One of the crew attached him to a safety harness before he was helped into the cage along with two other men. Nobody said anything as the ladder slowly rose; Sean suspected that every-one was feeling as anxious as he was. However, this wasn't only a rescue mission for him. He was trying to save the woman he loved.

His breath caught painfully but there was no point trying to deny how he felt any longer. He loved Molly and he wanted to be with her, but could he do so when it would mean breaking his promise to Claire? He sucked in a deep breath of air. Somehow he had to find a solution to this dilemma because one thing was certain: he couldn't face the thought of a future without Molly.

CHAPTER FOURTEEN

MOLLY COULD FEEL her fear rising as the minutes ticked past. How long had it been since the front wall of the building had collapsed? Ten minutes? Fifteen? Twenty, even? Surely something should be happening by now.

She went to the bedroom door but she could see very little from where she stood. She stepped tentatively into the room then stopped abruptly when she felt the floor give beneath her feet. She backed out of the door, her heart racing nineteen to the dozen as she realised just how serious the situation was. The whole building could collapse at any moment from the look of it and she, Karen and the baby would be trapped inside.

It was hard not to show her concern as she went to check on Karen. She was cradling baby Nicholas to her breast when Molly went into the sitting room and she looked hopefully up at her.

'Has the rescue team arrived?'

'Not yet, but I'm sure they won't be long now,'

Molly told her, crossing her fingers behind her back. Maybe it was a lie but it was better than worrying the poor soul to death by telling her the truth. 'How are you doing? Do you feel all right?'

'Fine.' Karen smiled down at the baby. 'I have this little fellow to look after and he's my main concern now.'

'He's beautiful,' Molly said truthfully. 'And, what's more, he's probably one of the first babies to be born on Christmas Day this year. That makes him even more special.'

'We certainly won't forget his birthday!' Karen declared, laughing. She sobered abruptly when there was a loud crash from the direction of the hall. 'Oh, what was that?'

'I'll go and see.'

Molly hurried to the door, her heart sinking when she saw that a large hole had appeared in the hall floor. It looked as though the floor of the apartment had given way and she could only pray that the damage wouldn't extend to the living room as well. She was just about to suggest to Karen that they moved into the bathroom when a light suddenly appeared through the living room window and the next second a metal cage holding three men swung into view.

Molly felt relief pour through her when she immediately recognised Sean amongst them. There was no time to check if he had seen her, however, because one of the other men was gesturing to her to keep away from the window. She hurried over to the sofa and crouched down beside Karen and the baby, shielding them as best she could as their rescuers broke the window. It took a couple of attempts to break through the toughened safety glass but at last they managed to gain entry. Molly rose unsteadily to her feet, unable to hide her relief when Sean came hurrying over to her.

'Are you all right? Please tell me you're not hurt!'

He gripped her shoulders and her racing heart beat all the faster when she saw the fear in his eyes. No one seeing it could doubt that he had been worried about her, deeply worried too. And that thought seemed to unleash all the emotions she had tried so hard to bury. She wanted Sean to worry about her. She wanted him to care about her safety and well-being as she cared about his. She wanted him to feel all those things when he looked at her because she loved him.

Molly took a deep breath as she finally faced up to the truth. For the past two years she had tried to fall *out* of love with him but she hadn't succeeded. She loved Sean every bit as much now as she had ever done, even if he could never love her.

'I'm fine. Really I am.' She forced herself to smile although there was an ache gnawing away inside her. Although there was no doubt in her mind that Sean cared about her, it didn't mean he loved her like he loved Claire. The thought that she could only ever be second best in his eyes hurt unbearably but she couldn't dwell on it. There was too much to do at the present time and she needed to focus on that. 'How soon can we get Karen and the baby out of here?'

'Straight away.' His expression was grim as he glanced at the other woman then turned back to her. 'The crew don't think the building is going to remain standing for very much longer so we need to get everyone out of here as quickly as possible.'

Molly nodded, not needing to hear anything more as she hurried over to Karen and helped her to her feet. One of the crew held the baby while another man helped Karen climb into the cradle, not an easy manoeuvre when there was a yawning drop beneath them. Once Karen was safely seated on the floor of the cradle, they carefully passed the baby to her and then helped Molly step on board. Sean followed next, shaking his head when she asked if they were waiting for the last crew member.

'The cradle will only hold three adults so they'll need to come back for him.'

It seemed to take for ever before they reached the ground although Molly knew for a fact that it was mere minutes. Her legs were trembling when she climbed out and she was glad of Sean's support as she walked shakily over to the ambulance. Karen's husband was already there, waiting for them, and he climbed in as well. Once everyone was safely on board, Sean turned to her.

'You're to go with them.' He shook his head when she opened her mouth to protest. 'No arguing, Molly. You need to get checked over at the hospital.'

'But I'm fine, Sean,' she began then stopped abruptly as he silenced her in the most effective way possible—with a kiss. Her head was whirling as she climbed into the back of the ambulance because, crazy though it sounded, that kiss had felt as though it had come straight from his heart. What did it mean? Was it possible that Sean loved her after all? She hugged the idea to her all the way back to the hospital, afraid to let it go in case it disappeared into the ether.

It was another half an hour before Sean was finally free to return to the hospital. All the casualties had been seen by then and either sent on their way or transferred to A&E. Amazingly, there had been no fatalities, which was a miracle considering the severity of the accident. The fire crew had the blaze under control now and the air accident investigators were on site. The people who lived in the apartments were being housed temporarily in a nearby hotel so at least they had somewhere clean and safe to sleep tonight. Sean turned to Mac as they left the site together.

'Thanks again for your help, Mac. We wouldn't have fared half as well if you hadn't been here.'

'I was glad to be able to help,' Mac told him, shaking his hand. He sighed as he glanced back at the ruined building. 'It makes you appreciate just how lucky you are when a thing like this happens, doesn't it? Bella used to live in one of those apartments. Thank heaven we moved out when she was expecting Grace. I don't know what I would have done if she'd been caught up in this.'

'Very scary,' Sean agreed soberly, inwardly shuddering at the thought. He understood only too well how it felt to know that the woman he loved was in danger and not be able to do anything about it.

'Too right!' Mac clapped him on the shoulder then headed over to his car. 'Oh, Merry Christmas! I'd forgotten it was Christmas Day in all the chaos.'

'And a Merry Christmas to you too,' Sean replied, smiling as he climbed into the car that was waiting to ferry him and the rest of the team back to the hospital. It was almost five a.m. by then which meant there was barely an hour left before the day shift arrived for duty. He knew that he would be expected to file a report about what had happened during the night but it would have to wait. There was something far more pressing he needed to do at this moment.

Molly was in the staffroom when he tracked her down. She was sitting slumped in a chair with her eyes closed and looked infinitely weary. She had obviously showered since she'd got back because her beautiful red-gold hair was still damp, the riotous curls tumbling around her face and giving her the appearance of one of Botticelli's famous cherubs.

Sean felt a huge wave of love sweep through him as he looked at her. He had come so close to losing her tonight and it had made him see just how much he loved her. He loved her with every fibre of his being, with his heart and his soul, and he wanted to spend the rest of his life showing her how he felt, but was it possible? Could he leave the past behind and look towards the future—a future which he longed for so very much?

He must have made some sort of a sound because her eyes opened. Sean felt his heart lift when he saw the love that burned in their depths. There wasn't a doubt in his mind that Molly loved him every bit as much as he loved her and it seemed almost too much to know that this kind and beautiful woman was prepared to love him after the way he had behaved towards her in the past.

'Hi!' Her voice was low, gentle, filled with so much love that Sean's heart overflowed with emotion.

'Hi, yourself,' he said, unable to hide how he felt. When she held out her hand, he didn't hesitate; he simply strode across the room and pulled her to her feet. Glancing up, he laughed softly as his eyes alighted on the decidedly wilted bunch of foliage pinned to the ceiling. 'Hmm. That seems propitious. Do you think someone's trying to tell us something?'

'Maybe. Although I doubt if we need anyone's help at this moment, do you?'

Raising herself on tiptoe, she pressed her mouth to his and he sighed deeply. The kiss was filled with so many emotions that he would have needed the best part of a lifetime to sort them all out but he didn't need to do that, did he? Each and every scrap of emotion simply led to one conclusion—that Molly loved him.

He kissed her back, letting his lips tell her exactly how he felt—how much he loved her; how scared he had been of losing her; how he longed for them to be together for ever; and how he feared it might not be possible. And she obviously understood. There was a wealth of sadness in her eyes when she drew back, a pain that cut him to the quick because he didn't want to hurt her, not when he simply wanted to love her.

'Will you come home with me, Sean?' she said quietly and he heard the tremor in her voice and hated himself all the more for making her feel like this. Molly should be rejoicing, filled with happiness at the thought of what the future held in store for them; she definitely shouldn't be experiencing this kind of heartache.

'Are you sure, sweetheart?' His voice caught and he had to force himself to continue but he had to make the situation perfectly clear. 'You must understand that I can't make any promises. I wish I could but...'

'I'm sure.' She pressed her fingers against his mouth, stopping the words because she didn't want to hear them. She gave him a tight little smile. 'I don't expect anything more than you feel able to give me.'

'Oh, Molly!'

Sean drew her to him and kissed her hungrily. That she could be so generous, so giving, was almost more than he could bear.

He let her go when the sound of footsteps alerted them to the fact that the day shift was arriving. He and Molly exchanged pleasantries with several members of staff, brushing aside their eager questions about what had gone on during the night by claiming that they were too exhausted to talk about it right then. Everyone seemed to accept it so that in a remarkably short time they were able to leave.

Sean led the way to his car, opening the door for her while she climbed inside. He slid behind the wheel and turned to her. 'Happy Christmas, Molly. Let's make this the best Christmas Day ever, shall we?'

'Yes, let's.'

She smiled back at him, her expression filled with so much love that he had to stop himself reaching out and hauling her into his arms. However, this wasn't the place, he reminded himself as he started the engine. They needed somewhere a lot more private than the car.

A shudder ran through him at the thought of what would happen when they got to Molly's house. He and Molly were going to make love and, although it

was what he wanted more than anything, he knew
that afterwards he would have to decide what he intended to do. It wasn't going to be an easy decision
but one thing was certain: he couldn't leave Molly
in a state of limbo. It wouldn't be fair.

Molly lay in her bed listening to the sound of the
shower running while she remembered all the other
times when this had happened. Sean would be taking a shower in the bathroom while she lay in her
bed and waited for him...

She blanked out the thought. She didn't want to
think about the past at this moment. Maybe she was
burying her head in the sand but she didn't want
any bad memories to taint what was about to happen. When the water stopped and Sean appeared in
the bedroom doorway with a towel wrapped around
his hips, she smiled. This was what mattered—what
happened right now. The past and the future were
unimportant.

'Feel better?' she asked as he came over to the
bed.

'Much. It's good to get all that muck out of my
hair.' He ran his hand over his wet hair, accidentally
showering her with water, and she squealed.

'Hey! I've already had a shower this morning. I
don't need another one, thank you very much.'

'Sure?' He grinned wickedly as he bent and licked
a stray drop of water off her shoulder.

'Uh-huh,' Molly muttered, trying to sound convincing. However, the feel of Sean's tongue licking her skin seemed to have robbed her of even the most basic ability to string several words together.

'Hmm, you don't sound *that* sure to me.'

He deliberately spattered another few drops of water onto her skin, his eyes holding hers as his tongue followed the path they made as they trickled from her shoulder to the edge of the sheet that covered her body. Molly held her breath when he paused then let it out in a whoosh when he pushed aside the sheet, his tongue gliding over her breast until it reached her nipple. Sensations flooded through her when he drew her nipple into his mouth and suckled it.

'Sean!'

His name was an explosion of both sound and feelings as it rushed from her lips and she felt him shudder, felt the hard pressure of his arousal against her hip. When he pushed the sheet completely off her so that his tongue could continue its journey, she didn't protest. Why would she when it was what she wanted, what she needed? She wanted Sean to explore her body and get to know all the dips and hollows again, as she would soon know him.

His tongue had reached her navel now and slowly began to circle it, dipping in and out of the tiny indentation. Molly's hands clenched because each gentle stroke of his tongue against her flesh was merely heightening her desire for an even greater intimacy. When he dragged off his towel and took her hand to wrap it around him, she gloried in the feel of him, so strong and vital beneath her fingers.

'I love you, Molly.' He whispered the words in her ear as he lay down beside her and took her in his arms. 'No matter what happens, I want you to know that this isn't just sex for me.' He kissed her tenderly. 'I love you so very much, my darling.'

'I love you too, Sean,' she told him simply, her heart breaking.

It was unbearably poignant to know that he loved her and still be so unsure about the future. It lent an added urgency to the way they came together. When Sean entered her with one powerful thrust, Molly clung to him, needing to savour every precious second. She had no idea what was going to happen in the future but she refused to allow it to spoil what was happening now. At this moment they had each other. They had everything.

CHAPTER FIFTEEN

THE SOUND OF church bells ringing woke him. Sean lay in bed, feeling strangely at peace with himself. He and Molly had made love not once but twice before they had fallen asleep and he knew that he would store the memory of what had happened in his heart for ever. There had been passion, yes, but as well as that there had been such tenderness that he felt different. Making love with Molly, knowing that there was love in his heart as well as in hers, had been a life-changing experience. Now he knew what he had to do. Knew what he *wanted* to do. And it was a relief to be so sure when he had felt so ambivalent these past weeks. Rolling over, he stroked her cheek, wanting to tell her his decision. Molly had a right to know as this was going to affect her life as much as his.

'Mmm, that feels nice,' she murmured, snuggling against him. 'Has anyone told you that you have magic fingers, Dr Fitzgerald?'

'Nobody who matters,' he replied, replacing his

hand with his lips. He trailed a line of butterfly-soft kisses from her ear to her jaw and back again then laughed. 'Come on, sleepy-head, wake up. It's Christmas Day and it's time to rise and shine.'

'Why? Has Santa been?' she retorted, wriggling even closer to him. She chuckled wickedly when she felt his very predictable response to her nearness. 'Maybe that's him knocking at the door right now. I wonder if he has a present for me.'

After a comment like that it was inevitable what would happen. Sean didn't need a second invitation as he gathered her into his arms and kissed her soundly. Their lovemaking was just as fulfilling and as magical this time too and he sighed as he rolled onto his side and looked at her with wonderment.

'How do you make me feel like this, Molly? Have you developed some kind of special powers that I never knew about before?'

'Yes.' She kissed him on the lips, her eyes gentle as she stared at him. 'It's the power of love. It makes everything magical.'

'Oh, sweetheart!' He kissed her this time, feeling desire roaring through him once more. It shouldn't have been possible after what had just happened but they made love again. They were both exhausted when they broke apart. Sean flopped onto his back and groaned.

'My heaven, woman, you're insatiable. You've worn me out!'

'Are you complaining?' she asked cheekily, laughing at him.

'Certainly not!' He grinned back at her. 'Although I may need a breather before you have your wicked way with me yet again.'

'Hmph. Some folk are never happy. It's a good job it's Christmas and the season of goodwill is all I can say.' She tossed back the quilt and got out of bed. 'I shall leave you to recover your strength while I make us some breakfast.'

'I could give it a miss,' Sean offered, grabbing hold of her hand as she went to walk past him. He chuckled because the sight of her naked body seemed to be doing wonders for his flagging libido. 'I may not be *quite* as exhausted as I thought.'

'Too late, stud.' She wriggled out of his grasp and picked up her dressing gown from the back of the chair. 'The only thing you're getting at this precise moment is coffee!'

'Spoilsport,' Sean declared as she swished out of the door with her nose in the air.

He smiled to himself as he sank back against the pillows. It felt marvellous to indulge in this kind of banter and feel so at ease. He had always felt a bit tense when they had been together before, aware that he shouldn't be encouraging any real sense of closeness, but it was different now. He and Molly could relax and enjoy being together without him constantly worrying that he was leading her on. It made it all the more imperative that he carried out that decision he had made.

Sean took a deep breath as he tossed back the quilt, knowing how hard it was going to be, not only for him but for Claire's parents as well. However, although he hated the thought of upsetting them, the fact was that he couldn't have Molly in his life until he had drawn a line under the past.

Molly put the finishing touches to the breakfast tray and nodded in satisfaction. Freshly squeezed orange juice, eggs Benedict and coffee. There was a platter of fresh fruit as well, although she wasn't sure if it would get eaten or not. As she recalled, breakfast in bed with Sean didn't necessarily involve eating.

Heat rushed through her as she picked up the tray and carried it along the hall. Making love with Sean had been everything she could have wished for. He was both a tender and a passionate lover and she loved how he made her feel. That he enjoyed making love to her wasn't in any doubt but was it enough to tip the scales her way? Maybe he had told her that he loved her but could he leave the past behind? Molly hoped so with every fibre of her being but, as she made her way upstairs, she could feel a sense of dread gathering in the pit of her stomach. A happy-ever-after wasn't guaranteed.

The bed was empty when she reached the bedroom. Molly put the tray on the bedside table, feeling her unease mounting when she heard the shower running again. Why was Sean taking another shower if they were planning to spend the day in bed? When he appeared, fully dressed, she knew that she was right to feel concerned. He was leaving and that didn't bode well, did it?

'Help yourself.' She gestured towards the tray, hoping that he couldn't tell how anxious she felt. It had to be his decision to stay or to go, although it was hard to take such a balanced view.

'It all looks delicious but just coffee for me. Thank you.' He picked up the pot and poured himself a mug of coffee although he made no attempt to drink it.

'Not hungry?' she said lightly, spooning some fruit into a bowl purely for something to do as she doubted if she would be able to eat it when her stomach was churning with nerves.

'Not really.' He took a deep breath and Molly's heart seemed to scrunch up inside her as she waited to hear what he had to say, although she already suspected that it wasn't going to be good news.

'I can't stay, Molly. I'm sorry but there's something I need to do.'

'I see,' she said flatly, leaving it up to him to tell her what was so important that it couldn't wait.

'Yes.' He put his cup back on the tray and reached for her hands. 'I need to speak to Claire's parents, and to my parents, as well, come to that. It's time I told them what really happened the night Claire died.' He squeezed her fingers. 'Then I can put it all behind me.'

'If that's what you want, Sean,' she said, her heart racing with a mixture of fear and excitement. Maybe she was presuming too much but the only reason she could think of why Sean would do such a thing was because of her. Because of them.

'It is.' He bent and kissed her gently on the lips. 'It's what I want more than anything, although I am not looking forward to telling everyone the truth. I know how upset they're going to be.'

The sadness in his eyes was so painful to see. Molly wrapped her arms around him and hugged him tight. 'Are you sure you want to do it today?' she asked quietly. 'I mean, it's Christmas Day and it might make it all the harder for them.'

'Do you think so?' He shook his head. 'I certainly don't want to make it any worse than it has to be for Claire's parents, so do you think I should leave it until tomorrow to go and see them?'

'It's up to you, of course, but it might be easier.' Molly bit her lip, wondering if she was wrong to interfere. It was Sean's decision, after all, but she couldn't bear to think of him piling stress onto stress unnecessarily.

'I think you're right. Christmas Day will be tough enough for them without me showing up and telling them this.' He made a deliberate attempt to lighten the mood, smiling as he glanced at the breakfast tray. 'In which case, I can sample the delights on offer.'

'Food delights, do you mean? Or some other kind?' Molly said, determined to play her part. Maybe it was only putting off the moment until he left her but it would be so good to have this day together, something to remember if things didn't work out as she hoped and prayed they would. She put that dispiriting thought out of her mind as Sean reached for her.

'Both. Although maybe we should start with the *other* delights and carry on from there.'

His mouth was hungry as he kissed her—hungry for her, not for the food that was on offer. Molly kissed him back, showing him through actions rather than words how she felt, how much she loved and needed him. They made love all over again and there was such intensity to their lovemaking that they both cried. Molly kissed away his tears and then he kissed away hers too before they settled down to eat their breakfast. The eggs Benedict were cold and the coffee lukewarm but it didn't matter; it still tasted like manna from heaven because they ate it together, sitting side by side on her bed. Molly prayed with all her heart that there would be other occasions like this in the future but she knew nothing was guaranteed. Until Sean had spoken to everyone then she couldn't be certain that they even had a future.

It was the one black spot in an otherwise wonderful day. After breakfast they went for a long walk down by the river, holding hands and simply enjoy-

ing being together. There were quite a lot of people
about—parents helping their offspring to ride their
brand new bikes, other couples walking hand in hand
like they were doing. Everyone was making the most
of Christmas Day, it seemed, and it felt good to be
a part of it.

When they got back to her house, Molly started
to prepare lunch and Sean helped her, although his
idea of helping tended to hold up proceedings. Molly
chuckled as she wriggled out of his arms after about
the tenth time he had kissed her.

'If you hope to eat today then you have to show
some restraint. Not that I'm complaining, mind you.
But it's rather difficult to peel sprouts when you're
kissing me like that—it's very distracting!'

'Sorry, Chef!' Sean held up his hands in apology.
'I shall behave myself from now on. Promise.'

'Good,' Molly said firmly, although he could tell
from the smile that twitched the corners of her gorgeous mouth that she had been enjoying his atten-
tions every bit as much as he had enjoyed lavishing
them on her. The thought made him groan and he
saw her look at him in surprise.

'What do you want me to do?' he said hurriedly
before he managed to break his promise to behave
himself. 'I'm a dab hand at peeling sprouts, if you'd
like me to do them.'

'All right. If your hands are otherwise occupied
then maybe we can eat Christmas dinner actually on
Christmas Day.' She handed him the bag of sprouts

along with a knife. 'Don't forget to put a cross on the bottom of each one, will you? It helps them cook faster.'

'Yes, Chef!'

Sean saluted smartly, laughing when she rolled her eyes in response. He set to with a will, nevertheless, amazed that something as boring as sprout peeling should be so enjoyable. But there again, why should he be surprised? he thought. Everything he did with Molly took on a whole different light and became much more fun. The thought simply strengthened his determination to sort out his life. No matter how difficult it turned out to be, he had to do it. For him and for Molly.

Especially for Molly.

It was the most wonderful Christmas Day Molly could remember since she was a child. Although they had done nothing more taxing than playing board games after they had finally eaten their dinner, it had been perfect. They had both been on night duty so they had driven into work together in Sean's car. Thankfully, it had been fairly quiet for once so both she and Sean had been able to file their reports about what had happened the previous night. She had even had time to pop up to the Maternity unit to visit Karen and baby Nicholas. Karen's husband was there as well and Molly brushed aside the couple's thanks for what she had done. As she told them truthfully, she had been only too pleased to help.

By the time she finished work, Molly was feeling far more confident about the future. Once again Sean stayed over at her house and they made love again. Although it didn't seem possible, each time they did so, it felt even more wonderful than the time before. She fell asleep, snuggled up against him, feeling happy and sated, and she was still smiling when she woke up in the early afternoon. Being here with Sean was the most perfect experience ever.

Rolling over, Molly went to tell him how she felt but the bed was empty and the sheet on his side was cold when she ran her hand across it. A frisson of alarm scudded through her as she hurriedly got up and dragged on her dressing gown. Surely Sean hadn't left without saying goodbye? Maybe it was silly but she wanted to hold him, kiss him, send him off to do what he had to do knowing how much she loved him.

She ran down the stairs and came to an abrupt halt when she found him in the kitchen, hunched over a cooling mug of coffee. He looked up when he heard her footsteps and smiled but she could see how tense he looked.

'Hi! I hope I didn't wake you up. I tried not to make too much noise.'

'No. It's time I got up,' she said quietly, pulling out

a chair. She took a quick breath but the words had to be said. 'Are you going over to see Claire's parents?'

'Yes. I've already phoned my parents and told them I'm coming.' He shrugged. 'It shouldn't take that long. They live just outside Leeds so it's a pretty straightforward drive along the motorway.'

'It shouldn't be that busy today either,' Molly murmured. 'With it being Boxing Day, there won't be as much traffic on the roads.'

'Probably not.' He pushed back his chair and stood up. 'I suppose I'd better get going. I'm in work tonight so I shall need to get back in time for my shift.'

'Of course.'

Molly bit her lip. She wanted to beg him not to go and stay with her but she knew that it would be wrong to do that. Sean had to deal with this in his own way and she mustn't try and stop him because she was afraid of the outcome. When he came around the table and pulled her into his arms, Molly hugged him tightly against her, willing him to feel how much she needed him even though she knew it wouldn't be fair to tell him so at this moment. She mustn't try to influence him in any way.

He didn't say a word as he let her go. Molly sank down onto a chair as he walked along the hall and let himself out of the house, fighting against the urge to run after him. She had to trust him to see this through to the end, no matter how hard it proved to be. Screwing up her eyes, she made a wish that everything would turn out the way she hoped it would. It was Christmas, after all—only good things should happen at this time of the year. But, no matter how hard she tried to cling to that thought, she couldn't stave off the feeling of dread that swept through her. If Sean didn't find the closure he needed then this might be the end for them.

There was no sign of Sean when Molly went into work that night. She had spent the remainder of the afternoon hoping he would phone her but there had been no word from him. She could only assume that he had done what he had intended to do, but it was impossible not to fear the worst. When he appeared some ten minutes after his shift should have started, he looked drawn and grey.

Molly was in the process of taking a case history from an elderly woman who had fainted while having tea with her family. Both her daughters were there and, as they each wanted to have their say about what had happened to their mother, Molly had no choice other than to sit there and listen to them. Nevertheless, she was painfully aware that Sean avoided looking her way as he led his first patient to Cubicles.

She finally sorted out the family and left them in a cubicle while she went to find Steph. It sounded like a severe case of indigestion to her but it wasn't her call and she would leave it to Steph to make the final decision.

Sean was sitting at the computer, updating his patient's notes, and he barely glanced at her. Molly bit her lip but she couldn't face the thought of having to wait any longer to hear what had happened.

'How did you get on?' she said quietly. 'Did you speak to Claire's parents?'

'Yes.' His tone was clipped, not an encouraging sign at all.

'So what happened?' she began then stopped when Jason came over to ask if she would help him with a patient who was refusing to have a booster Tetanus shot.

Molly could hardly refuse, so once she had spoken to Steph she went and sorted out the problem, by which time Sean had disappeared into Resus to deal with a man who had suffered a heart attack. By the time he had finished, she was busily stitching up a woman who had had an accident with a carving knife and cut her hand. And so it went on. Each time Sean was free, she was busy. There was no chance to talk to him, not that he gave any sign that he wanted to talk to her. In fact, it appeared that talking to her was the last thing on his mind and she could only draw her own conclusions from it. Sean had changed his mind and the sooner she accepted that it was over between them, the better.

Sean knew that Molly was desperate to talk to him but he needed time to get everything straight in his

head. What he had learned that day had rocked his
world. It was only when he saw how drawn Molly
looked as she signed out that he realised he had to
speak to her. The last thing he wanted was Molly
thinking that he had changed his mind about them.

'Can we talk?' he said softly, going over to her.

'If you're sure you want to.' Her eyes met his and
he inwardly winced when he saw the hurt they held.

'I am.'

He slid his hand under her elbow, ignoring the
curious looks they were attracting from the rest of
the staff. Let them think what they liked—it didn't
matter. The only thing that mattered was Molly and
making sure that she knew how much he loved her.
Maybe his world had been rocked but nothing could
change that.

The thought helped to relieve some of the shock
he had felt ever since he had spoken to both his and
Claire's parents. He led her to the car and helped her
inside then bent and looked into her eyes. 'I just want
to say that what happened today doesn't change a
thing. I love you, Molly. And I want to be with you
for ever.'

'But?' She gave a hoarse little laugh. 'There has
to be a "but" tagged onto the end of that statement.'

'There isn't.' He leant into the car and kissed the
tip of her nose. 'I love you and there are no "buts"
attached to how I feel either.'

'Then why have you been avoiding me all night

long? And don't say that you haven't because we both know it's true. You have done your best not to have to speak to me, Sean, haven't you?'

'Yes, I have,' he admitted. 'And I'm sorry.' He closed the door and walked round to the driver's side, although he didn't immediately start the engine. 'However, I was told something today that I never expected to hear. I needed to get it straight in my own head before I spoke to you.'

'Why? What did they tell you?'

'That Claire had been having an affair with someone she worked with and that the baby might not have been mine after all.'

'What?' Molly stared at him in shock, and he grimaced.

'I know. I was stunned too. I still am. I had no idea that Claire was seeing someone else. Crazy, isn't it?'

He started the engine and drove out of the car park, feeling echoes of the shock he had had that afternoon spreading through him once more. Surely he should have suspected that something had been going on, he thought as he headed along the bypass. Especially when he and Claire had kept arguing all the time. He sighed because it was easy to paint a very different picture of events with the benefit of hindsight. However, the truth was that he had never imagined for a second that Claire had been seeing someone else. He had been far too bound up in making a success of his career to focus on his relationship. He glanced at Molly and felt his heart well up with love. It was a mistake he would never make again.

By tacit consent, they didn't discuss the subject any more until they were back in Molly's house. Molly had needed a bit of time herself to absorb what Sean had told her. She led the way into the sitting room and sank down onto the sofa, wondering what to say to him. It must have been a terrible experience to discover that the woman he had loved so much had been unfaithful to him. Her heart ached at the thought.

'I'm so sorry, Sean,' she said gently as he dropped down into a chair. 'It must have been such a shock for you to hear that. What I don't understand is why your parents, or Claire's, didn't tell you the truth before now. I take it that they knew, so why did they keep it a secret for all these years?'

'Basically because they didn't want to hurt me any more. Both my and Claire's parents decided that it would be better if they didn't tell me immediately after Claire died. And, of course, the longer it went on, the harder it became to tell me the truth.' He shook his head. 'In a weird sort of a way, I can understand their logic but to have let it go on for so long…'

He stopped as though words had failed him, which they probably had. Molly touched his hand, wanting him to know that she was here for him. It was heart-rending to imagine what he must be going through. 'So how do you feel now that you know?' she said softly.

'I'm not sure, to be honest. Shocked, I suppose. Amazed that I never even suspected what was going on. And sad too, because Claire didn't feel able to tell me herself.'

'It must have been awful for you, Sean. I'm so sorry.'

'It wasn't pleasant and if I'd learned the truth even a couple of years ago then I would have been devastated. However, although I do feel shocked because it's completely altered my view of the past, I can see now that if Claire and I had got married then it would never have worked.'

'Really?' Molly exclaimed in surprise.

'Yes.' He captured her hand and raised it to his lips, dropping a gentle kiss on her knuckles. 'I loved Claire very much but I was never *in love* with her. We had grown up together and we were fond of one another, but love? No. It wasn't that. Not as I now understand it. Maybe she'd realised that too and that is why she had an affair. She sensed that what we had together wasn't the real thing.'

'Are you sure?' Molly had to swallow the knot in her throat. 'You've had a shock, Sean—you've already admitted that. So how can you be sure that your judgement hasn't been affected by it?'

'It's quite simple.' He smiled at her, his face filled with so much love that her heart started to race. 'I know how I feel about you, my darling, and it's very different from how I felt about Claire. I'm in love with you, mind, body and soul, and it is a world removed from anything I have ever felt before.' He stood up and drew her to her feet, enfolding her in his arms and holding her so close that she could feel his heart beating in time with hers.

'It's such a relief that everything is finally out in the open and I don't have this guilty secret burning a hole inside me any more. It means I can now move on, or I can do if you will agree to move on with me, Molly. Will you? Will you take a chance on me, let me love you and care for you for ever and ever?'

'For only as long as that?' she said teasingly.

'How about from here to eternity?' he suggested and then grimaced. 'Sorry! That's the most hackneyed line I could have come up with!'

'Don't you believe it.' She nestled against him, her heart overflowing with happiness. 'Funnily enough, it sounds absolutely perfect to me.'

Lifting her face, she kissed him, wanting to put the seal on their happiness. Maybe she had stopped believing in happy endings but she had been wrong to do so. She had her very own happy ending right here, although not just an ending but a beginning as well. The beginning of a wonderful new life, loving and living with Sean.

'I love you,' she whispered.

'And I love you too. So very, very much.'

Christmas Eve, one year later...

'Come on, sweetheart, you're nearly there! Just one more push and you'll do it.'

'You want to try pushing,' Molly muttered, screwing up her face as another contraction began. She clung tight hold of Sean's hand as she worked through it, her heart lifting when a second later she heard the tiny cry of a newborn baby. 'What is it—a boy or a girl?' she demanded, lifting herself up on her elbows.

'A boy—a beautiful, perfect little boy,' Sean told her, his deep voice choked with tears. Bending, he kissed her cheek. 'Thank you so much, my love. I didn't think I could be any happier since we got married but I was wrong. Having you and now our son is like having all my dreams come true.'

'Mine too,' she told him, smiling into his eyes.

They had married in the spring, shortly after Molly had discovered that she was pregnant. Sean was surprisingly old-fashioned about such things and had wanted their baby to be born into a traditional family setting. Everyone had been delighted, Sean's parents and hers—even Claire's parents had sent them a card on their wedding day. It felt as though everyone had moved on and now, with a new baby to celebrate, the future looked rosier than ever.

'So what are we going to call him?' Sean handed the squalling infant to her, perching on the edge of the bed so he could examine his new son's tiny fingers and toes. 'We've changed our minds so many times that I can't remember what we finally decided on.'

Molly laughed. 'It was Sam for a boy, but would you mind if we changed it?'

'Again?' Sean rolled his eyes. 'What to this time?'

'Joseph. It just seems fitting for the time of year, don't you think?'

'Mary and Joseph and the Nativity, you mean?' He nodded. 'Yes, I like it. Joseph Fitzgerald. It has a definite ring to it.'

He picked up the baby's hand and solemnly shook it. 'Welcome to the family, young Joseph. I know that you are going to be very happy because you have the best mum in the whole wide world.'

'And the best dad too,' Molly added, dropping a kiss on the baby's downy head.

* * * * *

HIS CHRISTMAS
BRIDE-TO-BE

BY
ABIGAIL GORDON

Published in Great Britain 2015
by Mills & Boon, an imprint of Harlequin (UK) Limited,
Eton House, 18-24 Paradise Road, Richmond, Surrey, TW9 1SR

© 2015 Abigail Gordon

ISBN: 978-0-263-24751-0

Printed and bound in Spain
by CPI, Barcelona

Dear Reader,

We are in Glenminster again, surrounded by the green hills of Gloucestershire. *His Christmas Bride-to-Be* is my second book in this series, in which I hope you will enjoy making the acquaintance of Glenn and Emma.

Both have known heartbreak, and both discover that love is waiting to bring joy back into their lives—as it so often does.

With best wishes for happy reading,

Abigail Gordon

For Glenn, Emma, and healthcare in all its many forms

CHAPTER ONE

THE TAXI THAT had brought her from the airport had gone, and surrounded by the baggage that contained her belongings Emma took a deep breath and looked around her.

When she'd been driven through the town centre it had been as if nothing had changed while she'd been gone for what seemed like a lifetime. The green hills of Gloucestershire still surrounded the place where she'd been born and had never imagined leaving. Everywhere the elegant Regency properties that Glenminster was renowned for still stood in gracious splendour to delight the eye, while, busy as always, the promenades and restaurants had shown that they still attracted the shoppers and the gourmets to the extent that they always had.

All that she had to do now was turn the key in the lock, open the door and step inside the property that had been her home for as long as she could remember, and of which she was now the sole owner. The act of doing so was not going to be easy. It felt like only yesterday that she had fled in the night, heartbroken and bewildered from what she'd been told, as if the years she'd spent in a land far away had never happened.

During all that time there had been no communication between herself and the man she'd always thought was her father, and now he was gone. Since receiving the news that he had died, all the hurts of long ago had come back. What he had done to her had been cruel. He'd taken away her identity; made her feel like a nobody. Turned the life she'd been living happily enough for twenty-plus years into nothingness.

He had been a moderate parent, never very affectionate, and she'd sometimes wondered why. He'd provided the answer to that by telling her on the night she'd left Glenminster in a state of total hurt and disbelief that he wasn't her father, that he'd married her mother to give her the respectability of having a husband and a father for her child when it was born as the result of an affair that was over.

Emma had directed the taxi driver to take her to lawyers in the town centre where the keys for the house had been held in waiting for when she made an appearance. Once she had received them she had been asked to call the following day to discuss the details of Jeremy Chalmers's will.

She'd been informed previously that he'd left

her the house, or she wouldn't have intended going straight there on her return. She was uncertain if she would be able to live in it for any length of time after her father had disowned her that night long ago in such a cruel manner, but it would be somewhere to stay in the beginning while she slotted herself back into life in Glenminster.

Back in the taxi once more, having been given the house keys, she'd given the driver the directions for the last lap of her journey back to her roots and had thought grimly that it was some homecoming.

Gazing down at the keys, the memory was starkly clear of how she'd packed her cases and left the place that was dear to her heart that same night, intending to start a new life to replace the one that Jeremy Chalmers had shattered and made to sound unclean.

Her only thought as she'd driven out of the town that lay at the foot of the Gloucestershire hills had been to go where she could use her medical skills to benefit the sick and suffering of somewhere like Africa and start a new life as far away as she could get.

Until then they had been contained in the role of a junior doctor in a large practice in the place where she had been happy and content, but that night the urge to leave Glenminster had been overwhelming.

The last thing Emma had done before departing had been to drop a note off at the home of Lydia Forrester, the practice manager, to explain that she was about to do something she'd always wanted to do,

work in Africa for one of the medical agencies, and
that had been it without further explanation.

Time spent out there had been a lot of things, fulfilling, enlightening, exhausting and *lonely.* If she
stayed and went back to work in the practice that
she'd known so well in the busy town centre, would
the memory of that night come crowding back, she
asked herself, or would it be like balm to her soul
to be back where she belonged and lonely no more?

Yet was *that* likely to be the case in the house
where it had happened and which was just a short
distance from the surgery where her stepfather had
been senior doctor?

Emma had joined the staff there as soon as she'd
got her degree in medicine and had been carefree
and happy until that awful day. The job had absorbed
her working hours and mixing happily with her own
age group in her free time had made up for the atmosphere at home, where there had just been Jeremy
Chalmers and herself, living in separate vacuums
most of the time.

She'd lost her gentle, caring mother too soon and
had been left with only him as family—a bridge-
playing golf fanatic in his free time, and at the surgery a popular GP with an eye for the opposite sex.
He had proved how much on the night when he'd told
her that she was going to have to move out, find her-

self somewhere to stay, as he was getting married again and his new wife wouldn't want her around.

'Fine,' she'd told him, quite happy to find a place of her own to settle in, but the way he'd said so uncaringly that he was going to replace her mother and that *she* was in the way had rankled and she'd said, 'I *am* your daughter, you know!'

He'd been to the golf club and had told her thickly, 'That is where you're wrong. I married your mother to give her respectability and you a father figure. You're not mine.'

'What?' she'd cried in disbelief. 'I don't believe you?'

'You have to. You've no choice,' he'd said, and added, turning the knife even more as he'd begun to climb the stairs, 'She never told me who your father was, so you can't go running to him.'

As the door swung back on its hinges at last, reality took over from the pain-filled past. Nothing had changed, Emma thought as she went from room to room. There had been no modernisation of any kind.

The new bride must have been easy to please. So where was she now that her father had died from a heart attack on the golf course? It was all very strange. Had the widow moved out at the thought of a new owner appearing?

It would be time to be concerned about that when she'd spoken to the person who had taken over the running of the practice after her father's death. The absence of the new woman who had been in his life could be shelved until she, Emma, had been brought up to date with the present situation there.

But first, before anything else, there was the matter of arranging a suitable farewell for the man she'd thought, for most of her life, was her father. Jeremy had been well known in the town and there would be many wanting to show their respects.

The first she had heard about his death had been a month after the event, when the organisation she was working for had contacted her in a remote region of Africa to inform her of it and had explained that back in the UK her presence was required to organise the funeral as she was his only heir and would need to be the executor of his will.

It was a chilly afternoon, winter was about to take over from a mellow autumn, and having become accustomed to tropical heat Emma was grateful to discover that it was warm inside the house with the old-fashioned radiators giving out welcome heat.

Once her unpacking was finished hunger began to gnaw at her and when she looked in the refrigerator she found it was stocked with the kind of food that had become just a memory while working in the heat and dust of Africa.

It was a comforting moment. Someone had been incredibly thoughtful and had pre-empted her needs

on arriving back home in such sad and gloomy circumstances, yet who had it been? There had been no
evidence of anyone living there as she'd unpacked
her clothes.

It was a Friday, and once she'd been to the law
firm the following morning the weekend was going
to be a long and empty affair until she'd got her
bearings. With that thought in mind she wrapped up
warmly, which wasn't the easiest of things to do as
all her clothes were for a hotter climate, and decided
to walk the short distance to the practice in the town
centre before it closed to see if there was anyone left
on the staff that she knew.

The darkness of a winter night was all around
Emma by the time she got there and the surgery was
closed with just an illuminated notice board by the
doorway to inform the public what the opening hours
were and what numbers to ring in an emergency.

As she turned away, about to retrace her steps, a
car door slammed shut nearby and in the light of a
streetlamp and the glare coming from the windows
of a couple of shops that were still open she saw a
man in a dark overcoat with keys in his hand walking towards the practice door with long strides.

On seeing her, he stopped and said briskly, 'The
surgery is closed, as you can see. It will be open
again at eight-thirty tomorrow morning and will
close at twelve, it being Saturday. So can *I* help you
at all?'

'Er, no, thank you, I'm fine,' she told him, taken aback by his manner and sudden appearance.

'Good. I haven't a lot of time to spare,' he explained. 'I just came back to pick up some paperwork, and after that have to be ready at any time to welcome back the prodigal daughter of our late head of the practice, which is a bind as I have a meal to organise when I get in.'

Emma was observing him wide-eyed. He was no one she recognised from the time when she'd been on the staff there and she thought he was in for a surprise.

'I have no idea who *you* are,' she told him, 'but obviously you're connected with the practice, so maybe I can save you one of the chores that you've just described. My name is Emma Chalmers. Does it ring a bell? I've returned to Glenminster to take possession of the property that my…er…father has left me *and* to find occupation as a doctor should I decide to stay.'

As he observed her, slack-jawed with surprise, she turned and began to walk back the way she'd come.

It was nine o'clock when the doorbell rang and Emma went to open the door cautiously because her knowledge of neighbours or local people was scant after her absence, so she slipped the safety chain into position before fully opening the door to her caller.

It was him again, the bossy man in the overcoat, on the doorstep and as she surveyed him blankly he said, 'You will guess why I'm here, I suppose.' She shook her head.

'I've come to say sorry for being such a pain when we met earlier. My only excuse is that I have my father living with me and he likes his meals on the dot as eating is one of his great pleasures in life.'

'Er, yes, I see,' she said, 'but why were you, as a stranger, going to be the one who welcomed me back? Surely there is someone still there who remembers me?'

'Possibly, but I am filling the slot that your father left and so was chosen to do the honours. Everyone will be pleased to see you again, I'm sure.'

'Hmm, maybe,' she commented doubtfully, with the thought in mind that there was still the matter of the missing wife to be sorted.

'We had a message from Jeremy's lawyers a couple of days ago,' he explained, 'to say that you would be arriving tomorrow, so back there when we met it didn't occur to me that you might be already here and installed in this place...which isn't very palatial, is it?'

Emma ignored the comment and said, 'I was fortunate when I arrived to find that the kind person with amazing foresight who had switched on the heating had also filled the refrigerator, as I was both cold and hungry after the journey and the change of climate.'

He was smiling. 'Lucky you, then.' Seeing her

amazing tan, he asked, 'How was Africa? I'm told that is where you've been. I'm behind on practice gossip as I've only taken over as head of the place since your father died.'

'It was hot, hard work, and amazing,' she said, and couldn't believe she would be sleeping in the house that she had never wanted to see again after the night when Jeremy had removed the scales from her eyes in such a brutal manner.

Her unexpected visitor was turning to go and said, 'I must make tracks.' Reaching out, he shook her hand briefly and said, 'The name is Glenn Bartlett.'

Taken aback by the gesture, Emma said, 'Where do *you* live?'

'In a converted barn on the edge of the town.'

'Sounds nice.'

'Yes, I suppose you could say that,' he replied without much enthusiasm, and wishing her good-bye he went.

Driving home in the dark winter night, Glenn Bartlett thought that Emma Chalmers was nothing like her father if the big photograph on the practice wall was anything to go by. Maybe she'd inherited her dark hair and hazel eyes from her mother, although did it really matter?

He was cringing at the way he'd called her the 'prodigal daughter' as he knew absolutely nothing about her except that she was Jeremy Chalmers's only relative, from the sound of things, and his moaning about how busy he was must have sounded pathetic. Would Emma Chalmers have wanted to hear the gripes of a complete stranger?

Yet they were true. Unbelievably, he'd made time that morning to switch the heating on for her, do a dash to the supermarket to fill the empty fridge in the house that she was coming to live in, and put a slow casserole in his oven for his and his father's evening meal.

Back where he had left her, Emma had found some clean bedding in one of the drawers and was making up the bed that had been hers for as long as she could remember, while at the same time remembering word for word what the stranger who had knocked on her door had said.

It would seem that, apart from the father that he'd mentioned, there was no other immediate family in his life, and where had he come from to take over in Jeremy's place? Whoever he was, he'd had style.

The next morning she awoke to a wintry sun outside her window and the feeling that she didn't want the day to get under way because she had little to look forward to except the visit to the law firm in the late morning. Her instinct was telling her not to expect any good news from that, except maybe some enlightenment regarding the missing wife.

* * *

When she arrived there she was told that Jeremy's car was hers for the taking in the scheme of things. She felt that explanations were due. It seemed that the man sitting opposite her in the office of the law firm was not aware that she wasn't a blood relation to the deceased until she explained, and when she did so Emma was told that under those circumstances she wasn't entitled to any of his estate, except the house, which he had willed to her when her mother had been alive.

'The car was all that he had left,' the partner of the law firm went on to say. 'There were no financial assets. It would seem that our man Dr Chalmers was something of a high-flyer.'

It was at that point Emma asked if he had married again, as that was what he had been contemplating, and if so his new wife would be his next of kin.

Observing her with raised brows, he said, 'Dr Chalmers didn't remarry, as far as we are aware. Maybe his sudden death prevented him from accomplishing such a thing. So if no one else comes forward to claim the car, it will be yours if you want it.'

Emma left the office feeling weary and confused about life in general.

A time check revealed that the practice building only minutes away would still be open and she decided to stop by and say hello to whoever was on duty, admitting to herself that if Dr Glenn Bartlett was one of them it would be an ideal moment to see him in a different light after being taken aback by his unexpected visit the night before.

He wasn't there, but there were those who knew her from previously and in the middle of carrying out their functions either waved or flashed a smile across until such time as they were free to talk.

As she looked around her Emma was aware that the place had been redecorated since she'd last seen it. The seating and fabrics were new and there was an atmosphere of busy contentment amongst staff that hadn't always been there when Jeremy Chalmers had reigned.

'Emma!' a voice cried from behind her, and when she turned she saw Lydia Forrester, the practice manager, who ran the business side of the place from an office downstairs, was beaming across at her.

'I hope you're back to stay,' she went on to say. 'I've missed you and wasn't happy about the way you disappeared into the night all that time ago. It was a relief to hear from your father's solicitors that you'd been located and were coming home to arrange Jeremy's funeral. He was very subdued for a long time after you left.'

'Did he marry again?' Emma questioned. 'I've wondered who was going to be the bride.'

'Marry!' Lydia exclaimed. 'Whatever makes you ask that?' She looked around her. 'How about us going down to my office for a coffee? They are too busy here to have time to talk. It will quieten down towards lunchtime, and then we can come back up.'

'Yes, that would be great,' Emma replied, and followed her downstairs.

Lydia was silent as she made the drink and produced biscuits to go with it, but once they were seated she said awkwardly, 'I would have been the bride, Emma. Your father was going to marry me. We had been seeing each other away from the practice for a few months and when he asked me to marry him I said yes, never expecting for a moment that he would want to throw you out of the house. When he confessed that he'd told you to find somewhere else to live and that you'd gone that same night I was appalled and called the wedding off. So, my dear, you have the missing bride here before you.'

'You!' Emma exclaimed incredulously, with the memory of Jeremy's hurtful revelations about him not being her father just as painful now as they'd been then. 'You gave up your chance of happiness because of me? I wouldn't have minded moving out, especially as it was you that he was intending to marry.'

She couldn't tell Lydia the rest of it. Why she'd gone in the night, feeling hurt and humiliated, desperate to get away from what she'd been told, but holding no blame against her mother. She'd dealt with women and teenage girls in the practice in the same position that her mother had been in and had sympathised with their problems.

The practice manager was smiling. 'Your disappearance saved me from what would have been a big mistake, marrying Jeremy. I'd never been married before. Had never wanted to, but as middle age was creeping up on me it was getting a bit lonely and… well you know the rest. But happiness doesn't come at the expense of the hurt of others…and ever since I've looked upon it as a lucky escape.'

'I'm so glad you've explained,' Emma told her. 'From the first moment of my return I've wondered why the house felt so empty and cheerless. I've felt that I couldn't possibly live in it under those conditions, but now I might change my mind and make it fit to stay here.'

Feet on the stairs and voices were coming down towards them. It was twelve o'clock Saturday lunchtime, the practice had closed, and as friends of yesterday and newcomers she had to get to know crowded round her, for the first time it felt like coming home.

'Where is Glenn this morning?' she heard someone ask, and before a reply was forthcoming he spoke from up above.

'Did I hear my name mentioned?' he asked from the top of the stairs, and as he came down towards them he smiled across at her and asked the assembled staff, 'So have you done anything about arranging a welcome night out for Dr Chalmers?'

'We were just about to,' someone said. 'It's why we're all gathered below decks, but first we need to know if Emma would like that sort of thing.'

'I would love it,' she told them with a glance at Lydia, who had brought some clarity into her life and was smiling across at her.

'So how about tonight, at one of the restaurants on the Promenade that has a dance floor?' Mark Davies, a young GP trainee and a stranger to her, suggested. 'Any excuse for food and fun.'

As the idea seemed to appeal to the rest of them it was arranged that they meet at the Barrington Bar at eight o'clock. As they all went home to make the best of what was left of Saturday, Emma felt that it was beginning to feel more like a homecoming, although she had no idea what to wear.

There had been no time or inclination to dress up where she'd been. It had been cotton cropped trousers and a loose shirt with a wide-brimmed hat to protect her face from the heat of the sun, and any clothes that she'd left in the wardrobe here would be reminders of the hurt that being told she had been living there on sufferance had caused. They would also smell stale.

So after a quick bite in a nearby snack bar she went clothes shopping for the evening ahead and found the experience exhilarating after the long gap of wearing attractive outfits. Her euphoria didn't last long.

There was the arranging of Jeremy's funeral that had to be her first priority after the weekend, and if she'd needed a reminder the amount of black outfits in the boutiques and big stores would have given her memory the necessary prod.

As she made her way homewards with a dark winter suit and matching accessories for the funeral, and, totally opposite, a turquoise mini-dress for the night ahead with silver shoes and a white fake-fur jacket, Emma was remembering that it was the new head of the practice who had prompted the staff to arrange the welcome-back occasion of the coming evening. Would he be there?

Glenn Bartlett knew her less than anyone and, having seen him in the smart black overcoat, she imagined that he would turn up well dressed.

He did come, looking more like an attractive member of the opposite sex than a sombre well-wisher, and suddenly the evening felt happy and carefree after her time of hurt and toiling in hot places.

For one thing, Lydia had solved the missing wife mystery that had been concerning Emma, and for another the surgery crowd, apart from a couple of newcomers, had been delighted to see her back in Glenminster. *And to feel wanted was a wonderful thing.*

The Barrington Bar, where they were gathered, was one of the town's high spots as it boasted good food in a smart restaurant area beside a dance floor with musicians who were a delight to the ear, and as she looked around her the new head of the practice said from behind her, 'So is it good to be back, Emma?'

'Yes,' she said, sparkling back at him, and he thought that the weary-looking occupant of what had been a drab, deserted house had come out of her shell with gusto. The dress, jacket and shoes were magical.

Some of the practice staff had brought partners with them but not so Glenn Bartlett. There was a look of solitariness about him, even though he was being friendly enough after their uncomfortable first meeting.

Did he live alone in the converted barn that he'd mentioned when he'd rung her bell last night? she wondered. Someone had said when they'd all been gathered at the practice earlier that he'd been taking his father with the big appetite home.

At that moment James Prentice, a young GP who had recently joined the practice, appeared at her side and asked if she would like to dance. As Emma smiled at him and took hold of his outstretched hand, the man by her side strolled towards the bar and once he'd been served seated himself at an empty table and gazed into space unsmilingly.

He'd been a fool to come, Glenn was thinking. The fact that he'd suggested a welcome homecoming for Jeremy Chalmers's daughter would have been enough to add to switching on the heating and filling the refrigerator in that ghastly place, without turning out for a night at the Barrington Bar. It would have been a tempting idea at one time but not now, never again.

If it hadn't been for the fact that Emma Chalmers had returned to the Cotswolds for a very sad occasion he would have left her to it, but common decency had required that he make sure she had food and warmth and the pleasure of tonight's gathering to make her feel welcome because she'd looked tired and joyless on her arrival, which was not surprising after a long flight and a funeral to arrange as soon as possible.

Glenn finished his drink and, rising from his seat, told those of his companions who were nearest that he was leaving, going home to enjoy the peace that his father's departure had restored.

Emma was still on the dance floor in her partner's arms and as she glanced across he waved a brief goodbye and was gone.

Back home he sat in silence, gazing out into the dark night with the memory of Jeremy Chalmers's last moments on the golf course starkly clear. He'd known him before stepping into the vacancy that his passing had left.

The then head of the practice and his father had met at university. Jeremy, who had been on the point of retiring, had invited his friend's son, also a doctor, to stay for the weekend to familiarise himself

with the running of the practice with a view to taking over as his replacement in the very near future
after the necessary procedures had been dealt with.

They'd gone for a round of golf after lunch at the
club and while on the course Jeremy had suffered
the heart attack that had proved fatal. In intense pain
he had managed to gasp out his last request and he,
Glenn, working on him desperately as he'd tried to
save him, had been stunned when he'd heard what
it was.

'I have a daughter,' he'd croaked between pain
spasms, 'and I upset her gravely some years ago, so
much so that she left to go where I don't know, except it wasn't in this country. Emma is a doctor and
most likely has gone to one of the hot spots where
they need as many medics as they can get.'

'Bring her home for me, Glenn, back to where
she was happy until I told her some unmentionable
things about me.'

His lips had been blue, his eyes glazing even as
the sound of an approaching ambulance could be
heard screeching towards them, and his last words
had been, 'Promise you will?'

'Yes, I promise,' he'd told him gravely, and then
his father's friend had died.

Now, sitting sombrely in the attractive sitting room
of the property he'd bought on the occasion of taking
over the practice, Glenn was remembering the time

and effort he'd put in to discover the whereabouts of the missing daughter. He was upset to think that he hadn't tuned in to who she was outside the surgery the night before.

Fortunately he'd made sure that the house that had been her home previously was warm and habitable a day early and had had food in the refrigerator. Then had gone the extra mile by suggesting that the folk from the practice make her welcome with an evening in one of Glenminster's high spots.

Now just one thing remained regarding his promise to her father, and when that was done maybe he would be able to have a life of his own once again. The task of locating Emma Chalmers had been mammoth.

He would be there for her at her father's funeral and once that ordeal was over he was going to step aside and let her get on with her life. The same way he intended to carry on with his own, which was empty of womankind and was going to stay that way.

Drawing the curtains across to shut out the night, he went slowly up the spiral staircase that graced the hallway of his home and lay on top of the bedcovers, his last concern before sleep claimed him being the stranger that he had reluctantly taken under his wing.

What was her story? he wondered. Had she been close to Jeremy and they'd rowed about something that had made her go off in a huff? From what he'd said in his dying moments, it had seemed that Jeremy had been the reason for Emma's departure and whatever it had been he'd had cause to regret it.

Since coming back to her roots she had never mentioned him, which was not a good omen, and what about the mother that she'd lost not so long before her hasty departure? What sort of a marriage had she and Jeremy had?

CHAPTER TWO

THERE WERE A few offers to see Emma home safely when the Barrington Bar closed at the stroke of midnight heralding the Sabbath, but Lydia forestalled them by saying, 'I'm in my car, Emma, and haven't been on the wine. Would you like a lift as I have to pass your place?' And added to the rest, 'That leaves two more empty places if anyone wants to join us.'

The offer was immediately taken up by older members of staff, one of the practice nurses and a receptionist, both of whom lived just a short distance away, and when they were eventually alone in the car Lydia said, 'So how has your first full day back in Glenminster felt?'

'Very strange,' Emma told her, 'and unexpectedly pleasant. But that feeling isn't going to last long when I start making the funeral arrangements for Jeremy. He wasn't my father. Did you know that, Lydia?'

'No, I didn't!' she gasped 'How long have you been aware of it?'

'Just as long as it took him to let me see how little

I meant to him—which was immediately after he'd said he wanted me gone, out of the way.'

The house was in sight and when Lydia stopped the car she said dejectedly, 'And all of that was because he wanted to marry me? Surely he didn't think I would allow him to hurt *you* so that he could have *me*. None of it brought him any joy, did it? Without even knowing about what he had said regarding him not being your father, I refused to go ahead with the wedding when he told me that he'd made it clear that you wouldn't be welcome around the place once we were married. Sadly, by that time Emma, you'd gone and not a single person knew where you were.

'Jeremy was with Glenn when he had the heart attack and made him promise to find you and bring you back to Glenminster to make up for all the hurt he'd caused you. So he did have a conscience of sorts, I suppose. Glenn, being the kind of guy who keeps his word, spent hours searching for you in every possible way until he finally located you. No doubt once the funeral is over he will be ready to get back to his own life, hoping that yours is sorted.'

Shaken to the core by what she'd been told about the man she'd been going to marry, Lydia was about to drive off into the night when Emma asked, 'Was it Dr Bartlett who saw to it that there was heating and food in the house?'

'Yes,' she was told. 'Glenn mentioned that he was going to deal with those things and you almost arrived before he'd done so by appearing a day early. Now, one last thing before I go—have you enjoyed tonight, Emma?'

'It was wonderful,' she said, 'and would have been even more so if I could have thanked Dr Bartlett for all he has done for me, but as I didn't know about it I shall make up for my lack of appreciation in the morning.'

Glenn was having a late breakfast when he saw Emma appear on Sunday morning, and as he watched her walk purposefully along the drive he sighed. What now? he wondered. He didn't have to wait long for an answer as once he had invited her inside she told him, 'I'm here to say thank you for all that you've done for me, Dr Bartlett. I had no idea until Lydia explained on the way home last night that my father had put upon you the burden of finding me, and that it was you who had made my homecoming as comfortable as possible with food and warmth. It must have all been very time-consuming.'

He was smiling, partly with relief because she wanted no more from him and because she was so easily pleased with what he'd done for her. At the beginning Emma Chalmers had just been a lost soul that Jeremy had asked him to find so that he could die in the hope that he, Glenn, would bring her back to where she belonged. Difficult as the process had sometimes been, he'd had no regrets in having to keep the promise he'd made.

Pointing to a comfortable chair by the fireside, he said, 'It was in a good cause, Emma, and having now met you I realise just how worthy it was. Whatever it was that Jeremy had done to you it was clear that he regretted it. I could tell that it lay heavily on his conscience, and as my last involvement in your affairs, if you need any assistance with the funeral arrangements, you have only to ask.'

She was smiling but there were tears on her lashes as she said, 'I will try not to involve you if I can, but thanks for the offer.'

As she rose from the chair, ready to depart, he said, 'My parents will be at the funeral. They are a crazy pair but their hearts are in the right place and I love them dearly. It was my dad who told Jeremy that I was a doctor and had come to live in the village after leaving a practice up north. So that was how I came to be with him on the day he died.

'Jeremy had been to see me and, having been told that I'd been doing a similar job to his in the place that I'd left, asked if I would be interested in replacing him at the practice in Glenminster as he was ready to retire. Once I'd seen it and been introduced to staff I was keen to take over, and that is how I come to be here.'

'Going through the usual formalities with the health services and the rest took a while but I had no regrets, and now we have his daughter back with us, so hopefully he will rest in peace. You don't resemble him at all, do you?' he commented.

He saw her flinch but her only comment gave nothing away.

'No,' she said in a low voice. 'I'm more like my mother.' Having no wish to start going down those sort of channels in the conversation, she said, 'Thanks again, Dr Bartlett, for all that you've done for both me *and* him.' On the point of leaving, she commented, 'Your home is lovely.'

He nodded. 'Yes, I suppose it is, and with the hills above and the delightful town below them, I am happy to be settled here.'

'So do you live alone, then?' she couldn't resist asking.

There was a glint in the deep blue eyes observing her and Emma wished she hadn't asked as his reply was short and purposeful, and to make it even more so he had opened the door and was waiting for her to depart as he delivered it. 'Yes. I prefer the solitary life. It is so much easier to deal with.'

She smiled a twisted smile and told him, 'I've had a lot of that sort of thing where I've been based over the last few years and to me it was not easy to cope with at all. Solitariness is something that takes all the colour out of life, so I'm afraid I can't agree with you on that.' And stepping out into the crisp Sunday morning, she walked briskly towards the town centre and the house on the edge of it that the man who hadn't been her father had left to her for reasons she didn't know.

There had been no generosity in Jeremy on that awful night and ever since she had needed a name that wasn't his: the name of the man who had made her mother pregnant. Did he even know that he had a daughter?

Common sense was butting in, taking over her thought processes. So what? You had a fantastic mother who loved and cherished you. Let that be balm to your soul, and as for that guy back there, doesn't every doctor long for peace after spending long hours of each day caring for the health of others? If you've never had the same yearning, you are unique.

Back at the property that Emma had admired, Glenn was facing up to the fact that his description of his home life must have sounded extremely boring. With a glance at the photograph on his bedside table he wondered what Jeremy's daughter would think of him if she knew why he needed to be alone.

Serena was gone, along with many others, taken from him by one of nature's cruel tricks, a huge tsunami, unexpected, unbelievable. Since then he had lived for two things only, caring for his parents and his job, and there were times when the job was the least exhausting of the two.

* * *

They'd been holidaying in one of the world's delightful faraway places when it had struck. The only reason he had survived was because he'd taken a book
with him to one of the resort's golden beaches and
had been engrossed in its contents, while Serena had
been doing her favourite thing, swimming to a rock
that was quite a way out and sunbathing there.

When the huge wall of water had come thunder-
ing towards them, sweeping everything out of the
way with its force, they'd both been caught up in it.
Glenn had been closer to land and had surfaced and
managed to hold onto driftwood before staggering
towards what had been left of the hotel where they'd
been staying. But of Serena, his wife, sunbathing on
the rock far out, she and others like her had disappeared and had never been found.

Weeks later, with all hope gone, Glenn had arrived
back but had been unable to bear to stay where they'd
lived together so happily. So he had moved to a new
job and a new house in the town where his parents
lived, telling the older folk that he didn't want his
affairs discussed amongst the residents of Glenminster, or anywhere else for that matter.

The only way he had coped after leaving the practice up north to join the one in the town centre had
been by giving his total commitment to his patients,
and when away from the practice shutting himself

into the converted barn that he'd bought and in the silence grieving for what he had lost.

That day on the golf course had been a one-off. Jeremy had persuaded Glenn to join him there for a round or two much against his inclination because it would be interrupting the quiet time that he allowed himself whenever possible.

When the other man had collapsed with a massive heart attack in the middle of the game and hadn't responded to Glenn's frantic efforts as they'd waited for an ambulance, Jeremy had begged him with his dying breath to find his daughter and bring her home to Glenminster. Though aghast at the request, as it had seemed that no one had known where she was, he had carried out Jeremy's wishes faithfully. Once the funeral was over Glenn was fully intent on returning to his reclusive evenings and weekends.

The fact that Emma, having only been back in her home town three days, had visited him on the third one had not been what he had expected. Neither was it what he was going to want once he began to live his own life again.

He'd seen to it that she was back home where she belonged and on a grey winter's day had made sure she would be warm and fed when she arrived. He had even gone so far as to make sure that she received a warm welcome home from the practice staff at the Barrington Bar, of all places, which had not been the kind of thing on his personal agenda. Once his duty had been done he had been off home to the peace that his bruised heart cried out for.

Only to find that Emma had good manners. On the quiet Sunday morning she hadn't picked up the phone to thank him for all that he'd done on her behalf, which until her chat with Lydia she'd had no knowledge of, but had come in person. So why was he feeling so edgy about it?

Was she going to want to come back into the practice? They needed another doctor. But was the daughter of chancer and man about town Jeremy Chalmers someone he would want around the place?

He spent the rest of the day clearing up fallen leaves in the garden and at last, satisfied that all was tidy, went inside when daylight began to fade and began to make himself a meal.

As he was on the point of putting a piece of steak under the grill the phone rang and when Glenn heard Emma's voice at the other end of the line he sighed. She didn't hear it, but his tone of voice when he replied was enough for her to know it would have been better to have waited until the following morning to report the conversation she'd just had with a funeral director.

'I'm sorry to disturb you again, Dr Bartlett,' she said. 'It is just that I've been speaking to the funeral firm, who have been waiting for me to appear with regard to a date for the funeral that has been unfortunately delayed because of my absence, and they pointed out that as my—er—father was so well known in the practice and around the town, maybe a Sunday would be the most suitable day. Then all the staff would be free and more of the townspeople would be able to attend, it not being a regular working day for most people.'

'Yes, good thinking,' he agreed, relieved that the final chapter of the sad episode on the golf course was to be soon for her sake as well as his. 'Why not call in at the practice tomorrow so that I can help you with the rest of the arrangements?'

There was silence at the other end of the line for a moment and then Emma said haltingly, 'Are you sure you don't mind me butting into your time there? I'm afraid that I've been in your face a lot since I returned.'

Glenn thought that she'd picked up on his moroseness and his desire to be free of his commitment to a man he'd hardly known, so he told her, 'No, not so. Once the funeral is organised and has taken place we can both get on with our lives.' But as the steak began to sizzle and the vegetables he intended having with it came to the boil Emma had one last thing to say and he almost groaned out loud.

'Just one thing and then I really will leave you to enjoy your Sunday evening. It is with regard to the food that you provided me with. How much am I in your debt?'

'You're not. You owe me nothing,' he said abruptly. 'It was part of the promise that I made to a dying man.'

Her response came fast. 'So let me make you a meal after the practice has closed tomorrow evening. It would save me butting into your lunch hour to discuss the arrangements for next Sunday.'

His reply was given at a similar speed. 'No! I've told you, Emma. You owe me nothing. I'll see you tomorrow at midday.' And as she rang off without further comment it was clear to her that he was more than eager for the role he had played during recent weeks to be at an end.

Glenn had been looking forward to the meal he'd cooked, but every time he thought about how uncivil he'd been when she'd wanted to thank him for what he'd done for her the food felt as if it would choke him.

Emma would have understood if you'd explained that you still mourn the loss of your wife under horrendous circumstances, he told himself, and that after a week at the surgery you want to be left in peace.

Pushing the plate away from him, he poured a glass of wine and went to sit in front of the log fire that was burning brightly in the sitting room. Gazing morosely at the dancing flames, Glenn admitted to himself that it was most unfair to transfer the pain of his shattered life to a stranger such as her.

He was behaving like a complete moron. Why in

heaven's name didn't he explain the reason for his behaviour and try to get it in perspective? Otherwise people would start asking questions that he didn't want to answer.

For one thing, Emma wouldn't want to feel that his attitude was another dark chapter of her life to add to the fact that she had to attend the funeral of a man who had confessed to causing her great hurt.

With determination to atone for the rebuff he'd handed out when she'd wanted to make him a meal, Glenn decided that he would call at her house on his way home the following evening if she didn't appear in the lunch hour, and do all he could to show Emma that he felt no ill will towards her. That his behaviour came from pain that never went away, so he needed to focus on work.

As his first appointment of the day arrived on the following morning he settled down to what he did best: looking after his patients.

The staff of the practice consisted of Lydia, the practice manager, six GPs with himself as senior, two trainee GPs, who were there to earn their accreditation after qualifying as doctors, and four incredible receptionists who held it all together.

Once the man who had been his predecessor had been laid to rest, the gloom that had hung over the practice might lighten. As a new era began, was Jeremy's prodigal daughter going to want to join the practice, or had he put her off completely? he wondered.

Back at the house the night before Emma had been deep in thought as she'd cleared away after a solitary meal, and they had not been happy thoughts. Did she want to be in the first funeral car on her own? There was no one who should rightly be with her. Her mother had left no relations, neither had Jeremy—and she had no knowledge of who her birth father might be.

Maybe Lydia would join her. If she did it would help to take away some of the dreadful lost and lonely feeling that she'd had ever since she'd been told with brutal clarity that the man she had always thought to be her father, in fact, was not.

The other concern on her mind was the fact that she was having a bad start in getting to know the man who had replaced Jeremy in the practice. She was experiencing a kind and thoughtful side to his character that was contradicted by his brusque attitude on occasion.

It was clear that Glenn was not a good mixer. It would be interesting to find out what sort of a man he was if she joined the practice staff. She did want to feel happy and fulfilled back in Glenminster, if that was possible.

She didn't want to return to the heat and endless toil of Africa until she had recharged her batteries in the place where she had grown up and where she'd

had a job she'd loved until the bubble of her contentment had burst.

With those thoughts in mind she presented herself at the practice in the lunch hour. When Glenn's
last morning patient had gone, and before the afternoon's sick and suffering began to arrive, he left his
consulting room and went to see if Emma had come,
as he'd asked her to. He was relieved to find her outside in the corridor deep in conversation with Lydia.

On seeing him the older woman suggested that
Emma come down to her office for a coffee before
she went, and left them together. So Glenn opened
the door that he'd just come through and when Emma
was seated on the opposite side of his desk at his invitation he asked, 'So how are you this morning?'
He followed it with another question. 'Are you any
nearer to knowing how you want the funeral to be
arranged?'

Emma was looking around her. The last time she'd
been in the room Jeremy had been seated where
Glenn was now. The memory of her last day in Glenminster came back so clearly it was making her feel
weak and disoriented, although Jeremy hadn't delivered the actual body blow until late that evening,
when he'd been drinking and had been about to climb
the stairs to sleep it off.

Glenn watched the colour drain from her face and
came round the desk to stand beside her, concerned.
But Emma was rallying, taking control of the black

moment from the past. Managing a wan smile as he gazed down at her anxiously, she said, 'I'm all right, it was just a memory of the last time I was in this room and what happened afterwards that knocked me sideways.'

Straightening up in the chair, she said, 'In answer to your question, I'm fine. I've just asked Lydia if she will join me in the one and only funeral car that will be needed instead of my being alone. I have no relatives that I could ask to keep me company on such a depressing occasion. Obviously there will be other people following in their cars, but that is how it will be for me.'

'And what did she say?' he asked uncomfortably, knowing that he should have given some thought to Emma's solitariness on the day instead of being so wrapped up in his own feelings.

'She said yes, that she will be with me.'

'Good. I hadn't realised just how alone you are, Emma,' he commented. 'If Lydia hadn't been able to do as you asked I would have volunteered. Though whether you would have wanted someone you hardly know with you on such an occasion seems unlikely.'

He glanced at a clock on the wall and commented, 'I can only give you half an hour before my after-noon patients start arriving so what exactly do you want to discuss?'

'I'm going to have an announcement in the local press, announcing that the funeral will be on Sunday at the crematorium at three o'clock, for the benefit of anyone wanting to take part in the service or just to watch,' she told him, 'and I'm arranging a meal for afterwards for the practice staff and any of his close friends.'

'That sounds fine,' he agreed. 'What about flowers?'

'No. Instead, I'd like donations to be made to the Heart Foundation, or locally to Horizon's Eye Hospital, which is an amazing place. Do you think those kind of arrangements will be suitable?' she enquired. She was ready to go and leave him to his busy afternoon, aware all the while that the time she had taken out of his lunch hour might leave no opportunity for him to have a snack or whatever he did for refreshment at that time of day.

But remembering Glenn Bartlett's rebuffs of the previous evening, there was no way she was going to concern herself about that. He was the one who'd suggested a chat in the lunch hour, and in the days when she'd been employed there she'd often missed her lunch due to pressure of work.

'Yes,' he told her, unaware of the thoughts going through her mind. 'Just one question. Am I right in presuming that it will all start from what is now your house?'

'Yes, of course,' she replied, the cold hand of dread clamping on her heart. Until the man she'd thought had been her father had been laid to rest she couldn't even contemplate what she was going to do in the future if Glenn didn't want her back at the surgery.

It was possible, taking note of his manner towards her, that he could be feeling that enough was enough. That having found her and brought her back to where Jeremy Chalmers had wanted her to be…and the rest of it, he'd had enough without her being forever in his sights.

Maybe after Sunday, in the relief that the slate had been wiped clean, she would be able to see everything more clearly. As far as she was concerned, it couldn't come quickly enough. So, getting up to go down to Lydia's office in the basement for the coffee that she'd suggested, Emma wished Glenn goodbye and left him deep in thought.

In the days that followed Emma felt as if she were in some sort of limbo. She wandered around the shops for suitable clothes to fill her wardrobe against winter's chill, while trying to ignore signs of the coming of Christmas already on view in some of them.

It was the last thing she wanted to contemplate, spending Christmas in the house that had been left to her in its present state. It had always been basic and she'd often wondered why her mother had never complained, but now she understood. Maybe Jeremy had expected gratitude instead of requests for a brighter home from the woman he had married to save her name.

She supposed she could give the place a make-over or alternatively put it up for sale and move to somewhere smaller and more modern and not so near the bustle of the town, but until Sunday's ordeal was over she couldn't contemplate the future.

It was done. The event that Emma had been dreading had taken place and, with Lydia beside her and Glenn Bartlett hovering nearby, she had coped. There had been a good turnout, as she'd expected, and now the staff of the practice and a few of Jeremy's golfing friends were gathered in a restaurant in the town centre for the meal she'd organised.

Emma was feeling that now the future was going to open out in front of her, though not as an exciting challenge. More as if it was hidden in a mist of uncertainty. As she caught the glance of the man who had brought her home from a foreign country to an uncertain future, she felt her colour rise at the thought of asking for a return to her previous position in the practice. He was so obviously wanting an end to their unwanted connection.

Did he ever smile? she wondered. If his expression was less closed and sombre he would be the most attractive man she'd ever met. His hair was dark russet, his eyes as blue as a summer sky—but always with no joy in them.

It seemed that he was unmarried, not in a relationship of any kind, and lived alone in his delightful property, with the occasional visit from his elderly parents.

Her smile was wry. It seemed as if neither of them was fulfilling their full potential. His life sounded almost hermit-like. Or was it that he had enough to think about with the job and being there for his folks? Although they sounded anything but fragile.

She was being observed in return. What was it that Jeremy Chalmers had done to cause his daughter the degree of hurt that he'd confessed to when he'd lain dying? Glenn asked himself. It had been enough to make her leave Glenminster and only be prepared to return in the event of his death.

Emma didn't come over as the weak and whingeing type. Whatever it was, she didn't carry her sorrows around with her, as he did. Maybe they weren't as dreadful as the burden he was carrying, having Serena there one moment and the next gone for ever. If they'd had a child to remember her by he might be coping better.

The funeral party were getting ready to leave. He got to his feet and joined them and as Emma shook hands and thanked them for their time and their support, he waited until they'd gone and asked, 'Do you want a lift home, Emma?'

She smiled. 'No, I'm fine. Lydia is going to take me, but thanks for the offer. And also thanks once again for the way you have been there for me, a stranger, at this awful time.' Her smile deepened. 'I promise I will not cause any more hassle in your life.'

Before he could explain that his moroseness came from coping with terrible grief every moment of every day, she had gone to where the practice manager was waiting for her, leaving him to return to the empty house that he had turned into his stronghold against life without Serena. For the first time since he had gone to live there Glenn was reluctant to turn the key in the lock and go inside, and when he did so, instead of its comforting peace, a heavy silence hung over every room.

CHAPTER THREE

WHEN EMMA AWOKE the next morning the first flickers of daylight were appearing on the wintry horizon and she thought that it would have been so much easier to have returned to Glenminster in summer, with long mellow days to provide some brightness to the occasion.

The feeling of closure of the day before was not so strong in the moment of awakening to the rest of her life, because in the background was, and always would be, the shadowy figure of the man who was her birth father.

But there were two things to look forward to that hopefully would not have any painful attachments to them. First, the opportunity, if Glenn Bartlett was agreeable, for her to apply for the GP vacancy at the practice where she'd been so happy and fulfilled before, and, second, house hunting for a modern apartment bought from the proceeds of the sale of the house that she had returned to so unwillingly.

With regard to the practice, Glenn couldn't stop

her from applying for the post, but his obvious eagerness to be left in peace after spending so much time on her and her affairs indicated that he might not be bubbling over at the thought of her being still in his life to some extent. The only way to pursue that matter was to get in touch and sound him out about joining the practice.

Before she did either of those things there was something she wanted to do first and that was to put flowers on her mother's grave in a nearby churchyard, knowing that it would have been sadly neglected during her absence as Jeremy hadn't been into that sort of thing.

It had been on her mind ever since she'd come back to Glenminster but she had needed to be clear of her responsibilities regarding *him* before bringing her life back to some degree of normality.

As she approached the grave with an array of winter flowers, Emma stopped in her tracks. It was clean and tidy but already had a display of roses gracing the centrepiece that looked as if they had been put there recently.

The only person she could think of who might have done that was Lydia from the practice. The two women had been great friends and she had called off the wedding when she'd discovered how Jeremy had been planning to treat her dead friend's daughter.

The church was open and rather than not place the flowers she'd brought on the grave Emma went inside and asked the verger if she could borrow a vase for a short while, and was told to help herself to any that were standing idle on the window sills.

When she'd arranged the flowers to her satisfaction and had placed them next to the others, she stood back and observed them gravely. For the first time since Jeremy had left her feeling lost and joyless there was peace in her heart and it was all due to an attractive stranger who had searched for her high and low to keep a promise he had made.

After leaving the cemetery Emma went to the garage where Jeremy's car had been kept awaiting her return to claim it. A large, black, showy model, it had no appeal whatsoever, and with the manager's agreement she changed it for something smaller and brighter. She came away with cash to spare and the feeling that for once everything was going right, or at least it would be once she'd thanked Lydia for looking after the grave in her absence.

She had to pass the practice on her way home and intended to stop to do that, and at the same time ask Glenn about the vacancy for another doctor.

She found them both having just come up from the monthly practice meeting in the basement. For once there was a smile on his face when he saw her and no sign of the weary tolerance of previous meetings. She decided that it must be the pleasure of being off the hook that was making him look happy to see her. But how was Glenn going to feel if she wanted to be back in the practice, always around in some form or other?

'I came to see you both for different reasons,' she told them, 'and won't keep either of you for more than a few moments.'

'Fine,' he said. 'I'll be in my consulting room when you've had your chat with Lydia,' and strolled off in that direction.

'Is anything wrong?' the practice manager asked anxiously.

'No. Not at all,' Emma told her. 'I've just been to put flowers on my mother's grave and there were already some there, beautiful cream roses, when I was expecting it to look totally neglected. I thought that only you would think to do that in my absence. So thank you, Lydia.'

'You're mistaken,' the practice manager told her gently. 'You are right in thinking I had a mind to keep it clean and with fresh flowers, but I haven't done so recently.'

'And you don't know who else might have done?' Emma asked incredulously.

'No. How very strange.'

'Isn't it? I shall have to keep a lookout for the mystery grave-visitor,' she said slowly, 'and will let you know when I discover who it is.'

When she knocked on the door of Glenn's consulting room and was told to enter she was still in a state of amazement. He said, 'What gives? You look as if you've seen a ghost.'

'Not exactly,' she told him, 'but something along those lines.'

'Nothing to do with me, I hope?'

'No. I came to ask if I could talk to you some time about the vacancy for another doctor here at the practice.'

'I see,' he replied thoughtfully. 'So what is wrong with now? The place is empty. We don't make appointments for the afternoon when we have the monthly practice meeting in the morning, so I am free and would like to hear what you have to say.'

'I would like to join the practice again if you would be happy about that,' she told him. 'I would never have left it in the first place if Jeremy hadn't told me something one night that hurt so much I just had to get away to face up to what it meant. I left the next morning.

'It is something I don't want to discuss, but as everyone else in the practice who was present at that time is aware of how I left without saying any goodbyes, I felt that I should explain the reason for my absence to you.'

'You don't have to explain anything to me about your private life, Emma,' he said levelly. 'Mine is buried deep in a black pit that I never seem to be able to climb out of. As to the rest of what you've said, I am concerned that you seem to think I wouldn't be happy to have you as part of the practice. If I have given you that impression, I'm sorry.

'The vacancy has arisen because one of our GPs has gone to live abroad unexpectedly with very little notice. Having once been employed here, you will be aware that in the town centre the pressure is always on. So shall we fix a starting date? And I will deal with any necessary paperwork regarding you coming back to us.'

He was observing her thoughtfully. 'Maybe you should give yourself time to unwind before you come. Your own health is just as important as the health of others, and stress is something that can wind one down into a dangerous state of exhaustion. I know because I've been there.'

Emma could feel tears threatening. The very person she had thought would be dubious about the idea of her rejoining the practice was being kind and thoughtful, so much so that if she didn't make a quick departure she would be weeping out her pain and loneliness in front of him.

'I'll be fine,' she told him hoarsely. 'I need to be with people of my own kind, Glenn, and after the sort of life I've been leading for the last few years nothing I have to deal with at the practice is going to stress me out. Thanks for being so considerate. It is a long time since anyone took the trouble to notice that I was there.' And before he had the chance to make any further comment she went, hurrying through the empty surgery with head bent.

He'd touched a nerve there, Glenn thought when Emma had gone. Had he been so wrapped up in his own sorrows that he hadn't noticed that Emma was not the calm unflappable person that she appeared to be on the outside? The few words of concern that he'd felt obliged to express had opened a floodgate of pain from somewhere. At least he had his parents to give his life some purpose, but there had been no mention of anyone close to her, or surely they would have been at yesterday's funeral.

Lydia knew Emma better than anyone else, it would seem. Maybe she could throw some light on the distress of a few moments ago. He found her on the point of leaving, ready to take advantage of the empty surgery, and asked, 'Can you spare a moment?'

'Yes,' was the reply. She liked the reserved but totally dependable head of the practice. After Jeremy's comings and goings and afternoons on the golf course when he should have been holding the place together Glenn Bartlett was a pleasure to work with.

'Just a quick question,' he said. 'I've had a chat with Emma about her joining the practice in the near future. It seems that she is keen to be back where she belonged before going to Africa and will be with us soon.'

'I am so glad about that,' Lydia said. 'She has had

a hard time over the last few years. Emma lost the mother that she adored when she was very young and ended up with just Jeremy in that dreadful house until he upset her so much that she left in the middle of the night. Until you found her no one knew where she was. I am sure she is going to be all right now, Glenn.'

'I hope so,' he said doubtfully, 'but when I suggested that she take some time to recover from the last couple of weeks and have a rest before stepping back into the practice she became so upset I wished I hadn't spoken. Why do you think that was?'

'It could have been because it is so long since anyone showed her any consideration,' was the reply, which was almost word for word what Emma had said.

Lydia could have told him how Emma had been informed that she was a nobody in the unkindest possible way, cast aside by the man she'd thought was her father, and it was his concern for her well-being that had broken through her reserve. But there was no way she was going to tell a virtual stranger about the tricks that life had played on someone that she was so fond of.

One of the reasons Lydia had agreed to marry Jeremy had been the desire to be a good stepmother to his motherless daughter, and also she'd been weary of returning to an empty house at the end of each day at the practice.

But he had been his own worst enemy when he'd been too quick to tell Emma that she was going to be in the way when he married for a second time, without divulging the name of his bride-to-be. When Emma had voiced a mild protest, in his drunkenness Jeremy had wiped out her identity, so much so that when he'd woken up the next morning she'd gone.

'I see,' Glenn said, breaking into her thoughts. 'I knew nothing about Emma as she was long gone when I joined the practice. Until Jeremy begged me to bring her back to where she belonged that day on the golf course. Having done as he asked, I have wanted to get back to my own life, such as it is. I will bear in mind what you have said, Lydia. I'm sorry to have kept you.'

'It has been good to talk,' she told him, and clutching her car keys disappeared into the winter night.

He was the last to leave, the rest of the staff having taken advantage of the absence of patients because of the meeting in the basement. When Glenn turned to go to where his car was parked, after securing the outer door of the building in the light of streetlamps, he was reminded of the night he'd first seen Emma hovering hesitantly outside the locked building and had mistaken her for a patient. He had never expected in that moment of meeting that her connection with the practice was going to be the same as his own to a lesser degree.

The thought of it was fine, just as long as his life

away from the place was not going to be a further-
ance of the responsibilities he had undertaken on her
behalf that day on the golf course.

It occurred to him that maybe some shuffling
around was required with regard to who was allo-
cated what consulting room. There a vacant one next
to his so maybe a transfer for one of the longer-serv-
ing members of the practice staff would work, with
Emma installed in a room further down the corridor.

As he left the practice Glenn was tempted to call
on her to make sure that she was all right after her
emotional outburst earlier. He pointed his car in the
direction of her house, but drove straight past on
observing the flashy vehicle that belonged to James
Prentice parked on the driveway.

Trust that one to be first in line when a new
woman appeared on the scene, he thought grimly,
with the memory of the trainee GP monopolising
Emma at the Barrington Bar on the night when the
members of the practice had gathered to welcome
her back home.

Yet why not? Just because his life was grey and
empty there was no reason why those who had a
zest for living should be denied the pleasure of it.
At least seeing Prentice's car outside Emma's house
had brought with it the relief of knowing that she
wasn't alone and sad back there after her emotional
exit from the practice earlier.

That line of reasoning lasted until he was pulling

up on his own drive and knew that he had to make sure that she was all right whether Prentice was there or not. He thought grimly that he really was carrying his promise to Jeremy Chalmers to the extreme. But he was already reversing and when he approached Emma's house once again he groaned at the sight of the same car still on the drive.

But the thought was there that maybe she hadn't invited him, that the pushy Prentice had invaded her privacy for some reason. After seeing him perform at the Barrington Bar the other night there were a few reasons why he had an uneasy feeling about him.

After parking across the road from the house, Glenn rang the doorbell and adopted a casual approach when the door was opened to him, but there was nothing casual about Emma's expression when she saw him standing there.

'Glenn!' she breathed, stepping back to let him in. 'Is everything all right?'

'Er...yes,' he told her. 'I just wanted to make sure that you'd arrived home safely and realise that I needn't have concerned myself as I see that you have Prentice here.'

'What gives you that idea?' she exclaimed. 'I'm on my own. I haven't seen James since that night at the Barrington Bar.'

'But the car on the drive,' he persisted. 'Surely it belongs to him?'

'Not to my knowledge. The only one out there

is mine. I did an exchange with the garage on the car that my…er…father left me, for something more trendy. I must have chosen a model similar to that of James without being aware of it as I've never seen his car.'

'Ah, I see,' he said uncomfortably, and followed it with, 'I'm sorry to have bothered you.' He was ready to get off, with the feeling that Emma must be totally weary of him fussing over her like some bore with nothing better to do when his day at the practice was over. Wasn't he supposed to be eager to get back to the days before Jeremy had gasped out his last wishes and placed the burden on him that he'd so wanted to relinquish?

'Have you eaten?' she asked softly.

'Er…no, but I intend to shortly.'

'I could make you a meal if you would let me,' she volunteered. 'I owe you such a lot, Glenn.'

'You owe me nothing,' he said with a wintry smile. 'Except maybe to cherish the life that I've brought you back to with every ounce of your being. Because it can all slip away when we least expect it to.'

With that comment he went striding off into the night to where he'd parked his car. As Emma closed the door slowly behind him his description of what his life was like came to mind. She wished she knew what it was that was hurting him so much, that was responsible for the black pit that he'd described.

But the chances of finding out were slim as Glenn was the most private person she'd ever met. The least she could do was to respect that privacy and get on with adjusting to life back at the practice.

Back home for the second time Glenn was squirming at the thought of the mistake he'd made regarding Emma's car. She must think him an interfering fusspot, he thought grimly. If they were going to be working together at the practice he needed to be around less in her private life.

Having been looking forward to the time when he could let her get on with it, he'd just made a complete fool of himself and it was not going to happen again.

Not in the mood for cooking, he made a sandwich and a mug of coffee and settled down by the fire, waiting for the silence of the room to wrap itself comfortingly around him as it always did. But not tonight, it seemed. The events of the day kept butting into his consciousness and he couldn't relax. The thought uppermost in his mind was that Emma Chalmers was beginning to be a disturbing influence in his life, which was something he could do without. Maybe agreeing to her coming back to the practice was *not* such a good idea.

There were other practices equally as busy as theirs that would welcome her with open arms on hearing the details of where she'd spent the last few years. But would she want to work for them? Had he brought Emma home to places she loved only to want her elsewhere?

The irony of the situation was that he who knew her the least out of the folks at the practice was the one she was having the most to do with. He hadn't intended it to be like that.

But recalling Lydia's veiled comments about Emma's past hurts and the practice manager's obvious desire to have her back amongst them, he was going to have to stick to the arrangement he'd made with Jeremy's daughter while keeping his distance at the same time.

If Glenn had spent a restless evening, so had Emma. It hurt that he hadn't let her offer him any hospitality. Not being aware of the chat he'd had with Lydia after she had left him in an emotional state the other day, Emma was unaware that his concerns on her behalf had been brought to the fore again when, on arriving at her house, he had thought that she had been socialising with the practice womaniser.

Walking slowly up the stairs to bed with the restlessness still upon him, Glenn stood in front of his and Serena's wedding picture on the dressing table and asked gently of his smiling bride 'Why couldn't you have stayed on the beach, you crazy woman?'

The next morning, with Emma's time her own until a date had been fixed for her to start at the practice, she went to check if the strange flowers were still on the grave beside the ones she'd put there. On discovering that they were, she decided that they were a one-off of some kind, and once faded would not be replaced.

With that reassurance in mind she went on her way to her next important errand, which was regarding house prices in the area. She came away having surprisingly developed a yearning to stay where she was and create something beautiful out of her house during the long winter months.

Glenminster was busy with early Christmas shoppers and Emma didn't want to linger too long anywhere near the practice with the memory of her visit the previous day. So she parked the car and went for a coffee in a bistro on the other side of town, where she sat hunched at one of the tables, drinking the steaming brew and digesting mentally the idea of giving a makeover to the drab place that was still her home and so convenient for the practice.

Just thinking about the two places made her impatient to be involved with them both. As if Glenn had read her mind, there was a brisk message waiting for her when she got back to ask how about her returning to the practice the following Monday. For the first time in what seemed like an eternity bells of joy rang in her heart.

She rang back immediately with a reply of just two words, 'Yes! Please!' And for the first time since meeting him she heard him laugh.

'That's good, then,' he told her. 'We look forward to seeing you on Monday next, if not before.' And was gone.

She spent the rest of the day with literature she'd picked up from a local builder while out and about earlier. The ideas suggested for modernising old properties were fascinating, so much so that it was evening before she knew it and Lydia was knocking on her door on her way home from the practice with the news that there were fresh flowers on the grave that hadn't been there the day before.

'After what you told me yesterday I took a stroll through the churchyard in the lunch hour and there they were,' she said.

'But I was there myself first thing!' Emma exclaimed.

'So it must have been after that. When you'd been and gone,' Lydia reasoned. 'But why now, when there was nothing like that all the time you were away? I used to put flowers on occasionally but there were never any others already in place.'

'Glenn goes through the churchyard as a short cut, instead of driving there, when he goes to visit old Mrs Benson. He might have seen someone bring the flowers. Shall I ask him?'

'No,' Emma said uncomfortably. 'I'll keep a lookout myself, he has been involved enough with my affairs and I think is weary of the hassle.' Then she took a leap in the dark. 'Why does he refer to his life so miserably, Lydia? What do you know about him?'

'Nothing,' was the reply. 'Nothing at all regarding his private life, but what I see on the job is a different thing. Glenn Bartlett is the best head of the practice ever. I've seen a few mediocre ones come and go in my time, including Jeremy.

'Which reminds me, Emma, do you have the urge to change your name from the one you thought was yours, considering the heartbreak he caused you, or stay with it to avoid questions?'

'What would be the point of changing it now?' she asked flatly, 'I could always change it to my mother's maiden name, I suppose, but everyone knows me as Chalmers. And as I haven't a clue what my birth father's name is or was, I can scarcely change it to that. If I ever found out, that would be the time to decide.'

'Yes, I guess so,' Lydia agreed, and on the point of departing suggested quizzically, 'With regard to what I came about, we will have to take turns watching out for the phantom flower-bringer, I'm afraid.'

'It will be someone who is putting flowers on the wrong grave and will realise their mistake sooner or later,' Emma said firmly, having no wish to discuss the matter further, and when Lydia had gone she picked up the brochures on home conversions once more.

But her concentration had diminished with the memory of Lydia's comments about Glenn now uppermost in her mind, and her eagerness to be back working in the practice overwhelmed her. Just seven days to go and she would be back where she'd been happiest amongst those of a like kind, and with her boss, the man who had brought her back to Glenminster. What more could she ask?

Over the next week Emma didn't hear from Glenn. And as the days passed, with no glimpses of him driving past on his home visits, or signs of him anywhere in the vicinity of the house where he lived the quiet life away from the surgery, Emma found she missed him. So by the time Monday morning came she was surprised how much she wanted to see him again.

She was to be disappointed. There was no sign of him in the practice building and Lydia met her with the news that Glenn was taking a break and would be back in a week's time. With a doctor short, her presence would be welcomed by the rest of the staff. As Lydia pointed out the consulting room that would be hers, Emma thought they wouldn't exactly be tripping over each other when he did put in an appearance, as it was just about as far away from his as it could be.

But there was no time for wishing and wondering. No sooner had she settled herself and her belongings in the room that was to be hers than patients allotted to her by the receptionists were beginning to appear.

She had a warm welcome for those she knew and a cautious approach for those she didn't, and the time flew with her disappointment regarding Glenn's absence forgotten.

But it returned at six o'clock with the switching off the lights and the locking of the doors. As Emma drove home in winter darkness there was the question of why, when Glenn had rung to tell her that she could start back at the practice today and that he would see her then, he hadn't kept his word.

Where was he and who was he with? she pondered. None of the rest of the staff had shown surprise at his absence so it must have been general knowledge to everyone except her that he would not be there on her first day back to welcome her as promised. But after all why should she know? She was just an additional staff member, a new member of the team, no one of particular importance.

The sea was calm, unbelievably so, but all his memories of it were of a gigantic wall of water sweeping everyone and everything before it into total destruction.

The rock where Serena had gone to sunbathe still rose majestically out of clear blue water, just as it had done on that day when his life had changed for ever.

The rebuilding of the hotel where he and Serena had been staying was finished. It had taken three years to make it fit to live in again and the same applied to the rest of the resort that had been their favourite holiday venue.

At long last he was coming to terms with what he had always felt to be the unfairness of being left to live the empty life that had been thrust upon him. He'd been back a few times since it had happened, looking for solace, for answers that might make his life worth living again, but none had ever been forthcoming. Even the strange friendship with Emma Chalmers, which had come out of nowhere and was pleasing enough in its own up-and-down sort of way, wasn't enough to take away the pain of loss.

She had been forced to cope with a loss of her own in the short time since he'd brought her back from Africa, but hadn't felt much grief as far as he could see.

He would be flying back home in the next few hours, feeling guilty at having not kept his promise to be there on her first day back at the practice. An early morning news item a week ago had alerted him to the fact that the rebuilding of the devastated holiday resort was complete. And that those who had lived there and lost everything in the disaster were returning in the hope that soon the tourist trade would be back and flourishing.

On hearing it, Glenn's first thought had been that he never wanted to go there again. But there had been others that followed it, the most overwhelming one being that he needed to say goodbye to the

place, and with it his farewell to the wife he had lost
so tragically.

His father had once given him good advice,
unwanted at the time. 'Let her go, Glenn. Serena
wouldn't want you to live a life of loneliness and
grief,' Jonas had urged, but Glenn had ignored him.
It was only today, seeing the sea calm and still, the
buildings rebuilt and the gardens back to their previous glory, where there had been carnage, that had
finally given him the will to let go.

They were waiting for him at the airport, the parents
that he loved, elderly and temperamental but mostly
on his wavelength. Typically his father's first comment was, 'You left that young daughter of Jeremy's
high and dry on her first day back at the practice.
Did you forget?'

'No. I didn't,' he told him. 'It was just that when
I heard about the rebuilding on the six o'clock news
that morning I knew I had to go. Everything else
seemed blurred and vague, and I got the first flight
of the day out there. I will speak to Emma in the
morning and I'm sure she will understand.'

'And?' his mother interrupted gently. 'How did
it feel to see it all made good again? Was the rock
still there?'

'Yes, it was,' he told her, 'and it was strange because seeing it comforted me. I felt that at last I could
say my goodbyes to Serena.'

'And you'll have a word with that girl of Jeremy's tomorrow?' his father insisted, tactless to the last.

'Yes, of course. I've said I will, haven't I?' he told him as the three of them boarded a waiting taxi. Emma wasn't going to lose any sleep over his absence, he thought. It was the job she coveted, not a washed-out widower like him.

But the time he'd just spent in a place that would be in the background of his life for ever had been well worth the effort. He was ready to accept what he had been given, make the best of it, and it was a major step forward. It was a pity that his father couldn't see it that way, instead of fussing about what he saw as letting down a comparative stranger.

It seemed that he had gone to the practice to pick up a prescription and seen Emma's expression when she'd discovered that his son was not around on her first morning at the practice, and like an elderly knight of old had taken up her cause. For heaven's sake, Lydia would have been there to make Emma welcome and young Prentice wouldn't have been far away, that was for sure.

When the taxi stopped outside the neat semi-detached where his parents lived Glenn paid the driver and then saw them safely inside before walking the short distance to his own home. On the way he had to pass the drab property that was Emma's residence and when he glanced across saw that in

spite of the fact that it was well gone midnight there
was a light on in an upstairs room, and he thought
wryly that maybe she had found it easier to find solace than he had.

She was very noticeable with her long dark hair
and big hazel eyes, he thought, and now that she was
back in civilisation who could blame her if she found
some of the men she was getting to know exciting
to spend time with.

Yet from what little he knew of Emma it was
strange that she should already be so close to someone of his gender after so short a time, if that was
the case. And he might have thought it stranger still
if he had known that Emma was propped up against
the pillows all alone, studying builders' estimates as
if there was no tomorrow.

As for himself, for the first time in ages he slept
the moment his head touched the pillow, unaware
that Emma's last thought before sleep had claimed
her had been of him and his disappointing absence
on her first day at the practice. It had taken some of
the pleasure out of her return to work, but not all of
it. She had slotted back in again as if she'd never been
away and hoped Glenn would approve whenever he
came back from where he had disappeared to.

CHAPTER FOUR

DESPITE THE LATENESS of his return the previous night Glenn was at his desk when Emma arrived at the practice the next morning. Having left the door of his consulting room open, he was watching for her arrival and called her in the moment she appeared.

Beckoning for her to take a seat, he asked levelly, 'So how did your first day go, Emma? Was it up to expectations? I had expected to be here, but something completely unexpected took me to foreign parts and I didn't get back until very late last night.'

'Yes, it was fine,' she told him, 'just like old times, only better since having worked abroad.'

'I passed your house on the last lap of my way home,' he said, 'and saw that one of your bedroom lights was on at that late hour, so it would seem that you are settling in amongst us satisfactorily.'

'Yes, I suppose you could say that,' she agreed coolly, 'if you would class leafing through a pile of builders' estimates as "settling in".'

Ignoring the implied rebuke, he said, 'You mean

you're considering giving your house a face-lift? All I can say to that is good thinking.'

'It will be my Christmas present to myself.'

He didn't like the sound of that. Surely Emma had someone to spend Christmas with? It was clear from the funeral that she had no close relatives.

But it was still some weeks away. There would be time for both their lives to change before then: his because of what had just happened in a faraway place, and Emma's because by then she would have found new friends and made her house beautiful.

Any other surmising had to wait as there were voices to be heard nearby, the waiting room was filling up, and as Emma turned to go to her own part of the busy practice he said, 'I'm here if you have any problems, so don't hesitate to ask.'

Glenn watched her colour rise at the reassurance he was offering and wondered if he had hit a sore spot of some kind. Had she thought that he was forgetting her past position in the practice and hinting that her absence over the last few years might have made her less than capable with her own kind?

If that was the case Emma would be so wrong. There was an air of efficiency about her that showed she knew what she was about, and he wasn't going to interfere regarding that.

She didn't reply to the offer he'd made, just smiled, and as she turned to go to her consulting

room he pressed the buzzer on his desk and the day
was under way.

In the early afternoon Glenn had a house call to
make at a farm high on a hillside. During the lunch
break he went to find Emma with the intention of
suggesting that she accompany him to renew her acquaintance with the more rural parts that the practice covered, now bare and leafless in winter's grip.

He discovered that she was nowhere around and
concluded that she'd gone to do a quick shop somewhere in her lunch hour, until Lydia, observing him
finding Emma missing, explained that she was most
likely to be found in the churchyard.

When he asked why, the answer was that her
mother's grave was there, and Glenn was immediately aware of the strange arrangement of her parents being buried in different places, as Jeremy had
been laid to rest in the local cemetery.

Not wanting to question Lydia further, he strolled
towards the church and, sure enough, Emma was
there, arranging fresh flowers on one of the graves,
and he wondered why, as there was an abundance
of them there already.

When his shadow fell across them she looked up,
startled, and asked, 'Have you come to tell me that
lunchtime is over?'

'No, not at all,' he said, feeling a little awkward
that he was interrupting something special. 'I'm driving up into the hills to do a home visit for my next

patient and thought you might like to renew your acquaintance with the green hills of Gloucestershire. They're as beautiful as ever above the Regency finery of Glenminster.

'My mother was born in this place, but when I came along they were living in Yorkshire because of my father's job. She was so homesick they christened me Glenn after the place she loved so much. At the first opportunity he brought her back to Glenminster and they've been here ever since.

'Not me, though. I met my wife when we were both studying medicine up north and when we married we stayed up there content with our lot until it all fell apart and I came back here to pick up the pieces.'

Emma was listening to what he had to say with wide eyes. Was this the same man who valued his privacy, wouldn't let her make him a meal, and now was putting the blame for his peculiarities on to a failed marriage?

'It would be a pleasure to be up amongst the hills again,' she told him, and with a last look at an abundance of cream roses on the grave she turned away and they walked back to the practice building in silence.

Once they were there Glenn said, 'Can you be ready in twenty minutes? Have you had some lunch?'

'Yes,' she told him, and feeling that she ought to explain said, 'The reason you found me beside my mother's grave is because since I've come back I've discovered that someone is mistakenly putting flowers on it and I need to know who they are.

'I thought it might be Lydia because the two of them were good friends. But it isn't and she is just as curious as I am, as I have no relatives that I know of.'

Glenn was observing her sombrely. What was it about Emma that brought out the need in him to look after her? It wasn't because his return to the place where his life had been resurrected a few days ago had made him want to find a replacement for Serena.

That had just brought some peace to the empty shell that he lived in. That being so, as they drove towards the farmhouse high up on the hillside where his patient lived, he felt free to offer his services with regard to the mystery mourner. He said, 'If there *is* someone bringing flowers in remembrance of your mother, we need to find out why, don't you think?'

'Yes, I suppose so,' she agreed. 'Yet it is a long time since she was taken from me, though not to someone else, it might seem, unless they're putting flowers on the wrong grave. The hurt is always there. I loved her so much, but today I don't want to think about the past. I just want to look and look and look at my favourite places.'

'And so you shall,' he promised, 'when we've seen the farmer and sorted out his health problems. You may remember him from before you went away. Does the name Jack Walsh ring a bell?'

Emma swivelled to face him in the confines of the

car. 'Yes, his son was in my class at school. What's wrong with his father?'

'An injury while harvesting that occurred during your absence. Every so often his spine seizes up and he has to go for hospital treatment. He won't make the effort until I insist on it, and with Christmas coming up he will be reluctant to miss the festivities. Luckily his wife, who knows him better than he knows himself, rang to say that he could hardly walk.'

'So who runs the place?' Emma asked.

'The rest of the family,' was the reply as he brought the car to a halt outside a farmhouse built from the local golden stone that was so popular amongst the builders and house owners of the area.

They found Jack Walsh reclining on a couch, watching television. When he spotted Emma he groaned.

'You're Jeremy's daughter, aren't you?' he asked. 'Come back, have you, now that he's gone?'

Glenn watched the colour drain from her face and anger spiralled inside him. 'Dr Chalmers is here to assist, not to be insulted!' he told him. 'So how about a demonstration of your mobility as that's what we're here to observe? Your wife thinks that it's worse.'

As Jack eased himself off the couch and, leaning on a stick, moved slowly across the room Emma was wishing herself miles away. There had been something in his comment regarding herself that had made her cringe because it had brought back the memory of that awful night when she'd fled from her home.

At that moment Mrs Walsh appeared and greeted them with a relieved smile and the conversation became medical again. Glenn sternly insisted that the regular physiotherapy sessions that Jack had been giving a miss should be started again immediately unless he wanted to be totally unable to enjoy the pleasures of Christmas.

'Your muscle control is very poor, more from lack of effort than anything else,' Emma told him when both doctors had examined the patient.

'Dr Chalmers is right,' Glenn told him, 'so back to the physiotherapy and we will see you again before Christmas is upon us.'

'Aye, if you say so,' Jack agreed irritably. 'It's all right for some.'

When they left the farm it was three o'clock and Glenn thought there wasn't going to be much time for Emma to renew her acquaintance with past memories. 'It will be dark soon,' he said. 'What would you like to do most in the time we have left before we need to return to the practice?'

Her answer was prompt. 'Watch a winter sunset on the horizon.'

'Right, we will do that, but from inside. How about afternoon tea, somewhere with a good view?'

She hesitated. 'Won't we be needed back at the practice?'

'Not for a couple of hours. My father is insisting

that I make it up to you for not being around on your first day there.' Glenn smiled as he drove into the parking area of a cosy-looking café. 'So here goes, afternoon tea up amongst the hills.'

They had a table near the window, the food was delicious, and as the winter sun sank below the skyline Emma thought it was the first time she'd felt really happy in years.

As he watched Emma, Glenn thought that this stranger that he had bought back to Glenminster was very easily pleased. She made no demands, just quietly got on with the life she had come back to, but he sensed that deep down she was hurting and it almost certainly had something to do with Jeremy.

A smile tugged at the corner of his mouth as he compared Emma's father to his own. His was a 'do-gooder', which was the main reason why his mother sometimes threw him out because he overdid it and his concern for others got her down. While she just wanted a pleasant retirement he was busy looking after all the waifs and strays of the neighbourhood. Glenn understood both their points of view.

He sometimes thought that if he could have given his parents a grandchild to love in their old age it would have been different, but a terrifying act of nature had put an end to that dream for always.

As they watched the sun go down he said, 'I am very impressed to hear that you're going to give the house a face-lift, Emma, but it will be a huge undertaking for you on your own, Why did Chalmers let it get so run-down? He was always smartly dressed, had a big car, and was never away from the golf club, so I'm told, yet the house is a mess.'

'It was just a place to sleep—that was how he saw it,' she told him, 'and if my mother ever asked for anything new, he wasn't interested.'

'Yes. I see,' he commented, and thought that all of that went with Chalmers's type. On the heels of that thought came another that he was already putting into words and thinking he was insane.

'If you decide to go ahead with the renovations, I will be only too pleased to help in any way I can,' he said gently. 'You have only to ask, Emma.'

He watched her colour rise as she turned to him in confusion and said, 'I wouldn't dream of involving you in doing anything like that, Glenn. You did enough in finding me and bringing me back home.'

'Yes, well, we'll see about that if and when the time comes,' he said. 'In the meantime, take everything one step at a time.'

What did he mean by that? she wondered. Was it a reference to her impulsive decision to give the house a makeover, or was Glenn aware that she was attracted to him—a lot?

It was time to change the subject, she thought as they drove back to the practice. 'I've loved being back amongst the hills, Glenn,' she said. 'Thank you for taking me with you. I thought it would be just a matter of a house call to a difficult patient, but it was much more than that.'

He smiled in response, and the thought came to him again that Emma didn't take a lot of pleasing.

But how long was she going to be pleased with him safe behind his touch-me-not barricades? He found himself worryingly close to thinking about her in a way he hadn't envisaged before, so bringing a lighter note into the moment he said, 'So can I tell my father that I have redeemed myself for being missing on your first day at the practice?'

'You can indeed,' Emma assured him. 'Today has been my first happy day in ages. I would be totally content if it weren't for the flowers that keep appearing on my mother's grave.'

'Yes, that I can understand,' he said gently. 'We need to do something about it. I sometimes use the churchyard as a short cut so will be on the lookout. And I'm sure Lydia will be keeping a close watch too, and of course you will be. So between us we should be able to come up with an answer sooner or later.'

When they arrived back at the practice Glenn had a patient waiting and Emma was involved with assisting the practice nurses with a cluster of school children brought in by their parents for the nasal flu spray vaccination, and for the rest of the afternoon the happy moments up on the hillside seemed far away. But in the quiet of the evening the memory of the time spent with Glenn was there again and with it the same amount of pleasure.

During the following fortnight the mystery of the flowers seemed to have gone away and Emma began to think that maybe it had been someone's mistake as no more strange blooms appeared. The only flowers on view were the ones that she took herself and she was relieved to discover that it was so.

But just when she had started to forget about them the flowers reappeared. Engrossed in her plans for renovating the house, Emma decided to ignore them. Not so Glenn and Lydia, who kept watch for a while, but without any success. Eventually Emma placed them on a grave that was always bare, only to find the unknown mourner not fazed by that as fresh flowers continued to arrive alongside her own.

With Christmas approaching and nothing to look forward to socially, Emma was pleased to hear that there was to be a staff party on the Saturday evening a week before the festive occasion. She felt that it called for something special to wear, especially if Glenn was going to be there. Although she had her doubts that he would be.

Ever since the afternoon spent with him up on the hillside Glenn had been distant when in her company and she wondered if he still spent every moment of his spare time closeted in his house. He had referred to the ending of his marriage with cold clarity and she wondered where his ex-wife was now.

Nevertheless, it didn't stop her from buying a dress that brought out the attractions of the dark sheen of her hair and pale smooth skin, and as the occasion drew near she resigned herself to being an odd one out in the hotel that had been chosen by those who knew the night life of the town, as it was now, far better than she did.

Lydia would be there and had suggested that they share a taxi to get there but had explained that she would be staying the night at the hotel after the party and so wouldn't be around for the home journey.

'But I'm sure that Glenn will give you a lift home if you ask him,' she'd said. 'He never stays over on those occasions. Just puts in a courtesy appearance and once the meal is over expresses his best wishes to the staff and goes back to the peace of that lovely house of his. That is if you don't want to stay long, of course. Otherwise it will need to be a taxi again,' she told her.

'Right, I'll remember that.' She wondered if deep down she really wanted to go. There were decisions to make about the house, alterations that she wanted done as soon as possible. A quiet night in would help to move the project along more quickly, but there was the beautiful new dress. She did want to wear it when Glenn would be there to see her in it…

* * *

In the meantime, as the days spent at the practice went too fast and were so busy, Glenn wasn't looking forward to Christmas any more than he had over the last few years. He may have made his peace regarding losing Serena, but the loneliness was still there.

Restless now in the quiet of his home, unable to relax, he knew he had to do something about it, but what? As head of the practice he was committed to going to the staff Christmas party, which was looming up in the near future. He realised with a combination of pleasure and pain that Emma would be there.

Glenn had shopped already for his Christmas gifts to his parents. As was the routine since losing Serena, he would be spending the two festive days with them at their house, with his mother doing all she could to brighten the occasion and his father restless and on edge because he longed for grandchildren and his son never did anything towards granting him his wish.

He had wondered a few times what Emma's Christmas would be like in that ghastly house on her own. If his two days of festivities were heavy going, hers would probably be worse, unless she had something planned that he knew nothing about.

As far as she was concerned, it still upset her that Glenn hadn't let her thank him for his kindness on the occasion of her return to Glenminster and she intended using the approaching festivities to make up for the lapse in some way.

As the days went by she was beginning to feel a loneliness that had never been there before at Christmastime, even while she'd worked abroad. Although it hadn't exactly been joyful in past years, with just Jeremy and herself to share the event with their opposing lifestyles and little in common, it hadn't felt as empty as this, she thought as she wandered around Glenminster's delightful shopping promenades for a gift for Lydia and a magical something to present to Glenn if he would accept it.

On one of her shopping trips she met Glenn's parents, and his father, Jonas, introduced her to Glenn's mother Olivia as 'Jeremy's daughter come back to the fold' and asked how she intended spending Christmas.

It was an awkward moment. Emma knew that he was always on the lookout for waifs and strays and didn't want to be classified as such, but was lost how to reply to the question. Luckily, Glenn's mum provided an escape route by saying that her husband was always looking for helpers with his good works and on Christmas Day was masterminding a free Yuletide lunch for the needy in the town centre.

'I would love to help with that,' Emma told him with complete honesty, 'either by cooking, serving, or helping generally.'

'I'll accept the offer,' he told her promptly with

gruff gratitude, 'but only on one condition—that you dine with us in the evening.'

Emma felt her colour rise at the thought of Glenn's expression when he discovered that she was going to be part of his Christmas celebrations—if that was the correct word to describe the foursome that his father had suggested. Uneasy at the thought, Emma made a weak acceptance of the invitation and braced herself for explaining how it had come about to Glenn the next time they came face to face, which turned out to be the following morning at the practice.

Glenn had been engrossed in a report he'd received from the endocrine clinic in Glenminster's main hospital concerning a patient whose calcium levels had been rising dangerously over past months, according to his recent tests. When he looked up to see Emma standing in front of him she looked very serious, so he asked her what was wrong.

'It's about Christmas Day,' she said awkwardly. 'Your father has invited me to dine with the three of you in the evening and I really don't want to intrude, but hesitate to offend him.'

'I didn't know that you were on visiting terms with my folks,' he commented dryly. 'How did that come about?'

'I offered to assist with the Christmas lunch he's organising for the lonely and needy folks around the place, and the invitation to dine with your parents and yourself in the evening became part of the arrangement.'

'So why the fuss? If you don't want to do that, tell him so. My dad is a great guy for organising other people's lives, whether they want him to or not. But he means well and when it comes to the lonely or isolated he excels himself.'

'And is that how you see me?' she said quietly. As a pathetic loner? You don't know the half of it.' And on that comment she went to her consulting room and prepared to face the day.

When Emma had gone Glenn squirmed at the way he'd been so offhand with her. What was he thinking? The thought of her beside him on such a special day of the year was magical. It would help to take away some of the emptiness that he lived with, but instead of telling her how much he needed her he had sent her away after showing little interest in her plea for his advice. And as the morning progressed there was no opportunity to tell her how much he would like her to be there on the evening of Christmas Day.

The flowers were still appearing on the grave and Emma had decided that if in some way her mother was conscious of them and content to receive them, she was going to let the mystery of them lie like a blessing. So that lunchtime she went into the church-yard as she sometimes did and spent a few quiet moments there to calm the confusion of her conversation with Glenn earlier.

As she turned to go he was there, seemingly having read her mind. Observing her quizzically, he said, 'Do you ever regret coming back to Glenminster, Emma?'

'No, of course not,' she said immediately. 'I belong here and nowhere else, but there are unsolved questions I have to live with.'

'Such as the mystery flowers?'

'Yes, that in part; but bigger issues than that haunt me. I envy you your parents, Glenn. You are so fortunate to have them here in your life every moment of every day. Although I am so sorry that your marriage didn't work.'

'Is that what you think?' he exclaimed. 'That I'm divorced or something of the sort?'

'Well—yes, I assumed.'

'I'm not divorced, Emma,' said Glenn. 'My wife is dead. Swept away in a tsunami when we were on holiday some years ago.'

'Oh, how awful for you!' she breathed. 'I had no idea. Do, please, forgive me for jumping to the wrong conclusion.'

'It's an understandable mistake to make,' he said. 'Only my parents know what happened and at my express request they don't discuss my affairs with anyone. It's something I don't like to talk about, and I would be obliged if you would do the same.'

'Yes, of course,' she told him, still stunned by what he had told her. 'I really am so very sorry,

Glenn. If ever there is anything I can do to help, do please say so.'

He was smiling a tight smile. 'There *is* one thing. In spite of my having put the dampener on it earlier, how about you sitting beside me on Christmas Day night to please my parents? I'll pick you up at seven o'clock if that's all right.'

'Er…yes,' she replied, wondering what he would say next to amaze her, and asked hesitantly, 'What shall I bring?'

'Just yourself will do fine,' she was told, and with a glance at the clock in the church tower high above them added, 'We had better get back to our patients or we'll have a queue.'

Emma smiled across at him, happier than she'd felt for ages. The invitation to join Glenn and his family for a Christmas meal made her feel more wanted than she had done in a long time. But poor Glenn! What he'd had to say about the loss of his wife was heartbreaking and explained so many of the things about him that had previously puzzled her.

It was the day of the staff party and with that and Christmas the following week, with all the excitement and nostalgia that entailed, there was a lovely heart-warming atmosphere in the surgery. Everyone was looking forward to the festive season and a well-earned rest. It was midday and most of the staff had already gone to enjoy their weekend when a phone call came through to say that Jack Walsh needed to see a doctor urgently. Glenn sighed. Jack had a high temperature and it sounded as if he might have some sort of infection. After checking that the building was empty, he locked up and went to his car, ready to drive up to the remote farm.

At that moment Emma drove onto the practice forecourt and he observed her in surprise. Having noted that her consulting room was empty, Glenn had taken it for granted that, like the rest of the staff, she had gone to enjoy the weekend ahead.

As she got out of her car he wound his window down and asked in surprise, 'Where have you been? Everywhere is locked up. I'm off to see Jack Walsh at the hill farm. He has a high temperature and from what his wife says seems to be heading for something serious.'

'Can I go along with you?' she asked. 'I missed the hills so much while I was away and loved it the other time you took me up there.'

'I would have thought that you'd have lots of nice things planned for the rest of the day,' he said. 'Come, by all means, if you wish, but it won't be much fun up there on a day like this. There is a definite nip in the air and the sky is dark and lowering.'

Emma was already easing herself into the passenger seat beside him and flashed him a smile. 'It's a case of anything to get out of my stately home,' she teased, and he could understand that.

'Where have you been?' Glenn asked as he drove off the forecourt of the practice.

'To see a child with 'flu,' she replied. 'I hope I don't get it for Christmas.'

So do I, he thought. The party later that night and having Emma with him at his parents' house on Christmas Day were beginning to stand out in his mind like stars in a dark sky.

By the time he pulled up at the Walsh farm it was snowing. Large flakes were falling all around them, silently forming a white carpet that was getting thicker by the moment. Glenn said, 'Are you wishing you hadn't come? We could be snowed in up here and it's the staff party tonight.'

The question had an answer that was making her heart beat faster. Emma wanted to be wherever Glenn was, be it the smart hotel where the staff party was to be held or on the Walshs' ramshackle farm, so as Mrs Walsh opened the door, Emma's smile was serene.

'Doctor, he's bad this time,' she said worriedly, as she led the way to a drab bedroom on the ground floor of the building. 'He's hot as fire, his breathing is difficult, and he isn't talking sense.'

'How long has he been like this?' Glenn asked, as he bent over the feverish figure on the bed.

'He's gradually been getting worse since yesterday,' was the reply.

Glenn frowned.

'It could be pneumonia or something worse,' he said when the two doctors had finished examining him. 'I'm going to phone for an ambulance and hope that it will be able to get here before this place becomes inaccessible.' He sent a wry smile in Emma's direction. 'So much for life in the fast lane.'

'I don't mind,' she told him, and she really didn't as long as she was with him. Although Glenn was still an unknown quantity as far as she was concerned. Since they'd met he'd wanted nothing of her or from her, and as far as she knew nothing had changed.

It was still early afternoon. They might get to the party yet if the snow eased off and an ambulance managed to get through. She would still be able to wear the dress that she'd been hoping would make Glenn see her how she wanted him to.

CHAPTER FIVE

AN HOUR LATER an ambulance did come trundling through the snow with its siren screeching. After a quick word from Glenn the sick man was taken on board and was on his way to the nearest hospital, leaving the two doctors to get back to civilisation the best they could.

After a mile of careful driving with visibility almost nil the car became stuck in a snowdrift. Glenn had been worried when they'd set off, but now anxiety on Emma's behalf spiralled as there was no signal when he tried to phone for help. He got out to assess the situation and was hit straight away by the severe cold.

'I should never have let you come with me!' he said when he opened the door to ease himself back in. 'I suggest that you climb over onto the back seat and if I leave the engine running you may be able to keep warm while I dig us out of this mess. I keep a couple of shovels in the boot for situations such as this.'

'Give me one and I'll help,' she said immediately.

He shook his head. 'No! You stay put and keep trying to get a signal on the phone while I'm out there, digging.'

As she was about to protest at his refusal to let her assist he said tightly, 'Do as I say, will you?' And she obeyed meekly.

A short time later he got back behind the wheel but had no luck—the car was still stuck. He groaned as he climbed into the back seat beside her and asked grimly if she'd been able to get a signal.

When she shook her head Glenn held out his arms and when Emma made no move towards him he said dryly, 'I don't bite. I am merely offering body warmth because the car heater doesn't seem to be working.'

With a wry smile she went into his hold and as he held her close against his chest, in spite of the snow drifting silently and thickly around the car, she had never felt so safe in her life before. Beside her, Glenn was thinking that it was the first time he had held a woman in his arms since he'd lost Serena and it was arousing all the passions he had kept so tightly under control ever since.

Because it wasn't just any member of the opposite sex he was holding close. It was the daughter that Jeremy Chalmers had confessed to having done some great hurt to as he'd been dying, and he, Glenn, would very much like to know what it was.

'So tell me what it was that Jeremy did to you

that hurt so much,' he said gently, when they'd sat in silence for a while.

Her face clouded and Glenn thought she was going to refuse, but after a pause she sighed. 'He had been out drinking and came home late. Then he told me that I would have to move out of the only home I'd ever known. That he was getting married for a second time and that I was not welcome to stay where I had lived all my life,' Emma said. 'And when I protested that I was his daughter and didn't deserve such treatment, he informed me that he was not my father. He had married my lovely mother to give her respectability, and her child—me—a name. And as a final hurtful truth he told me that he had no idea who my father was, that my mother had never told him, so I was a nobody.

'Unable to bear the thought of staying in Glenminster after listening to his nastiness, I left during the night and had no intention of ever returning until you got in touch and brought me back to the place I loved.'

She turned, looked up at him from the circle of his arms and said softly, 'I will always bless you for that, Glenn.'

Emma's mouth was only an inch or two away. It would be so easy to kiss her, he thought achingly, kiss away the hurts that Jeremy had caused in his spiteful drunkenness, and make love to her in the privacy of the snowbound car.

Tilting her chin with gentle fingers, he looked down at her upturned face and it was there, the feeling of togetherness that she aroused in him, and letting desire take hold of his senses he kissed her just once long and tenderly, then it was gone, swept away by the happenings of the past that still had him in their grip.

The mighty wall of water surging towards him that, when it had taken its toll of the holiday resort, had also taken Serena, along with many others, and ever since he'd carried with him the guilt of being spared when she had been lost.

The torment of the thoughts that wouldn't allow him to hold Emma any closer was broken by the sound of some sort of vehicle approaching through the swirling white flakes and she cried, 'It sounds like a truck of some sort, Glenn!'

Relief washed over him, mixed with regret that he hadn't taken advantage of the magical moments when he'd held her in his arms, but her safety had to come first and he said, 'It's a snow plough, Emma. We might get to the staff party after all if they can pull us out of this drift.'

At that moment a voice could be heard across the divide between the two vehicles.

'Are you folks OK?' a voice called. 'The ambulance crew phoned to say you might have problems getting back to civilisation, so we're here to clear the way for you to drive back to Glenminster.'

'Yes, we're fine,' Glenn told them. 'But the drifts

around the car were getting a bit worrying, so the sooner you can get us moving again the more grateful we will be. We're so thankful for your help. Where have you come from?'

'We're from a farm not far away,' was the reply. 'The police and local council know I have one of these things and we have an arrangement that I come out to tow folks like you out of the drifts.' The young guy seated beside him jumped down onto the snow with ropes in his hands and attached them to the front of Glenn's car. 'This is my son. He knows what he's doing. We'll soon have you free and on your way.' When the car suddenly lurched forward onto level ground they knew that it wasn't a vain promise.

As he thanked them before moving slowly onto the main road that would take them back to the town Glenn said, 'If ever I can do you a favour you have only to ask.'

The farmer laughed from high up on the driving seat of the snow plough and said, 'I could do with something for my indigestion.'

'So shall we see you at the surgery on Monday morning, then?' Glenn grinned.

'You might,' was the reply as the man went trundling off into the distance.

On the way back Glenn was silent. Emma wondered if he was already regretting those moments when they'd been so close, surrounded by drifting snow with the moment to themselves. As if he sensed her thoughts he said, 'That wasn't the best drive back, was it?'

Stung, she replied, 'I thought that some of it was very pleasant.'

'Yes, maybe,' he said, 'but circumstances can sometimes create illusions that are not meant to be.'

Her house had come into sight and when Glenn stopped the car outside he said, 'So are you going to the party? There is still time. I'm going as I have no choice. As head of the practice I have to keep putting in an appearance at these sorts of things, but I don't intend to stay long.'

'Yes, I'm going,' she told him. 'I was looking forward to it, but suddenly it has become a chore.' She felt like telling him that she'd bought a special dress for the occasion, but wouldn't be wearing it after the way he'd put the dampener on those magical moments in the car.

'That's good, then,' he said, ignoring her downbeat comment.

Without her there the event would mean nothing to him in spite the downturn in his mood.

As Emma watched him drive off into the night the memory of being in his arms on the back seat of the car was warming her blood, bringing desire again into the moment.

Yet how crazy had that been, acknowledging their attraction to each other at such a time. The memory came to mind of the Sunday morning when she'd gone to his house to thank him for all that he had done in preparation for her arrival and had asked if he lived alone.

'Yes, I do,' he'd told her, and had sent her on her way with the feeling that he was a loner and preferred it that way. Since then she had got to know him better and, knowing that he had lost his wife in the most awful circumstances, she decided if she let herself fall in love with a man who still lived in the past she must be crazy.

By the time Lydia arrived to pick her up, Emma had changed her mind about the dress. She would wear it after all. Whatever Glenn thought of their relationship, there was no call for her to dress down because he wasn't interested in her. She owed it to herself, if no one else, and was determined to enjoy the evening no matter what.

Glenn's spirits rose as he caught his first glimpse of her coming out of the cloakroom, having dispensed with her warm winter coat. How could he not want her? Emma was special, dark-haired with smooth creamy skin, curves in all the right places, and tonight she looked bewitching in a black dress with silver trimmings. So why couldn't he tell her he was sorry about what he'd said on the way home from the farm? Why couldn't he give them both a chance to get to know one another better?

Yet Glenn found he couldn't. As their glances held he turned away and went to chat to other staff members who didn't have the same effect on him as Emma did. As the evening progressed his only communication with her was to ask briefly if she was all right after the snow hazard they'd encountered. Emma's brief response that she was fine gave him no further encouragement, so he left her chatting to James and wished him miles away.

Glenn got up to leave after the meal and to say goodbye to Lydia and Emma, who were seated nearby. 'Why are you going so soon?' Lydia asked.

'It's been a long day,' he said, his smooth tone covering up his turbulent feelings. 'Has Emma told you we had to be rescued from a snowdrift by a local farmer and his son in their snow plough?'

'Er...no,' Lydia replied, and he smiled tightly.

'Maybe you didn't think it worth mentioning,' he said, turning to where Emma was sitting.

'Some parts of it were and some weren't,' she told him quietly, intent on not revealing the hurt of his comments on the way home.

'Ah, yes,' he said, and looked deep into her eyes. 'I'm sorry if I offended you, Emma.'

'It's forgotten,' she said, and wished it was true. But she *had* felt hurt and there was no way she wanted that to become common knowledge.

Glenn left then, striding purposefully towards the door. Heads turned at the sight of his looks and stature and Emma swallowed hard. His leaving felt like another rebuke in her empty life and she wished she had stayed at home and planned the alterations to her house instead.

'What have you done to upset Glenn?' Lydia asked curiously, breaking into her thoughts.

'Nothing at all,' she said tightly, and added, in a moment of sheer misery, 'Why does no one ever want me, Lydia? First there was my unknown father, who can't have wanted either my mother or me, then Jeremy told me to leave, and now Glenn, who I admire and respect, wants me to keep my distance.'

'I don't know about the rest of it,' Lydia said comfortingly, 'but for some reason Glenn has no wish to settle down, which is a shame because I've never seen him look at any other member of our sex like he looks at you. Try not to be too sad, Emma.'

As she listened to what Lydia had to say she remembered Glenn confiding in her about how he had lost his wife and requesting her not to discuss it with anyone. She couldn't tell Lydia what she knew so without further comment, when James appeared at her side once more she excused herself and let him take her onto the dance floor just once more. Then she rang for a taxi.

On the way home she did a foolish thing. Instead of letting the taxi driver take her straight home, Emma asked him to drop her off beside the church and beneath the light of a full moon made her way towards the grave, curious to see if any more flowers had been left there.

As she drew nearer she saw someone standing motionless beside it and increased her pace. But by the time she got there whoever it was had gone and as the quiet night surrounded her once again she looked down at the grave and they were there again, flowers from someone who must have known her mother.

As Emma walked the short distance to her dismal home she wished that Glenn was by her side and for once her wish was granted. He pulled up beside her from nowhere and without speaking opened the car door for her to get in.

Once she was seated he asked, 'Emma, what happened to the taxi that you set off for home in? Lydia rang me to say that you had left the party early too and she was worried about you. So I went round to your place to make sure you were safe and found it in darkness.'

'Yes, I know,' she admitted meekly. 'It was a crazy thing to do but as the taxi was about to go past the church I had a sudden urge to check if any more flowers had been put on the grave. So I paid the driver and went to see.'

'And?' he questioned.

'There was someone standing beside it in the moonlight, Glenn, but by the time I was near enough to see them clearly they'd gone. When I looked down fresh flowers had been put in the vases.'

'And did you have time to see what gender this person was?' he asked. 'It's unlikely a woman would be found in a churchyard after dark.'

'No,' she told him. 'It is as I said. They'd gone by the time I got to the grave. Maybe they heard my footsteps on the flagged path.'

'Has it made you nervous?'

'A bit, I suppose, but it was my own fault.'

The car was already pointing in the direction of Glenn's house. Emma sat bolt upright in shock when he suddenly said, 'I'm going to take you to my place for the night. I never feel easy about you being in that house on your own after dark, and just in case the person in the graveyard saw you, or already knows where you live, we aren't going to take any chances.'

'Do you have a spare room?' she enquired faintly.

'Yes, of course I have! I've got two, as a matter fact, and you'll be quite safe in whichever one you prefer.'

'You know that I'll be green with envy while I'm inside your house, don't you?' she teased.

'There's no need to be,' he parried back. 'Like they say, a home is where the heart is and mine is in a place far away.'

Glenn watched the light go out of her eyes and the colour drain from her face and wished he hadn't been so clumsy.

You are crazy to have brought her here, he told himself as he put his key in the lock when they arrived at the converted barn that appealed to her so much. Especially after the way the two of you were up there in the snowdrift. She's beautiful and kind. For pity's sake, don't hurt her because you've been hurt. Emma has had enough sadness in her life already. Don't get involved in promising her something that you aren't able to give.

When he turned to face her, though, he was smiling, and as she observed him questioningly he said, totally out of context, 'The dress is lovely, Emma. Just so right for your colouring. I intended telling you that at the party but the opportunity didn't present itself.' Unaware of what had been in his mind just a few moments ago, she asked a question that he would rather not have had to answer.

'What was your wife like, Glenn?' she asked, and his smile disappeared.

'I have her photograph in my bedroom. If you would like to see it I'll bring it down,' he volunteered.

'Only if you want to,' she told him. He went upstairs and brought the picture back, and as Emma observed the smiling golden-haired woman in the photograph she could understand his abiding affection for her. But if Glenn's wife had loved him as much as he loved her, surely she would have wanted him to find happiness again with the right person?

Her own track record of not being wanted meant that she certainly wasn't at the top of anyone's yearning-for list. She could only imagine that happening in her dreams.

Emma was unaware that Glenn was watching her, taking in her every expression. He felt full of tenderness for her, but someone like Emma deserved better than him. Despite that, as he listened to her telling him gently that his wife had been very beautiful, for once he was more enraptured by a woman other than Serena.

As Emma handed the photograph back to him Glenn said, 'If you'd like to come upstairs I'll show you the guest room. Feel free to get up whenever you like in the morning. It's Sunday, so there's no rush. Would you like a hot drink before you settle for the night?'

'Er…no, thanks,' she replied. 'I had plenty to eat and drink at the party. Glenn, I'm sorry that I've caused you concern by my actions. It was stupid of me to go into the churchyard at that hour. I don't know what possessed me,' she added guiltily. 'I won't stay for breakfast. I'll leave early so as not to cause further disruption of your organised life, and see you back at the practice on Monday.'

'I don't think so,' he said. 'Breakfast is part of the arrangement of you sleeping safe and sound beneath my roof for once.'

* * *

It had been a long day and Emma was tired, but sleep was evading her because the events of the day had been so strange. It seemed unbelievable to her that Glenn could be sleeping only feet away in the master bedroom of his converted barn. His last comment before he'd closed the door had been to tell her she would find a selection of nightwear in the dressing-table drawers.

And now wearing a long chaste-looking nightdress of white cotton that seemed more like something that belonged to his mother than Glenn's cherished wife, Emma was sleepless still because the very idea of being so near yet so far from him in every other way during the night hours was incredible. And in the morning there would be joy in her heart when she went downstairs and he was there.

Glenn's bedroom door was wide open when Emma sallied forth fully dressed the next morning and she smiled at the thought of seeing him. It would be just two people getting to know each other, sharing their different joys and sorrows, she thought, and what could be wrong with that?

What *was* wrong with it was that Glenn was nowhere to be seen anywhere in the house. She went from room to room with the minutes ticking by, but there was no sign of him. There was no kettle boiling or bacon sizzling to create a breakfast atmosphere.

Outside, the drive and gardens were also deserted, and Glenn's car was nowhere to be seen. The only thing that *was* of interest were brochures about holidaying in Italy on the hall table, and she wondered if Glenn was planning a trip abroad.

Surely he hadn't already gone and in a rush to be off had forgotten she was there from the night before? It would fit in with how she saw herself as someone of little importance.

Though why should she be so quick to expect that he had left her like that? Glenn was thoughtful and caring. But annoyance was building up inside her and in her confusion she was hurting because he had insisted on her staying the night and now he was gone and she didn't know where.

Reaching for her topcoat hanging up in the hall, Emma gathered the few belongings that she'd had with her from the staff party. Two could play at that game, she thought tearfully and stepped out onto the drive, intending to make her way home on foot. Only to be brought to a halt when Glenn's car appeared. Within a matter of seconds he was out of it and observing her with a questioning smile that was the final irritation of the morning.

'I'm sorry, Emma,' he said. 'You must think me very rude to have been missing when you came down for breakfast.' She observed him in chilly silence. 'I got my timing wrong, I'm afraid. My mother phoned me before daybreak to say that Dad wasn't well. He's got some sort of throat infection and has a temperature, so she asked me to go and examine him.

'As there is rarely anything serious when they ring me on these occasions I went straight away, without disturbing you or leaving a message. I expected to be back within a very short time, only to get there and find him unwell with what seems like tonsillitis.

'So I had to write out a prescription and go and pick it up at an all-night chemist. I have promised to call again later. Could I persuade you to come back inside for some breakfast?'

She didn't say yes or no, just asked tightly, 'So why didn't you wake me up or leave a note? I would have been only too willing to have gone with you and done anything to help that I could.'

'What, after the day that you'd had?' he protested. 'Being insulted by that insolent Walsh fellow at the farm, and then caught in a snowdrift, followed by enduring my miserable comments on the way home?

'I scare myself sometimes when reality hits me. It takes me out of my safe cocoon and reminds me that life has to go on, that I'm not the only one who lost someone they loved on that dreadful occasion.'

He took her hand and drew her gently towards the door, wide open behind her, and once they were inside he unbuttoned her coat, slipped it off her shoulders and, holding her close, asked, 'So what would madam like for breakfast?'

'I'm not hungry,' she told him, stiffening in his

arms. She wasn't hungry, for food anyway, reassurance maybe, and Glenn was offering a plateful of that.

'I can't believe it,' he said gently, and planted a butterfly kiss on her cheek. 'How about that for starters, followed by food, glorious food?'

She was smiling now, the feeling of being left out in the cold disappearing, and when they'd eaten and she'd helped him tidy the kitchen Emma went with Glenn to visit his parents. She envied him the closeness of his small family.

If there was just one person *she* could call family and give her love and affection to now that her mother was gone, she would be content. But there was no one.

'You are so lucky to have your parents still with you,' she told Glenn as he drove her home in the quiet Sunday morning. 'I lost my mother some years ago and Jeremy wanted me gone as soon as he found someone to replace her.'

Glenn didn't comment but rage swept over him in a hot tide at the thought of what Jeremy had done to Emma. It wasn't surprising he'd been desperate to go to his maker with a clean slate. As far as Glenn was concerned, the man had done him a favour by asking him to find her, wherever she might be.

But his attraction to Emma was something new in his life and he was going to have to decide where he was going from this moment in time. Glenn would have liked to have spent the rest of the day with her, but once he had satisfied himself regarding his father's condition Emma had explained that she was expecting the builder to call with regard to the alterations she was planning and wanted to be there when he arrived.

'So, until tomorrow at the practice,' Glenn said, as he braked the car in front of her house, and with colour rising Emma thanked him for his hospitality, kissed him lightly on the cheek and was gone, leaving him to go back to make sure that his father really was improving with the touch of her lips against his skin feeling like a combination of a promise and a goodbye.

The patient *was* feeling better, his temperature was down, the inflammation in his throat reducing. Typically Jonas was now in a more upward mood with his thoughts turning to the event he was planning for the old and lonely on Christmas Day and wanting to know if Emma was still available to keep her promise of assisting.

'Yes, as far as I know,' Glenn told him. 'The surgery will be closed so she should be free, unless she has changed her mind.'

'And is she still going to dine with us in the evening?' his mother questioned.

'I suppose the same applies,' he said dryly, and left it at that, knowing that if Emma kept her promise and came to eat with them as arranged, whatever else there was between them it would be the best Christmas he'd had since he'd lost Serena. Which led him to wonder how was he going to make her aware of his feelings. He wanted to, needed to, because if nothing ever came of their attraction to each other, at least she had brought some joy into his empty life.

It was Monday morning and Emma was feeling miserable because the builder's quote for her requirements had been far above what she could afford, but she was excited about something else.

She'd noticed during her stay at Glenn's house that the one next to his was for sale and she'd gone home with an idea. It was of a similar design, though smaller, but just as attractive, and when the builder had left without an order Emma had rung the estate agents who were handling the sale and had discovered that it would cost less to buy it than do the extensive amount of work that her own property would need.

With excitement mounting, she'd asked the estate agents if they would be interested in selling hers as well. If things worked out, she hoped she would be able to buy the house next to Glenn's, which was empty at present.

It would be heavenly to live in a place like that. She'd been unable to stop thinking about it for what was left of the weekend. But would she be able to sell her own monstrosity? And, more importantly, would Glenn want her as a neighbour?

'How did you find your father when you checked on him again yesterday?' was Emma's first comment when they met up on Monday morning in the passage outside their respective consulting rooms.

'Much better,' Glenn replied. 'And to prove it he was asking if you are still available to help with his Christmas Day event. My mother also wanted to know if you will be joining us as planned later in the evening.'

'The answer to both those questions is yes,' said Emma. 'I'm looking forward to both very much.'

'How did you fare with the builder?' he wanted to know, concealing the pleasure that her reply had given him. 'Did he go away with a big order?' When she shook her head Glenn asked in surprise, 'Why ever not? I thought you were all set for a big face-lift for your house?'

'His quote was too high,' Emma explained, 'and I've had a change of plan over the weekend.'

'Meaning what?'

'I've put my house up for sale and I'm going to buy the one next to yours if it is still on the market when I've sold mine.'

'I see,' he said in a monotone. 'And where has that idea originated from?'

'I've liked where you live from the word go, and

something small but similar would be just right for my requirements.'

'And what if yours is still unsold when a buyer turns up for the one next to mine?' he asked in the same flat tone. 'What do you do then?'

'I'll worry about that when and if it happens,' Emma said, and called in her first patient of the day without further discussion.

CHAPTER SIX

EMMA'S FIRST PATIENT the next day was Anna Marsden, who had been in recently for her yearly check-up and was now back to have a chat about the results.

Newly retired from the position of manageress of Glenminster's largest womenswear boutique, Anna and her husband had been looking forward to a stress-free retirement. So Emma was not relishing having to let her know that the tests had shown that Anna had a type of blood clotting that showed signs of leukaemia and was going to need further investigation and treatment.

Anna's reaction to the news was typical of her. She listened to what Emma had to say and then responded calmly, 'Where do I go from here?'

'You have an appointment next Monday at the hospital,' Emma told her. 'Once you've chatted to the doctors there, you will have a clearer idea of what is involved.'

The woman seated across from her in the small consulting room smiled a twisted smile. 'Yes, of course, and at least I'll be able to have a lie-in when I feel like it now that I'm retired.'

When Anna left, the morning took its usual course of a steady flow of the sick and suffering coming and going. It gave Emma no time to question Glenn's reaction to the possibility that she might one day be living in the house next to his.

But in the lunch hour when Emma had a moment to spare and think about it properly, it became clear to her that although they'd spent some quality time together over the weekend he was still living in the past. There was no way she wanted to be in the background, chipping away at his love for the wife he had lost.

Yet it wasn't going to stop her from buying the house next to his if the opportunity presented itself. If Glenn was going to resent having her so near in his free time as well as being around constantly at the practice she would just have to accept the fact and get on with her life.

Glenn had just returned from visiting a patient who lived at the other end of the church graveyard from where the practice was. He popped in to inform her briefly that while there had been no sign of anyone hanging around the grave in the light of day, there had been fresh roses in one of the vases. Emma's niggling feeling of unease came flooding back.

With Christmas just a week away and her rash promise to spend some of the time with Glenn and his family hanging over her, Emma went to shop for the event on her way home that evening with little enthusiasm. She would be dining on one of the special nights of the year with people she hardly knew and could see it being an ordeal.

The daytime activity she'd volunteered for was different because she would be doing something useful in helping Glenn's father to bring some light into the darkness of other folks' lives. She wondered what his son would be doing while they were so employed. Putting up a fence between his house and the one next door?

Jonas had asked her if she could be at the community hall in the town centre for eight o'clock on the morning of Christmas Day as there were turkeys to be cooked in its spacious kitchens, along with all the other trappings. Within minutes of arriving Emma was at work along with a group of other volunteers who were mostly known to her from the practice, plus a couple of strangers. Glenn's father introduced her to one of them. His name was Alex Mowbray and he had lived in Glenminster many years ago before going to live abroad with his sick wife.

'I never wanted to leave this place,' Alex said, 'but my wife had a long-term serious illness. She wanted to move where it was warmer so I had no choice but to take her to live abroad.

'She died recently and my yearning to come back to Glenminster clocked in. So here I am, getting to know old friends who are still around and remembering with sadness those who are not.'

He seemed a decent sort, Emma thought as Alex Mowbray went back to his allotted task of preparing the vegetables that would be served with the turkey. Tall, with silver hair and kind blue eyes, he was easy to talk to, which was more than she could say for the man she was falling in love with. When she looked up, Glenn was there, having just arrived with a carload of provisions for the meal and an overwhelming urge to be near her.

So he wasn't going to be shut away in his castle for the day, like she'd expected, Emma thought joyfully. For at least part of the time he would be where she could see him.

Having unloaded the produce he'd brought, Glenn was beside Emma in a flash, smiling at the chef's hat she was wearing and asking if she was all set for the evening.

'Yes, if you still want me there,' she said. 'You didn't seem enthralled when I told you that I might be coming to live in the house next to yours.'

'That was merely the surprise,' he protested, 'and also because I don't take well to my secluded life being invaded.' It didn't seem like the moment to tell Emma that he wanted her living with him in his house, not in the small dwelling next to it.

Glenn looked around him. 'Dad is beckoning. He's going to tell me not to interfere with the workers. I'd better be off as I'm in charge of making sure that anyone unable to walk has transport to get here, which is going to involve half the practice staff making their cars available.'

'And I thought that you wouldn't be getting drawn into today's event,' she teased.

'What! With a father like mine?' He laughed and was gone again, leaving Emma to observe his father and Alex, who had appeared in their midst, chatting amicably as they performed their chosen tasks. Meanwhile Glenn and whoever was available from the practice staff were organising the transport that was going to be needed.

It was almost time for lunch and the kitchen staff were taking a short break before the diners arrived when Glenn's father informed Emma that he had invited their new acquaintance to dine with them that evening.

'Alex Mowbray lives alone,' he said, 'and that shouldn't happen to anyone at this time of year, so I've invited him to join us tonight.'

'Have you told your wife?' Emma teased, and he smiled.

'Yes, but she knows what I'm like. Olivia would be surprised if I *hadn't* invited someone else as well as you.'

'Is Glenn going to be happy, having me there?'

she asked haltingly. 'I'm tuned in to how much he cherishes his privacy.'

'It has been difficult for him since he lost Serena,' his father said, 'especially in such a dreadful way. May I be allowed to say that since he brought you back to Glenminster out of nowhere, his mother and I have begun to hope.'

'I don't think you should if you don't mind me saying so,' Emma told him. 'We get on well most of the time, but the barriers that Glenn lives behind are not going to come down with me, I'm afraid.'

Glenn appeared at that moment with an elderly couple that he'd driven to the community hall and cast a quick glance at his father and Emma in a deep discussion that tailed off while he was finding seats for his passengers.

When Glenn had done that, he turned to go for his next lot of guests and found Emma beside him, smiling her pleasure at being near him again.

'So how many more journeys do you have to make?' she asked, and there was no smile in return.

'Just a couple,' Glenn replied, and then said, 'I hope that there's a table set for all the kind folk who have been doing the chauffeuring at my request.'

'Yes, of course,' she assured him, 'and tonight your parents will have another stranger at their table. Your father has also invited Alex Mowbray, who has recently returned from abroad after many years away.'

'Fine,' he said, and was off to pick up the last of the guests without giving her time to reply.

After the Christmas dinner was over, the guests had departed and the volunteers had tidied the place up, Emma began the short walk home. She hadn't wanted to take up a parking space, which would be in big demand, at the community hall so she'd walked there earlier. She could have waited for a lift from Glenn but along with the other car drivers he was busy taking guests home, while his father had gone to take the hall keys back.

Emma had only been on the way a matter of minutes when Alex's car pulled up beside her. Winding the window down, he asked, 'Can I give you a lift?'

'Er...yes, if it won't be out of your way, Mr Mowbray,' she said, deciding she'd like to get to know this amiable stranger better. 'I live just a short distance down the road.'

As she settled herself in the passenger seat next to him he said, 'So you'll know Waverly House, then?'

'Yes, I do,' she told him. 'It is a beautiful old property.'

'Yes, indeed,' Alex agreed. 'It was where my wife and I lived before we moved abroad and I have gained much comfort in finding it for sale and bringing it back to its former glory. Although sadly there will be no one for me to leave it to as we were never able to have children because of her health problems.'

What a charming man, Emma thought as she thanked him for the lift and went to prepare for the day's next big event. This time it would be Glenn who would be driving her to her destination and as she showered and dressed for the occasion the promise of the evening ahead was like a precious Christmas gift, probably the only one she was likely to receive.

But that didn't matter as long as Glenn liked what she had bought for him. She would never forget as long as she lived how he had painstakingly found her and persuaded her to come home. She could scarcely believe he was now the centre of her universe.

Glenn had said he would call for her at seven o'clock and as the clock climbed slowly towards that time every moment felt magical. Until it went past seven, then eight, and was teetering on nine. He must have had better things to do and had changed his mind about picking her up she thought dejectedly.

The phone rang at last and her heart skipped a beat when she heard Glenn's voice. 'I am so sorry, Emma,' he said contritely. 'I was involved in a pile-up as I was leaving the town centre.'

Her heart missed a beat. 'Are you hurt?' she gasped.

'No. I just had to help treat the casualties, who are now safely in A and E. I should be with you in minutes so don't run away.'

'Does your mother know?' Emma asked.

'Yes. She's been holding the meal back but is now ready to serve when we put in an appearance. I couldn't get in touch with you earlier as the accident occurred on the bottom road and I couldn't get a signal. We had to drive the casualties ourselves until we were higher up and then ambulances came speeding out to them. All the time I kept thinking that you would be judging me as yet another person letting you down. Tell me truthfully, did you?'

'Er…yes,' Emma said with painful honesty, 'because I know that in spite of our friendship you prefer to be alone, and I do understand that, Glenn.'

There was silence for a moment and then he said, 'I'll be with you in a matter of minutes—and be prepared. Dad is going to be wearing his Father Christmas outfit.'

As she watched for his car Emma felt ashamed for being so quick to judge him. She knew Glenn was decent and honourable and she loved him, she thought glumly. But the chances of her love being returned were not evenly balanced.

Glenn was as good as his word and his car pulled up outside within a matter of minutes. Emma saw immediately that what must have been a smart suit was ripped and bloodstained, but he was unharmed. In her relief at seeing that he wasn't hurt she leaned across the passenger seat and kissed his grimy cheek. 'Please, forgive me for doubting you,' she said softly.

'Of course,' Glenn said, reflecting that if he wasn't

so scruffy and if his parents weren't patiently waiting for them to arrive, he might stop the car and show Emma how much she affected him. Within minutes they were pulling up outside his parents' house.

'Helping in an emergency such as tonight's is the penalty of being a doctor,' Glenn said, as his mother held him close for a moment.

Alex nodded his agreement.

Glenn's father was helping Emma to take off her coat and when it was done he kissed her cheek lightly beneath the mistletoe and she felt tears prick her eyes.

They were a lovely family, she thought wistfully. What a shame that their daughter-in-law hadn't lived to give them grandchildren.

Glenn had disappeared in the direction of the bathroom and minutes later he appeared scrubbed and clean in casual clothes. They sat down to eat with a small gift from their hostess beside each plate, leaving Emma to wonder when she would get the chance to give Glenn what she had bought for him.

It came when the meal was over and the two of them were clearing away while the older folks relaxed after their exertions of the day in front of the sitting-room fire.

'I have something for you, Glenn,' she said awkwardly. He looked at her questioningly, and she said, 'Christmas seems an appropriate occasion to show my gratitude for all that you have done for me.' Taking a small gift-wrapped box out of her handbag, she offered it to him.

Glenn didn't accept it at first, leaving her standing with it in her hand. After a moment's silence he took it from her and said in a low voice, 'Whatever it is that you want to give me there is no need, Emma. What I did for you I would have done for anyone.'

'Yes. I know,' she said, feeling hurt that he had put her in her place. 'If you don't want to accept it, fine. The gift doesn't carry with it any commitments, just my grateful thanks.' She left him with the small package unopened in his hand and went to join the others, the question uppermost in her mind being how soon she could go home without causing offence.

When she'd gone back into the lounge Glenn groaned at his tactlessness. Why couldn't he have explained to Emma that he couldn't bear the thought of hurting her at some time or other by letting his dedication to Serena's memory come between them?

He had something for her that he was going to present in privacy tomorrow. He had already asked Emma out to lunch and he wanted to put his present where it belonged on her finger. But he knew that their relationship was not the usual kind and had no idea how she would react when she saw his gift.

When Glenn removed the wrappings and Emma's gift was revealed he swallowed hard. It was a gold pocket watch. He had admired a similar one belonging to a patient and Emma had remembered.

He opened the sitting-room door and when she looked up he beckoned to her. Unobserved by the others, who were engrossed in a carol service on television, she went to join him in the hall.

Taking her hand in his, he said softly, 'Your gift is lovely, Emma. I am a tactless clod.' Pointing to the mistletoe sprig above their heads, he bent and kissed her long and lingeringly. He would have continued to do so if he hadn't heard movement coming from the sitting room because the programme they had been watching had come to an end.

Opening the door, Glenn smiled at them and said, 'Anyone for coffee?'

'Not for me, thanks,' Alex said. 'I came on foot and don't want to be too late getting back.'

'I'll be taking Emma home shortly,' Glenn said, 'and could drop you off after I've seen her safely home.'

Alex smiled. 'In that case, a coffee would be most acceptable.' And Emma thought, So much for the kiss. Apart from the time spent in the kitchen clearing up after the meal and the magical moments in the hall when Glenn had kissed her, they hadn't been alone for a moment all day. And now he was making sure they weren't by taking her home first.

There was the dry taste of anguish in her mouth, but pride stiffened her resolve and when Alex asked if that would be all right with her Emma flashed him a smile and said, 'Yes, of course.' And the matter was settled.

The fact that Glenn had spent no thought with regard to a Christmas gift for her was immaterial. Emma hadn't given him the watch expecting something in return. But it couldn't help bringing back that feeling of being of no importance, which had never gone away since the night Jeremy had told her she wasn't his and he wanted her gone.

They were outside her house and as she opened the car door and stepped onto the drive Glenn went round to her side and said in a low voice, 'It's late. I want to see you safely inside before I go. Emma, the reason I'm dropping you off first is because I want to know more about this stranger who has appeared out of nowhere. You have lived here a lot longer than I have, yet he isn't familiar to you, is he?'

'No, but Glenminster is a town, not a village where folks are much more likely to know each other,' she said. 'And from what Alex says, he has been long gone from here.' She glanced across to where he was waiting patiently for Glenn to get behind the steering-wheel again. 'All I know is that he seems a really nice man, and that he's rebought the house he used to live in and has refurbished it. It's a dream of a place.'

Emma instantly mellowed and, smiling at Glenn,

said, 'I will be ready at twelve, as requested.' As the
door closed behind her he got back into the car and
drove off with his mind full of questions that had
no answers.

When Glenn came for her the next day Emma was
wearing the white fake-fur jacket and turquoise dress
that she'd appeared in on that first night when everyone from the practice had welcomed her back to
Glenminster. His heartbeat quickened at the thought
of what he was going to say to her over lunch.

'So what did you find out about Alex Mowbray?'
she asked, when they were seated at the table that
had been reserved for them in the Barrington Bar.

'Not a lot,' Glenn said. 'Except that he is a really
nice guy who kept the faith with a sick wife but always wanted to come back here if the opportunity
arose.'

'Do you know what was wrong with her?' asked
Emma.

'Yes, advanced Parkinson's disease, which, as we
both know, is an illness that doesn't carry with it an
early death. The years must have crept by before he
was able to come back to the place he loved best. But
I didn't bring you here to talk about Alex,' he said
with a change of subject. Now it was Glenn's turn
to produce a small gift-wrapped box, which he put
on the table in front of her.

'I know you must have thought me mean for not

having a gift for you yesterday,' he explained, 'but I couldn't give you this then as what I have to ask you is private and very personal.' She sat watching him, transfixed by the moment, and he said, 'Maybe you would like to unwrap it to understand me better.'

'Yes, of course,' croaked Emma. She went weak at the knees when she saw that resting in a small velvet box was a solitaire diamond ring. It has happened at last, she thought joyfully. He wants me, he loves me. I can't believe it!

His next comment brought her back down to earth. 'I may never be able to be to you what you want me to be,' Glenn said gravely. 'To be totally committed I would have to give myself to you whole-heartedly, and I can't guarantee that I can do that by shutting Serena out of my life. So would you accept second best? I care for you a lot, Emma, I really do. And maybe one day I can be the way you want me to be.'

'No,' she breathed, and watched him flinch. 'I've had enough of being second best. I want to be with a man who will cherish me and who I can love in return, without making do with what is on offer. I only want your ring on my finger because you can't live without me and if that isn't so I will do without.'

Emma was getting to her feet and picking up her belongings, desperate to escape from the awful moment of humiliation. When she'd collected her coat from the cloakroom she went into the foyer and flagged down a passing taxi to take her home, leaving Glenn to stare stonily at the ring she had cast aside.

Lying on top of the bed covers, gazing blankly up at the ceiling, Emma heard Glenn's car pull up in the drive below and turned her face into the pillows to deaden the sound of the doorbell when it rang. It continued for some minutes and then stopped, and she heard him drive off into the afternoon. When she went onto the landing and looked down into the hallway the box with the ring inside was lying on the doormat. It was then that the tears came as she went down slowly, picked it up, and without opening it again placed it in a nearby drawer.

When Glenn's father was driving past Glenn's house in the late afternoon he saw his son's car parked outside so stopped to have a chat. 'Where's Emma?' he asked in surprise. 'We thought that you weren't coming to us today because you had plans to spend it with her.'

'Yes, I did,' said Glenn, 'but it would seem that I presumed too much and she doesn't want my company.'

'I see,' Jonas replied, and asked disappointedly, 'What makes you think that?'

'I was a tactless fool, expecting too much of her,'

Glenn replied bleakly, 'wanting what was best for me instead of her, and she refused.'

'Serena loved you,' his father said. 'Do you honestly think she would want you to cut yourself off from finding love again because she was taken?'

'Probably not,' Glenn agreed, 'but I still feel guilty because she wanted us to holiday somewhere else for a change, and I preferred to go to our usual place. She only went along with it to please me.'

'Yes, but you weren't to know that a tsunami was on its way that day,' Jonas protested.

'There is no answer to any of it,' Glenn replied. 'We've been through this discussion too often. I'll be fine here, getting some paperwork done, and will pop round for a bit later on if that's all right.'

'You know it is,' his father said. 'You've fed me often enough when your mother has had her fill of me. So we'll see you later, unless you've made friends with Emma again in the meantime.'

As if! Glenn thought bleakly. Emma brought out all his protective instincts one moment and the next stirred the heat of desire in him, and he wasn't getting any of it right.

When his father had gone Glenn left what he'd been doing and went for a brisk walk in the winter afternoon. He met Alex, doing the same thing. When he saw him Alex hailed him in his usual friendly manner and Glenn said, 'Are you looking forward to spending New Year in Glenminster?'

'You bet I am,' Alex said. 'I've wanted that for years. I was never able to come back to my roots until my wife passed away. I always had many precious memories of this place but it isn't the same as actually being here.'

'And I'm just the opposite,' Glenn told him. 'My memories are all in a faraway place and the last of them is not good.'

Having turned the screw on his heartstrings once again, Glenn went on his way with the thought that, like Alex, Emma was delighted to be back in their homeland, despite the gloomy nature of her return.

Unlike the two men, Emma was huddled beside the fire in her dismal sitting room with no inclination to move. The phone rang and Lydia's bright and cheerful voice came over the line.

'How are you fixed for coming to join me and mine for supper this evening?' she asked, and into the silence that followed she continued, 'I have visitors with me, relatives on holiday from Canada who have called unexpectedly, and I could do with some support.'

'Er…yes, I'm free tonight,' Emma told her reluctantly. 'What time do you want me there?'

'Seven o'clock, if that's all right,' Lydia replied.

'Yes, no problem,' she agreed, trying to sound enthusiastic.

When Lydia went on to say that she'd been try-

ing to get in touch with Glenn to invite him round
to give the occasion some support it was a relief for
Emma to hear that she hadn't been able to contact
him. The events of earlier in the day were still like
a knife thrust in her heart.

Asked if she'd seen anything of Glenn, it hurt to
admit that they'd met briefly at midday, but she had
no idea what his plans were for the rest of it. With a
sinking feeling inside she said goodbye to her friend
and wondered where she was going to find the zest
to socialise with Lydia's relatives.

CHAPTER SEVEN

WHEN GLENN RETURNED from his cheerless walk he found a message from Lydia awaiting him, and his reaction to it was the same as Emma's. The last thing he wanted to do was chat to strangers but Lydia was a tower of strength at the practice and a good friend so he didn't want to let her down.

The least he could do was help her to entertain her visitors and if Emma was there it would be a bonus. Even if she didn't want to have anything to do with him, just to be able to see her would help to lessen the nightmare he had managed to create for himself in the season of goodwill.

Emma was the first person Glenn saw when he arrived at Lydia's home. She was looking pale but composed with a wintry smile for him when he greeted her, which was in keeping with the weather outside and the misery he was experiencing inside being near her again.

What had she done with the ring? he wondered.

She'd put it with the rubbish in the waste bin most likely. Someone at the waste-disposal place might get a pleasant surprise, and if they did, good for them, as Glenn didn't want to see a reminder of his big mistake ever again.

He hoped and prayed that Emma wouldn't do a disappearing act again, as she'd done after Jeremy's hurtful treatment of her. He needed to be able to see her at the practice and around the place like he needed to breathe.

The Canadians were a pleasant lot, easy to get on with, and as the night progressed with a buffet that Lydia had arranged and lots of chatter Emma began to relax. At least the evening was proving to be a good opportunity for her to meet up with Glenn before seeing him at the practice when Christmas was over.

They had both walked the short distance to Lydia's house, thinking that driving wasn't a good idea if the wine was going to be flowing. At the first opportunity Glenn said to her in a low voice, 'No walking home alone, Emma. If you don't want me around, ring for a taxi.'

Emma nodded mutely as tiredness lay upon her like a heavy shawl after the day's events. There was no chance that she was going to opt for walking anywhere, she decided, and hoped that Lydia's guests might be feeling the same, having travelled quite some distance to see their hostess.

Yet it was midnight before the party was over and, doing as Glenn had suggested, Emma rang for a taxi. As it was the festive season there were long queues and it was going to be some time before her request was dealt with.

Glenn was observing her expression and guessed what the problem was. As they said goodbye to Lydia and her guests and went out into the night beneath a star-filled sky he said, 'You're going to have to let me walk you home, Emma.'

'I'll be fine on my own,' she told him flatly, and almost tripped over a tree root outside the house, but he caught her as she fell. As Glenn looked down at her in the circle of his arms he said, 'If you don't want me at your side on the way home I will be just a few paces behind you until you put the key in the door of your house. I will only leave you when you are safe inside. We still don't know the identity of the person who seems to have an endless supply of cream roses.'

As they set off, with Glenn walking a few paces behind, as promised, he said, 'There must have been other men in your mother's life, like the man who fathered you, for instance, and then disappeared.'

'If there were I never knew about them because I always thought that Jeremy was my father,' Emma said bleakly. 'And I had no reason to question it until that awful night when he put me straight and made me feel so unwanted.'

Glenn ached to hold her close, wanted to cradle her to him instead of bringing up the rear, but after the dreadful mistake he'd made in showing Emma the ring and telling her she could only expect to be second best, hoping she could cope with that, he'd known that he had blown it with her. And rightly so, as far as she was concerned.

Glenn had said what he had because of the dread of not making Emma as happy, as she deserved, because in the dark corners of his mind there was always the memory of what had happened to Serena making him slow to make another commitment that he might fall down on. And yet it was Emma who was always the centre of his imaginings.

When they stopped at Emma's door she put the key in the lock and said meaningfully, 'You've seen me home safely, Glenn, and now my key is in the door.' She added, as it swung back on its hinges, 'So the only thing left to say is...goodnight!'

'Yes, all right, I get the message,' he said levelly. 'I just wanted to be honest with you, Emma, that's all.' He was striding off into the dark night when she called him back. When he turned round, Emma was standing holding the box, which she'd taken out of the drawer in the hall. 'You will need this when you find someone willing to accept second best,' she said tautly, giving it back to him. And as Glenn looked down at it bleakly, lying on the palm of his hand, the door was closed against him and Emma was walking slowly up the stairs to her lonely bed.

It was New Year's Eve and Emma was greeting the occasion with little enthusiasm. She had nothing planned and was intending to spend it alone in any case when the phone rang. It was Glenn's mother, to ask whether, if she wasn't booked to go anywhere, she would like to join them for supper as they welcomed in another year on the calendar.

When Olivia said that there would be just the three of them there—Jonas, Glenn and herself—the vision of Glenn insisting on her not going home alone came once again and she excused herself by pleading a headache and having an early night.

It didn't get her far. Olivia must have reported their conversation because minutes later Glenn was on the line, wanting to know if she had any medication for the headache, and if she didn't could he bring something round?

'I'll be fine,' she told him. 'I'm hugging a hot-water bottle and expect to be asleep in moments.' She knew that if he came round, and doctor that he was guessed that there was nothing wrong with her, it would be very hurtful for his parents. She liked them both a lot and didn't want to upset them.

'All right,' Glenn said. 'I don't expect you would

have wanted to come in any case, but my parents aren't aware that we are not communicating so you will have to make allowances for them. They both set great store with the coming of a new year and are disappointed that you won't be there to share the moment with us. As far as the headache goes, if it starts to give you any problems I'll come round—*as a doctor, of course,*' was his parting comment, which left her feeling even more miserable.

Once the New Year was firmly established Emma didn't see much of anyone socially, except for Alex, who seemed to be the most agile out-and-about person amongst those who lived nearby. Emma had the feeling that the wanderer who had returned to Glenminster couldn't settle in his gracious house so she invited him round for coffee a couple of times.

Alex was an interesting person to talk to and she could imagine him being a loving father if ever he'd been blessed with children. Glenn would too, she mused ruefully. He had all the time in the world for the little ones who were brought to the practice by their parents with childish ailments.

Emma's closeness with Glenn had died after the business of the ill-fated proposal and although the days went by in a flash, the nights were long and lonely.

There had been a few viewers interested in her house. She had to show them round at weekends as her weekdays were swallowed up by the demands of her job. But she had received no offers for it so far. With the idea of living next door to Glenn no longer in her mind, she wasn't pushing for anything in particular yet she was still leaving her property on the market as daylight hours were becoming longer and Easter was on the calendar. Soon those who sought a change of residence would be out and about.

Glenn observed her from a distance. At the practice Emma was still a dedicated doctor, putting her patients before anything else, but on the rare occasions when he saw her out of hours she had little to say and looked pale and remote. So much so that he wondered how long he could stand having to live with the evidence of how much he had hurt her.

Glenn cringed every time he thought back to his blundering proposal. It now seemed arrogant and hurtful, like a request for the best of both worlds. It also registered that she was seeing more of Alex Mowbray than him when she was away from the practice.

Yet Glenn was aware that sometimes young, insecure women often turned to older men for comfort and reassurance. Although the way that Emma had sent him packing didn't exactly indicate insecurity, more like outrage if anything.

The house next door to Glenn had been sold, but the board outside hers indicated no buyers as yet. Right now he would give anything for Emma to live near if he couldn't have her with him.

Flowers were still being placed on her mother's grave by an unknown hand and it seemed as if Emma was accepting the fact without further questioning. It was as if she was past caring. But Glenn wasn't prepared to let it rest at that. It was spooky and required an answer for Emma's sake, but short of him camping out in the churchyard it was almost as if the unknown visitor knew when to visit the grave and when not to.

And for Emma, who was all alone in the world—or at least didn't appear to have any other family—Glenn felt that if only he could bring a feeling of belonging into her life he would have done something to make up for his own lack of commitment.

Glenn was beginning to think of Serena less and Emma more but maybe that was because of the situation he found himself in: wanting Emma but afraid to give his heart to her completely and betray his love for his wife that he carried like a sacred torch.

There was one occasion when the flame of their attraction was ignited to fever pitch when Emma had driven to a hotel in the Gloucestershire hills to relieve the boredom of an empty weekend and Glenn was out walking with rucksack and walking boots for the same reason.

Easter would soon be upon them and with the awakening of plants and flowers and a pale sun above, the day had brought out those, like themselves, who loved the countryside.

Emma was about to order afternoon tea when his

shadow fell across the table where she was seated out in the open, and he said gravely, 'Do you mind if I join you?'

'Er...no,' she said weakly, as the sight of him so near and unexpected made her blood warm and made her cheeks go pink.

A waitress was hovering to take their order and when that was done Glenn took the pack off his back and, facing her across the table, asked, 'So how are you, Emma? What brings you up here?'

She shrugged slender shoulders and told him, 'For the lack of anything else to do, I suppose. When the practice closed for the weekend at lunchtime I felt that I just had to get some fresh clean air after the long winter.'

'Me too,' Glenn agreed. 'Although I'm surprised not to find Alex with you. He told me once that he comes up here a lot to revive old memories, whatever they might be.'

'He's a lovely man,' she commented. 'But lonely, I feel. Alex once said that he came back because all his most precious memories are here. Whatever they might be, he was obviously happy in Glenminster, which is more than either of us can say, isn't it?'

As soon as she'd thrown that comment into the conversation Emma couldn't believe she'd said it. She'd given Glenn an opening for more aggravation and he was quick to respond.

'Which, I suppose, is my fault for being too faithful to the wife I lost?' he said, and got to his feet just as the waitress was bringing the food.

Emma felt the wetness of tears on her cheeks as he slung the bag he'd been carrying onto his back again and, leaving ample money on the table to pay for what they had ordered, set off back down the track on which he had come up.

She was on her feet, running after him. She caught up with him at the side of a deserted hayloft belonging to one of the farms. When Glenn turned to face her, Emma said breathlessly, 'Forgive me for my lack of understanding, Glenn, and for forgetting how you brought me back out of limbo. I will never forget that, no matter what.'

Her glance went to the hayloft, a close and sheltered place where they could be alone for a while. As if reading her mind, Glenn said, 'If ever I made love to you it would be on our wedding night, not in somewhere like that. Do you understand?'

'Yes, I do,' she said in a low voice. 'I understand perfectly and you have no idea how much it hurts to know how little chance there is of that.'

Glenn nodded and without speaking pointed himself homewards on the hillside, while she walked back to her car with dragging feet.

Following a miserable weekend that had seemed never-ending to Emma, they met again on Monday morning when she knocked on the door of his consulting room. After he opened it Emma said, before she choked on the words, 'I am sorry about what I said on Saturday, Glenn, and do hope you will forgive me.'

He reached out, took her hand in his, and pulled her into the room, closing the door behind her. 'There is nothing to forgive,' he said gently. 'I was too quick off the mark, Emma. But I have to tell you that you would be better off with someone unlike me, whose heart and mind are free from pain and sorrow.

'You are young and beautiful and deserve someone who isn't living in the past. It worries me that you are so alone, without family, with just a few friends. If we continue as we are doing one day you will wish that you'd never met me, because all your chances of happiness will be gone, lost in a relationship without roots, like your mother's was, from what I can gather. Do you really have no idea at all who your father was, or is? Have you ever seen your birth certificate?'

'No,' she said. 'I've never had any need to look for it, before now, and assumed Jeremy's name was on it. But I can't find it anywhere, so maybe my real father's name is included. I should get a copy and see what comes to light.'

'Yes,' Glenn agreed. 'It can't do any harm. You need to go to the register office where you were born to apply for a copy. You will have to pay for it, together with postage, on the spot. I'm told that it doesn't take long to arrive.

'I'll come along to give you moral support if you like and will be there for you when it arrives.' Then, as the surgery doors were opened at that moment at the start of another busy day, they separated, each with a mind full of questions that needed answers. And in the middle of it all Glenn prayed that the information Emma received from her birth certificate would bring some degree of contentment into her life and help to take away the loneliness.

They went the next day in their lunch hour to the local register office to fill in the necessary paperwork for a copy of her birth certificate, and when they came out of the building Emma was smiling because, thanks to Glenn, hope had been born inside her. He pointed to a café across the road and said, 'How about a quick bite before we go back to the practice?'

'Yes, please,' she told him, and as they settled themselves at a table by the window Alex passed by on the other side of the street. He observed them and thought what a happy couple they made. He would have liked to go across and join them but didn't want to butt in and went on his way.

It was true. Emma had been happy on that day, just being with Glenn and knowing that soon one of the blank chapters of her life might be opened up to her. Her happiness lasted until the certificate she was waiting for arrived, with the information regarding her father described as 'unknown'.

It had been amongst her mail one morning and she had badly needed Glenn to hold onto for support. But he was missing from the practice that day, having to be present at the monthly meeting of senior medical staff in the town that was held in the board room of its biggest hospital. Without him the day seemed never-ending.

Glenn rang just as she was about to leave for home to see if she'd heard anything about her birth certificate. When she told him tearfully that she had, he told her to stay where she was at the practice, which was now empty as all the other staff had gone home. His meeting was over so he could be with her in minutes. Emma obeyed with the feeling that her life was keeping to its familiar pattern of emptiness.

When Glenn came striding in he held out his arms and Emma wept out her disappointment as he stroked her hair gently and asked, 'So what did it actually say?' As if he didn't know.

'It said "unknown",' she told him wearily, and as she looked up at him he bent and kissed her, gently at first and then with kisses that made her forget everything except that she was where she wanted to be.

When he released her from his hold and they locked up and went out into the dark street, it was as if the winter moon above was shining more brightly amongst a sky full of stars. Turning to her, Glenn asked softly, 'Shall we find somewhere to eat, Emma?'

'Yes,' she said, but when she looked up into his eyes she saw regret there and knew he was wishing they could be back to the way they had been before, which was not on kissing terms. Although there had been no lack of tenderness and desire while she'd been in his arms.

There was a restaurant not far away and Glenn steered her towards it, devastated that the thing that Emma so much needed to know hadn't been forthcoming. He was also cross with himself for allowing her to hope for something again.

'Would you like to stay at my place tonight?' he asked when they left the restaurant. 'I don't like to think of you all alone with such a disappointment to cope with.'

The offer was tempting, but there was no way that she wanted to be so close to him yet out of bounds, so reluctantly she said with a catch in her voice, 'Thanks for the offer, Glenn, but I'll be fine. I might do some searching around the house to see if there is anything that might guide me to who my father was. I doubt it, though, because the last thing that Jeremy said after taking the ground from under my feet was that my mother had never told him the name of the man who

had made her pregnant. So I don't see her leaving
any names or addresses around, do you?'

Glenn sighed. 'No, not really, I suppose, and are
we really saying that she married Jeremy and put up
with him for twenty-plus years so you would have
a father?'

'Yes, it seems to have been that way,' said Emma
sadly, 'and I never knew anything different until Jeremy enlightened me.'

'What did your mother die from, Emma?'

'She was frail, probably from unhappiness that
she never let me see, and had a heart problem that
culminated in a sudden serious heart attack one day.
She was rushed to hospital but it was too late to save
her, which left Jeremy and me to jog along as best
we could with nothing at all in common.'

They had parked their cars not far from the place
where they'd gone to order the birth certificate, and
Glenn was only sorry that it had proved fruitless.
There was nothing more to say, it was time to say
goodbye, but he wasn't willing to give up on it. He
said, 'If you don't want to stay at my place, shall I
stay with you at yours?'

She flashed him a tired smile. 'No, I'll be fine.
Don't worry about me.'

'All right,' he agreed. He couldn't blame her if she
wanted to hold him at bay, but he still couldn't help
feeling concerned. 'I'll go, but only if you promise
that you will ring me if you need me at any time dur-

ing the night, and that you will come to me for breakfast before we start at the practice. Otherwise I will
come to your place to fetch you. Right? Understood?'

'Yes,' she replied. Despite her anxieties about
their relationship, his concern on her behalf felt like
healing balm. Feeling better, she drove off into the
night.

Glenn stopped off at his parents' house on the way
home and asked if either of them knew of anyone
who might have had an affair with Emma's mother
before she'd married Jeremy Chalmers.

They both looked at him blankly, and Jonas said,
'No, we don't. Emma's mum was local, while Jeremy
came from somewhere near where she'd worked before Emma was born. Emma was just a toddler when
he came as head of the practice.'

And his mother chipped in with, 'Why do you
want to know something like that?'

'It was just that I was curious,' he told her, 'because Emma tells me that she and Jeremy weren't
at all close.'

Olivia laughed. 'So aren't you the lucky one to
have people like us as your parents?'

'I certainly am,' he replied, holding her close,
while his father's comment was to the effect of when
was he going to give them some grandchildren? At
other times the question had irritated him because
of his devotion to Serena's memory, but this time it

had its appeal as suddenly the thought of having a little girl or boy who looked like Emma was firing his imagination.

When Emma appeared at his door the next morning, geared up for the coming day amongst the sick folk of Glenminster, Glenn breathed a sigh of relief.

He hadn't slept well at all because he'd kept imagining her being sad and lonely in the night hours and now, observing Emma, she looked the more rested of the two of them.

Glenn had gone to the trouble of making a cooked breakfast with all the trimmings, which was the last thing he would ever normally contemplate on a working day. When she saw what was on offer Emma said, 'Glenn, this is delightful. I will enjoy every mouthful.' How great it would be if they could have breakfast together every day after sleeping in the same bed, she thought. Her colour rose at the idea, and then their glances held. He smiled across at her and said, 'We must do this again some time.'

'Yes,' she said, glowing at the thought, 'that would be lovely.' And suddenly the misery of the previous day seemed far away. That was until they got to work and Lydia told them that on arriving at the practice she had seen an abundance of fresh flowers on the grave. And the same question about who the mysterious person who had known her mother could possibly be haunted Emma once more.

Glenn was close behind her and as he watched the colour fade from her face the determination within him to solve the mystery once and for all hardened. Anything to take away the hurt Emma felt every time it happened, even if he had to stay up all night.

There had to be a reason why the flowers were always cream roses, especially when golden daffodils and hyacinths were in bloom and there was cherry blossom on the trees. These roses were hothouse-grown, and if they were chosen for a special reason Emma had no knowledge of it.

Observing the number of blooms that had been put there only minutes ago it seemed logical to expect that it would be some time before the phantom mourner came again. When he or she did Glenn was determined he was going to be ready.

'Who can it possibly be, Glenn?' Emma said as they went inside the practice together. 'I know all my mother's friends and none of them frequent the graveyard or relieve the florists of most of their stock in one go.'

'I don't know,' Glenn said grimly, 'but I'm going to find out, and when I do they will have some explaining to do.' His voice softened. 'You don't deserve this, Emma. I want you to be happy and carefree.' She stared at him doubtfully, and he added, 'Yes, I know I haven't been helping that along much, but I have the matter in hand.'

It was only as they separated, each to their own consulting room, that Emma wondered what that meant.

It was half-term and quite a few parents were there with their young ones for various reasons. As ever on days like this the sound of young voices and small feet came from the play area of the practice, put there to keep the young patients happy until their names were called.

There was also the sound of fretful crying from one little one who had just arrived with worried parents. Glenn must have heard it as he came out of his consulting room as the patient he'd just seen was leaving and told them to take their little girl inside immediately.

Not long after he came out and told Reception in a low voice, 'We need an ambulance fast.' He turned to Emma, who was nearby and had heard the little one's crying. 'I suspect meningitis. The dreaded red rash is there and the other symptoms also make it look likely.'

His comments brought a sudden hush amongst those who were near enough to have heard what he'd said. After the ambulance had been and gone, with siren blaring as it sped on its way, a sombre silence hung over those who were still waiting to be seen.

After the dreadful beginning the day settled into a more normal routine and as the ills of winter became the main topic of conversation in the waiting room someone who had been absent for a while turned up in the form of James Prentice. He had been on a two-month course up north in a hospital there and was back with a new girlfriend in tow and expecting everyone to be as bowled over by her as he was.

With just a momentary lull following his arrival and a few quick handshakes for the new woman in his life because everyone was so busy, James left after announcing that they were getting engaged and would be in the Barrington Bar that evening if anyone would like to join them for a drink.

'That would seem to be a whirlwind romance,' Glenn said whimsically, as he and Emma were about to leave the practice at the end of what had been a very busy day. 'Are you intending to go to this evening's get-together? I shall go for a while to represent the practice but won't be staying long as I've got paperwork to deal with. I never seem to have the time to get to it during the day. So I can give you a lift there but can't promise to be able to bring you back.'

'Thanks for the offer,' she told him. 'I would appreciate it as my car is due for servicing. I can get a taxi to take me home if you've gone when I'm ready to leave. So what time will you pick me up?'

'Is seven o'clock all right?'

'Er…yes,' she replied absently with her mind elsewhere. 'Have we any report yet on the little girl with suspected meningitis?'

'It came through just a few moments ago,' Glenn said. 'She does have it, but they are hopeful that it was caught in time, so she should avoid any serious complications and she'll recover.'

'Poor little one,' Emma said sadly. 'I hate to hear of a child suffering.'

'I'm afraid that goes with the job,' Glenn said, 'but there is the other side to what we do for sick children—we make them well again in most cases because of our treatment and care.' Suddenly feeling that he was walking on eggshells, he said, 'Do you ever want children, Emma?'

She swivelled to face him. 'Yes, of course,' she said immediately. 'To have someone that I belong to and who belongs to me would be a dream come true. But I can't produce them without some assistance, I'm afraid.'

'Were you and Serena planning on having a family?' she asked with a casual sort of interest that was meant to preclude any kind of offence.

He took her breath away with his response.

'Yes, we wanted children,' Glenn told her, 'and we'd already done something towards that end. Serena was four months pregnant when that tsunami came out of nowhere. Mine was a double loss, so can you blame me for doing nothing about it when my parents bemoan their lack of grandchildren? I never told them about the pregnancy. I felt they had enough to cope with with the loss of their daughter-in-law.'

Emma's eyes were big and tears hung on her lashes as she turned to face him, stunned to hear that Glenn had been carrying around an even bigger burden than she'd known. Reaching out, she stroked the hard line of his jaw tenderly and with a groan he pulled her into his arms and held her close. And in that moment Emma knew that if he should never want her to be permanently in his life she would abide by it. That there would never be any other man that she would love as she loved him.

CHAPTER EIGHT

WHEN GLENN CALLED for her, as promised, at seven o'clock Emma was ready but showing little enthusiasm for the unexpected get-together that James had arranged. Observing her expression, he said wryly, 'Something tells me that we're not going to be the life and soul of the party tonight.

'I'm sorry, Emma, I would never have told you about the baby if the subject hadn't come up, and I don't want it to put a blight on your life too. I've learned to live with it. In these kinds of situations one has no choice. At least there's one bright side to tonight's event.'

'And what's that?' she questioned.

'Now he's engaged, Prentice will stop hanging around you. One day the right man will come along and you will find the happiness that you deserve.'

'Don't preach to me, Glenn,' Emma said tightly. 'You've made it clear that I'm not part of your agenda. And as I've already had the unpleasant experience of being told I wasn't wanted by my stepfather, the two together are enough to make me shy away from any future relationships on a permanent basis.'

'Wow! What did I do to deserve that?' he asked, swivelling to face her. 'I was merely referring to the many surprises that life always has in store and thinking how much Jeremy hurt you. I don't want to follow it with something similar.'

When there was no reply forthcoming, he asked, 'So, are you coming or not? Like I said, I'm going but not for long, and the night will be gone if we don't make a move.'

'Yes, I'm coming,' Emma told him, not willing to miss spending some time with Glenn regardless of what she'd said before. So soon they were amongst the rest of the staff, drinking champagne and toasting the newly betrothed couple with smiles that gave no hint of any inward turmoil.

An hour later, when Glenn said reluctantly that he was ready for the off and reminded her to travel home by taxi, with no detours near the church, he added, 'I am determined to find this mysterious person who puts the flowers on your mother's grave so frequently. In the meantime, Emma, don't let it upset you.

'You'll be the first to know when I solve the mystery and I think you will feel better if you keep away from it for a while.'

Emma nodded, ashamed of her earlier outburst, and with that, Glenn was gone.

As he drove the short distance home Glenn was remembering what he'd said to Emma about the grave. It was true that so far he was clueless, and a graveyard wasn't the best place to hang out, but he had to sort it out for her sake.

He felt sure he was missing something that was staring him in the face. And somehow it had to be connected with Emma—but what? Was it from her past, or her mother's? And if it was, how did he unravel the mystery? There must still be people around in Glenminster who had known Emma's mother and who she was seeing before she fell pregnant.

What about his parents, for instance? He'd already tried to sound them out, to no avail. But they'd lived in Glenminster as long as he could remember and his father had always socialised a lot. Maybe he should have another go at sounding him out and seeing if he came up with anything of interest? Mind you, knowing his dad, Jonas would have said if there was anything that he, Glenn, ought to know in connection with his friendship with Emma. Besides, his parents didn't know about the cream roses that graced the grave so regularly.

When he arrived home Glenn put the problem to the back of his mind while he attended to the demands of the practice. But once that was done it was there again, the niggling worry that there might be something that was going to cause Emma pain one day if he didn't pin it down for her.

From the size of the floral display it could be two to three weeks before the next visit from the mystery mourner. Whoever it was must have had a great deal of regard for the woman buried there, and would surely come back. Hopefully, by then he might have a plan ready that would bring the person into the open.

In the meantime, there was a severe cough doing the rounds that had some of the patients barking in the waiting room, and amongst the elderly, who were only just warming up after winter's chill, there were cases of bronchitis, while for the rest there was a virus here and there, and always a full list.

But during each busy day Glenn could rely on Emma and the practice team with their skills and dedication to their professions. He was more content than he had been for a long time, until the cream roses began to droop and he knew the time was approaching when he might come face to face with the person who might somehow be connected with Emma. He really hoped he could come up with a solution to the problem.

But would Emma want to meet the person who must have known her mother so well that they brought flowers so often and in such a secretive manner? Would he if it were him? Whoever it was, they had given Emma no means of discovering his or her identity.

Having no wish to spend twenty-four hours of every day in the churchyard, Glenn had changed his consulting room with that of one of the other doctors because it overlooked the grave in question. He'd also asked the vicar to keep an eye open for anyone bringing flowers to it around the time he thought they were due.

But as the days went by no one went anywhere near the grave for any reason whatsoever. The only folks around seemed to be just local people taking the same short cut that he did when he went to visit his elderly patient on the road that led past the church. In the end Glenn had to accept that maybe the strange behaviour of the person he sought had just been a joke or a fad, and that there was no cause for concern on his part.

As the time continued to pass uneventfully Glenn had to tell Emma when she asked that so far it seemed that either the person knew they were being watched and had given up the practice of leaving flowers on the grave, had gone to live elsewhere, or it had been some kind of a long-term mistake. Emma had accepted his comments at face value but deep down wanted an answer, a name to set her mind at rest.

The first thing Glenn did on arriving at the practice the morning after that conversation was to go into the churchyard to inspect the grave. He was relieved to find it still empty of fresh blooms, but by lunchtime they were there again. He thought that, short of keeping watch out in the cold all the time, the mystery could go on for ever and he had patients already arriving who needed his time much more than a display of cream roses.

Emma had seen Glenn go across and when he came back could tell from his expression that the flower person had returned from wherever they had been. Observing how much it upset her, Glenn knew that he couldn't proceed with his plans for the Easter weekend if it meant leaving her behind in that sort of a situation.

With Easter approaching had come light and brightness after winter's dark days. Before the mystery flowers had reappeared Emma's spirits had been lifted for quite some time, while Glenn had been considering doing what he always did at Easter.

The practice would be closed for the long weekend and he had intended following his usual routine and spending the time in Italy, where he was in the habit of renting a house on the Amalfi coast that belonged to a friend from his college days.

He always found the change of scene therapeutic and restful, but this time he felt that he couldn't relax knowing that he would be leaving Emma behind to cope with her dark moments and that he was responsible for some of them.

As the time drew nearer he wondered what sort of a reception he would get if he invited her to join him for the Easter break purely as a friend, putting aside all other thoughts and just enjoying themselves in the magic of Italy.

Knowing that he wouldn't rest until he'd asked her, Glenn waited until they were the first arrivals at the practice one morning and asked if she had a moment to spare.

'Well, yes,' Emma said laughingly, as her glance went around the empty waiting room and on the forecourt outside, and he wondered how long her lightheartedness would last when she heard what he had to say.

It seemed as if he had reason to worry as Emma's smile had disappeared within seconds and she was shaking her head. 'I don't think so,' she said in a low voice. 'That part of Italy is incredibly romantic and beautiful and I would love to go there, Glenn, but feel that it would be more sensible to stay at home. Thank you for inviting me and I hope you have a lovely time.'

He gave a twisted smile and, not wanting to give up easily, said, 'Do you think either of us will have a "lovely time" in one of the world's most beautiful places if we are on our own?'

'No, I suppose not,' she agreed weakly, and decided that it was only four days in Italy they were discussing, not a lifetime. And it *would* be a relief to be away from the mystery of the never-ending flowers on the grave.

'When would we fly out if I came?' Emma asked doubtfully.

'Thursday night, so as to be already there for Good Friday,' Glenn replied, and hoped that she was weakening.

The house had four bedrooms so Emma could have her choice, and there was no likelihood of him being missing when she woke up as when he was there he was always on the patio, soaking up the sun, at an early hour.

'So do I book you a flight for Thursday night or not?' Glenn asked patiently, as the practice began to come alive with the sound of voices inside and out.

'Er…yes… I suppose so,' Emma said. 'It would be a brief change of scene and I need something like that.' And before he could comment further she went to where her first patient of the day was waiting.

So much for enthusiasm, he thought, but at least she'd said yes.

Enthusiasm was more in evidence when Glenn called to pick her up on the Thursday night to go to the airport. There was a smile for him and as he observed Emma's outfit of leggings with a smart silk shirt above them and her weekend case, waiting to go into the boot of his car, his spirits lifted.

They chatted easily enough during the flight and he hid a smile at Emma's expression when she saw the house. It was a very attractive residence, overlooking the sea, and moonlight was shining on the water. It was already quite late after their evening flight.

'There are four bedrooms,' Glenn told her. 'Choose whichever one you want. There's a chef who lives nearby who comes in to do the food, so for a short time we shall be living in style. I've got a hire car due to arrive tomorrow, so shall we drive along the beautiful Amalfi coast? Or do you want to just laze about as we've got here so late?'

'It all sounds fantastic,' Emma said. 'I was crazy not to want to come, but nothing seems right in my life any more except my job at the practice. I am totally content with that. But the mystery of the flowers gets me down and…'

'Go on, say it,' Glenn told her. 'You don't get much joy out of me either. I know what you thought about my proposal. I must have been out of my mind to be so patronising. I hope that one day you can forgive me, Emma.'

'I think I already have,' Emma replied. 'It was wrong of me on that occasion not to take into account the memory of how Serena died and how difficult that must be to live with all the time.'

Glenn was smiling. 'So shall we put all our sad thoughts to one side and enjoy our time together for the next few days?'

'Yes, why not?' Emma agreed, and kissing him lightly on the cheek went slowly up the stairs to the bedroom she had chosen, content to know that Glenn would be near while she slept. Anything further than that would happen only if they both wanted it to, and finally it seemed as if that might be the case.

The following morning they swam in the pool and lay in the sun and the day dawdled along contentedly with every glance, every touch a promise. When it was time to go up to change for the evening meal Glenn bypassed his room and followed Emma into hers. He slipped the towelling robe that she'd been wearing by the pool off her shoulders and kissed every part of her that wasn't covered by her swim-suit until she was melting at his touch. It was like coming in out of the wilderness to happiness and joy.

But the telephone on the bedside table had other ideas and when Glenn released her to answer its strident ring Emma saw his expression change. Her heart missed a beat as he said, 'We'll get the first flight out and go straight to the hospital.' As he re-placed the receiver he said grimly, 'That was my mother. Dad climbed a tall tree in the garden this afternoon to rescue their cat, which had gone up it to escape next door's dog. When it wouldn't come down he stretched an inch too far to reach it, over-balanced and fell down onto the stone path below.'

'And?' Emma questioned anxiously.

'He's in hospital with a fractured arm and leg and my mother needs me, I'm afraid.'

'Yes, of course,' Emma agreed immediately, with a vision of his energetic father hurt and fretful. 'I'll tell the chef that we have to leave while you book a flight.'

'So much for our special time together,' Glenn said flatly. 'I was going to suggest that we go along the Amalfi coast tomorrow. Do you think it wasn't meant to be?'

'No, of course not,' Emma told him gently. 'At present your parents have to come first.'

'Yes, of course,' he agreed, 'but it is typical of Dad that he thinks he can shin up a tree at his age without getting stuck. He sees himself as Superman, thinks that he's invincible. Apparently while he was lying at the bottom of it the cat came down of its own accord without any trouble and ran off.'

They found Jonas sitting up in bed, looking bruised and crestfallen to have been the cause of them having to fly home so soon. Emma told him gently that there was no blame attached to what he had done, and said to Glenn that he was lucky to have a father to love and cherish him. In the silence that followed there was no one amongst them who wanted to contradict that.

A nurse was hovering with the comment that the patient needed some rest and would be in a better condition for chatting the following day, and as they prepared to leave, Jonas said to Glenn, 'Be sure to come tomorrow. We need to talk, and it will give your mother a chance to rest.'

'Yes, sure,' he agreed, 'and in the meantime don't go climbing any more trees.'

'You might be thanking me for climbing that tree soon,' was the reply, and they left the patient in the care of the nurse and took Glenn's mother home to rest.

'I didn't want to bring you back from your break,' Olivia said, 'but Jonas insisted and made such a fuss he was causing alarm amongst the nursing staff.' She turned to Emma. 'You must think us a strange family, my dear.'

'As someone who hasn't got one, I envy you more than words can say,' she replied, and felt like weeping.

'I want you to stay at my place tonight,' Glenn told Emma as they drove the short distance to his house after seeing his mother safely settled. 'Not for any other reason than I want you to be where I know you are near. It has been a strange day. Only hours ago we were in Italy and then we got that phone call. Did you think Dad was OK when we got there? He seemed strange, don't you think?'

'Yes,' Emma agreed. 'It was as if he knew something that we weren't aware of, unless he was suffering from concussion.'

'We'll have to see what tomorrow brings,' Glenn said. 'Are you hungry? We haven't eaten in ages.'

'Just coffee and a biscuit will suit me fine,' Emma said softly. 'Thank goodness that it's Saturday to-morrow.'

'I couldn't agree more,' Glenn said, and added, 'The guest room is ready, just help yourself to any-thing you find there. I'll bring your case up so that you have your own nightwear available if you would prefer it. Emma, there won't be any locked doors between us.'

'Good,' she said. 'So if I'm up first am I allowed to bring you a cup of tea?'

'Yes, of course, but I haven't brought you here to wait on me. I just want you where you are safe and free from care, and I never feel that you are either of those things in that house of yours.'

'I can't do anything about that until I find a buyer,' Emma said, 'and I'm sure you will agree that it isn't the usual "desirable residence" that the average house hunter is seeking.'

She was asleep within moments of settling into Glenn's guest room this time and when she awoke the next morning, with a bright sun shining up above, the memories of the day before came back—the de-lights of Amalfi and Capri that hadn't materialised, the moment when Glenn had caressed her and held her close, only to have it taken from them by the news of his father's fall from the tree that had caused their hasty return to Glenminster.

What would today bring? Emma wondered. Some degree of recovery for Glenn's father hopefully, but he was elderly and a fall of that severity could have serious after-effects.

When she went down to breakfast, having showered and changed into fresh casual clothes, Glenn was on to the hospital, asking when it would be convenient to visit his father who, it seemed, had been restless in the night and impatient to see his son.

'Shall I drop you off at your place on my way to the hospital when we've had breakfast?' Glenn suggested, after assuring the hospital that he would be there as soon as possible.

'Yes, that would suit me fine,' Emma told him. 'It would give you some private time with your family and I can check the post and get in touch with the estate agent to see if there have been any viewings of the house while I've been away. Before we separate, would you like to come there for a meal this evening? It's time that I offered you some hospitality for a change.'

Glenn hesitated for a second and then said, 'That would be great, Emma, but I'm not sure what the day is going to bring with regard to my father. Can we put that on hold for the time being?'

'Yes, of course,' she agreed, with the feeling that maybe Glenn was relieved that their closeness of the last couple of days was being slowed down by un-expected circumstances. And she was back to her feeling of aloneness, knowing that he was the only person who could change that.

There was no mail when Emma arrived back at the house, which was not surprising considering the short time she'd been away, but a phone message from the estate agent was waiting to the effect that there had been a viewer in her absence who might be interested in her property, but instead of feeling uplifted at the thought, Emma's feeling of being sur-plus to requirements gained momentum.

When Glenn arrived at the hospital two things were obvious. The first was that his father was in full control of all his faculties, and the second was his eagerness to pass on to his son the reason why he had actually fallen from the tree, which in the first instance sounded less believable than Glenn could have imagined.

'I fell because Pusscat had taken herself high up onto one of the branches to get away from next door's dog,' Jonas explained, 'and as I was reaching for her and in full control of the situation I glimpsed someone going past on the pavement across the way, carrying a large bunch of cream roses. And as I stretched myself further along the branch to get a better look, it gave way.'

'So you didn't see who it was, which gender?' Glenn asked.

'No. All I saw after that was stars as I hit the ground.'

'Did you manage to see what this person was wearing?'

'Only a glimpse before I lost my balance. It seemed like a long grey belted raincoat with a pull-down hat as it was raining at the time, and then I was falling.' Jonas was nearly back to his usual self. 'But I shall expect to be referred to as Sherlock in any future confrontations.'

'You're amazing,' Glenn told him gently, 'to risk life and limb like that for Emma's sake.'

'Aye, maybe,' he replied, 'but I didn't find out who the cream roses were from, did I?'

'Not yet, but it's a lead that we can follow.'

The nurse that Glenn had spoken to on the phone was near and she said gently, 'It is time to rest now that you have seen your son, Mr Bartlett. The doctor is on his way to see how you are this morning and we don't want you tired or overexcited, do we?'

'You're not going to raise any false hopes for Emma, are you?' was his father's last comment as Glenn prepared to leave.

'No, not until I have the right answer,' Glenn replied, and added as he left, 'And now do as the nurse says, Dad, and get some rest.'

On the way home, Glenn stopped off at the church

to check if flowers had been recently placed on the grave, and sure enough they were there. But who had brought them and why was something he had yet to discover.

The wording on the gravestone referred to Emma's mother's maiden name, rather than her married one, which was strange. It had a sound of Jeremy about it, and meant that anyone knowing Helena from the distant past would have no knowledge that Emma was her daughter.

It was not surprising that Emma hadn't known about her real father until Jeremy had told her the truth so brutally and she had fled Glenminster until he had tracked her down and brought her home.

On his way home Glenn called to see Emma to make sure she was all right after he had left her so abruptly to visit his father, but there was no answer when he rang the doorbell. As midday was approaching he stopped off at one of the places where they had lunched a couple of times in the hope that she might be there.

But it was not to be, and despite his efforts he couldn't find her. So once he had eaten he went to report the patient's progress to his mother, who had been having a quiet morning knowing that he would have seen his father. She was preparing to go in later for the afternoon visiting.

'Where's Emma?' she wanted to know. 'I was

so sorry to have dragged you both away from the delights of Italy after such a short stay.'

'I would have been sorry if you hadn't,' he told her, 'and so would Emma. She is somewhere around but I'm not sure where. I've just called at her place but she wasn't there. She stayed at my house last night as I didn't want her going back to that dismal place of hers after Italy.'

Emma was in the town centre at the offices of the estate agent, following up the message that she'd received about an interested viewer of her house. When she got there she discovered that they had seen the house a second time that morning and had made an offer.

'Really?' she exclaimed. 'I can hardly believe it.'

The estate agent explained that the house was big and well built even if it wasn't exactly the last word in design, which had helped it to sell. He asked if she was going to accept the offer.

'Yes, please,' she said. The thought uppermost in her mind was that with money in the bank she would be free to go where she wanted. And if Glenn continued to keep her at a distance, she could start again somewhere new, where there was no pain or longing.

CHAPTER NINE

EMMA RANG GLENN that evening and the lift in her voice said she had good news of some sort to impart.

'I've got a buyer for the house,' she told him, and there was silence for a moment.

'Wow!' he exclaimed. 'Fast work! Well done! And where are you planning to move to?'

Your house, with you, Emma would have liked to say, but it would seem that thought hadn't occurred to him, or surely he would have suggested it?

'I have no idea at the moment,' she replied. 'I only learned this afternoon that I had a buyer.'

'Yes, of course,' Glenn said. 'Why don't I come round and take you to dine somewhere nice to celebrate the occasion? Would you like that, Emma?'

Would she like it? Of course she would! 'Yes, that would be nice,' Emma said. 'I'll need some time to get ready, though.'

'How long?'

'An hour or so. But what about your father, Glenn? Oughtn't we to go to evening visiting instead?'

'We'll go to the hospital first and dine afterwards, if that is all right with you.'

'Yes, I'd love to do that. Your family are amazing,' Emma said. 'I do so envy you, Glenn.'

He wanted to tell Emma about the person in the grey raincoat carrying the flowers, but he was worried that it might spoil their evening. There would be time enough to tell her when he'd eventually found the identity of the mystery donator.

Emma had dressed with care in a wraparound cream silk dress that enhanced the dark attraction of her hair and eyes, and with complementary jewellery to match and shoes that brought her almost level with Glenn's height. She surveyed herself before answering his ring on the doorbell. She thought she must be crazy to think there was anything other than mild interest from Glenn. Ever since they'd had to leave Italy he had seemed withdrawn. And yet she still felt compelled to dress with care. Yes, she really must be crazy.

Her efforts, it seemed, did not go unnoticed. When Glenn saw her, there was longing in his glance, tenderness around his mouth and hope was born in her again, briefly. But it faded when he commented that, it being a mild evening, she might not need the jacket she'd brought with her. And in the car as they drove to the hospital there was no closeness, just the same small talk.

* * *

Jonas shot Glenn a questioning look when they appeared and when his son shook his head, the patient tutted his impatience. He reached for a fruit drink that was standing on the locker next to his bed, and as Emma chatted with Olivia, who had come back for evening visiting, Glenn whispered, 'I'm working on it, Dad. Woe betide anyone wearing a grey raincoat who comes into my line of vision! But it might have to wait until we have another shower. It could be a garment that only comes out in wet weather. And there's also the fact that it might just be a coincidence. You could have seen someone with the same kind of flowers.'

'Yes, I know,' Jonas said, 'and I'm fidgety. I want to be out of this place to help you find this person, but the doctor says not yet.'

'A rest for once will do you no harm,' Glenn told him, 'and I'll be in touch the moment I have any news, all right?'

'Yes. Now, go and enjoy your evening and perhaps you could drop your mother off on the way to wherever you are going.'

'Of course,' Glenn said, and thought how fortunate he was to have both of his parents still fit and well, apart from his father's injuries. Thankfully the fall from the tree hadn't done too much damage and he was responding satisfactorily to treatment. If only there was a family like his for Emma, where she could feel loved and wanted.

He could give Emma one that was theirs alone if she would only let him, but she needed to know where she came from before that and just who it was who was so interested in her mother's grave.

Glenn had booked a table at a restaurant on one of the tasteful shopping promenades that Glenminster was famed for and as they waited to be served, he said, 'So tell me what your mother was like, Emma. Do you resemble her at all?'

'No, not in any way,' she said. 'Mum was blonde with blue eyes, while my hair is dark and my eyes are hazel. We were of a similar build but that's the only resemblance. Why do you ask?'

'Just curiosity, that's all,' Glenn said easily. 'What sort of a job did she have before she had you?'

'She was secretary to the manager of one of the big banks in Glenminster, but had to give it up when I was born. Jeremy told me on the night I left that she had only married him to gain respectability and to give me a father.'

'And did you believe him?'

'It might have been true in one way, but she certainly paid the price for it. He ruled the roost and was prone to remind her frequently how much she was indebted to him, which I didn't understand at the time because I had no reason to think that he wasn't my father.'

'So you really have no idea who your birth father could be? No special friends of your mother's?'

'No, I'm afraid not,' Emma said regretfully. 'I remember when I was small my mother cried a lot. As I grew older we were very close, like sisters almost, but she never breathed a word. And after she died I jogged along with Jeremy's fads and fancies, having no idea that he wasn't my father. Until, as I told you, he wanted to remarry, told me to go, and when I protested, put me well and truly in the picture with such devastating results.'

'The low-life!' he gritted. 'But why didn't he remarry?'

'It was Lydia that he wanted to marry, but as soon as she realised how he had treated me she called it off.'

The food they had ordered was being placed in front of them and when Glenn smiled across at her, Emma said, 'Glenn, why all the questions? Are they why you suggested that we dine out tonight?'

'Not especially. I was just interested, that's all, and felt that you know a lot more about me than I do about you.'

'And does that matter?' Emma asked.

'It might do at some time in the future.'

'Such as…?'

'There are lots of times when the foundations of our lives are of interest to others.'

Emma gave up on that pronouncement and turned her attention to the food, while Glenn reflected that once he had found out the identity of the visitor to her mother's grave and presented them to her, he was going to say something to her that was getting to be long overdue. In the meantime just to have her near was absolutely magical.

When they left the restaurant they walked slowly to the car, holding hands beneath an Easter moon, and Emma's doubts and uncertainties melted away until Glenn pulled up outside her house, kissed her gently on the cheek and said, 'If I'm not around tomorrow, I'll see you at the practice on Tuesday.'

'So you don't want to come in for a coffee?' Emma asked.

Glenn shook his head. 'No, because if I do it will be much more than that I want.' He drove off into the night without further comment, leaving her to wonder what he could possibly mean.

It was busy at the practice on the Tuesday morning after the Easter weekend and Glenn had been hoping that he might have had some good news regarding the long grey raincoat to impart to his father. But ever since Jonas had fallen out of the tree the sun hadn't stopped shining, and there had been no call to ask Emma if she could identify its owner.

Besides, Glenn hadn't wanted to mention it to her yet in the vain hope that he might be able to present a complete answer to the question that was eating at him so much.

Quite a few of the regular patients were missing, having been away for the holiday weekend, and as Glenn drove past the mainline railway station on his way back to the practice after a house call in the late morning he saw a few of them homeward bound, unloading themselves and their luggage from a London train. It was then that he spotted the likeable Alex Mowbray amongst them, *and he was wearing a grey belted raincoat.*

As Alex went to join the taxi queue outside the station Glenn pulled up beside him and asked if he wanted a lift, and the offer was gratefully accepted.

'I've been to London a few times over the last couple of months,' Alex explained, as Glenn pulled away from the pavement, 'seeing the shows and generally getting to know the place again after a long absence, but it isn't much fun when one is alone and I'm soon back here in the place I love the most.'

'There is a lot to be said for family life,' Glenn said conversationally. 'I'm fortunate that I still have my parents close by, unlike poor Emma Chalmers— she has no one. Her mother died a few years ago and she has never known who her father is.'

'I hadn't realised that," said Alex. 'Poor Emma, that's very sad.'

'Jeremy Chalmers was Emma's stepfather, he filled the gap left in Emma and Helena's lives when Emma's real father left Helena pregnant, and she never knew the difference. Until in a moment of spite Jeremy enlightened Emma about her true father and she flew the nest to get away from him.'

The colour had drained from the face of the man beside him. 'You are telling me that I have a daughter, is that it?' Alex croaked. 'That I made Helena pregnant on the one and only occasion we made love? It was the night that I was due to leave the UK. I left the next morning to take my sick wife to a gentler climate.

'Helena and I loved each other deeply but my duty was to the woman that I was married to and it was only when she passed away recently that it felt right for me to come back to Glenminster.

'But how did you find out about us? I had prayed that I might find Helena still here and was devastated when it was not to be. I have found solace in putting her favourite flowers on her grave. And then I got to know Emma through your father, with no idea she was my daughter. Glenn, take me to her, please, I beg you!'

Glenn smiled. 'Emma will be busy at the practice at this moment, but if you could wait until tonight I could arrange for the two of you to meet in privacy at my house. It's thanks to my father I've discovered the truth and you have found the daughter you never knew you had.'

'He saw you walking down the road, carrying cream roses, while he was at the top of a tree, trying to get his cat down. He fell off in his excitement and ended up in hospital. But before he fell he noted the raincoat that you're wearing.'

'I can't believe this is happening to me,' Alex said brokenly. 'I have been lonely for so long.'

'Not any more when Emma knows who you are,' Glenn promised. 'Seven o'clock at my place?'

'Yes, absolutely,' Alex agreed, and as his house came into sight he smiled. 'This will be Emma's one day.'

When Glenn arrived back at the practice he told Emma that he would be entertaining a visitor that evening and hoped that she would join them as they would very much like to meet her. Emma's spirits plunged downwards as her first thought was that Glenn had found someone to replace Serena and wanted to break it to her gently.

But she dredged up a smile and asked, 'What time do you want me there?'

'Is seven o'clock all right?'

'Yes, that will be fine,' Emma agreed, and went back to her patients with the thought uppermost in her mind that whatever he had in store for her she would not let him see tears.

When she arrived at the stated time she saw a car on the drive next to his that looked familiar, though she wasn't sure why. Although why it really mattered when she had to get through the evening she didn't know. The sooner this ordeal was over the better.

When Glenn opened the door to her he was smiling, and as she stepped inside he said, 'Someone is waiting to be introduced to you, Emma.' But as she followed him into the sitting room the only person present was Alex Mowbray, who was beaming across at her, and after greeting him she turned to Glenn and said, 'I don't understand. I already know Alex. We are good friends.'

'Er...yes, you do know him,' he agreed. 'You know him as a friend, but Alex is something else as well that you have no idea of. So I'm going to leave him to tell you what that is.' As Emma gazed at him in bewilderment he left them alone with each other and closed the door behind him.

When Glenn had gone, Alex pointed to the sofa and said gently, 'Come and sit by me, Emma, while I tell you something that is wonderful and amazing.' She did as Alex asked, observing him in puzzlement, and he continued, 'I have discovered today from Glenn that we are not just good friends, you and I, but we are also blood relations.'

'How can that be?' Emma asked in amazement. 'I have no family, Alex, none at all.'

'Yes, you have,' Alex said gently. 'Your mother and I loved each other very much, but I had a sick wife I was committed to and Helena and I knew that nothing could come of our love for each other. But on the night before I left this country with my wife, your mother and I slept together.

'I must have made her pregnant, and in keeping with the vows we'd made never to see each other again she didn't get in touch to tell me what had happened. Never betrayed the vow we'd made to keep our love for each other secret for my wife's sake, and it was only today, when Glenn gave me a lift from the station, that my life became worth living again.

'When my wife died only a few months ago I came straight here, but saw the grave and knew I was too late to be with Helena. So I resorted to putting cream roses, her favourite flowers, on it, and would have continued to do so if Glenn's father hadn't seen me on my way there on Good Friday with more flowers. So can you accept me as your father, Emma, someone who will love and cherish you always?'

'Yes, of course,' she said tearfully. 'I have been so lonely, and I liked you from the moment that we met, but never dreamt that we might be related. We have Glenn to thank for this.'

'And my dad, don't forget,' Glenn said, as he came in with flutes of champagne. 'There will be no holding him down after this. So shall we drink to Alex being one of the family and there to give you away, as fathers do, on our wedding day?'

'Yes, please,' she said softly, as all her doubts and fears disappeared, and as they raised their glasses the father that Emma had never known wiped a tear from his eye.

* * *

After Alex had gone, quietly radiant, and they were settled in front of the fire, holding hands, Emma said, 'I've thought since we came back from Italy that you were relieved to have an escape route in the form of your father's accident presenting itself to avoid spending time with me, and I am so ashamed.'

'Don't be,' Glenn said gently. 'It was perfectly understandable. The words have been on my lips constantly but I made myself wait until I'd solved the puzzle of the flowers. I can't believe what a wonderful solution it turned out to be.'

'I will never forget that you gave me a family,' Emma said softly, 'and one day hopefully there will be another one, yours and mine, to gladden the hearts of their grandparents. Serena if we have a girl child and Jonas for a boy?'

'Yes, please,' Glenn said, with his arms around her, holding her close in what felt like the safest place on earth. 'And I have some more news concerning Dad. Mum rang earlier to say that he has been discharged from the hospital. They let her take him home with her after this evening's visiting.

'Shall we go round there and tell them the good news that Alex is going to be part of the family for evermore, and that one day they may be granted their greatest wish of the patter of tiny feet all around them?'

'Yes,' Emma said joyfully. 'Your father deserves

to hear something good after what happened to him, and your mother will be delighted to know that you and I love each other, and that we are going to spend the rest of our lives together.'

'You came out of nowhere and captured my heart, brought me joy out of sadness at Christmastime,' Glenn told her. 'Would you be prepared to wait until it comes round again for a Christmas wedding?'

'Yes, that would be lovely,' Emma said without hesitation, smiling up at him with the promise of all the happiness to come in her bright hazel gaze, 'just as long as I can live here with you from this day on, which is something I've always wanted.'

'That goes without saying,' he said tenderly. 'Where else would I want you to be but in my home, in my heart?'

When his parents had heard all their news, they rejoiced to hear that not only was Alex Emma's father but he would be at the engagement party that the two doctors were planning on having with family, friends and the practice staff in the near future. It seemed that Jonas's glimpse of him before the branch had given way had provided the answer to the mystery of the cream roses, and in spite of his injuries he was a very happy man.

Emma and Glenn had decided to hold their engagement party at Glenn's house with outside caterers in charge of refreshments. When they went into work the next day they amazed everyone except Lydia by announcing their engagement and inviting them to celebrate it with them some time in the near future. For the rest of the day it was the main topic of conversation.

That evening, wanting to have all ends tied up of what was going to be one of the happiest times of his life, Glenn said, 'What kind of a ring would you like, Emma? Something other than that ill-fated solitaire diamond that I made such a hash of when I produced it?'

Emma smiled across at him. 'I would like the diamond if you still have it,' she said softly. When Glenn looked at her in surprise she added, 'I have realised since that the way you explained it when you offered it to me was because you cared about me, and needed to make me see how much you would never want to let your painful past hurt me as it hurts you. I misjudged you, Glenn. So if you still have it, that is the ring I would like to wear.'

'You are incredible,' he said gently, 'and, yes, I have still got it in a drawer in my bedroom, so shall I go and get it?'

'Yes, please,' Emma told him, happy that the dark moment from the past was turning into a joyful one, and when Glenn took her hand and placed the sparkling ring on her finger, there was brightness all around them.

* * *

The engagement party was like a dream coming true for them as they greeted their guests on an evening in early June, and when Alex arrived and held her close for a fatherly moment, Emma's contentment was complete.

She had been round to his place on a few occasions to get to know him and it was always a time of fulfilment and thankfulness when she thought of how Glenn had brought him to her out of nowhere and into her life.

It seemed that Alex had been the bank manager of one of the biggest banks in Glenminster and Helena had been his secretary. They had fallen deeply in love with the knowledge that there had been no future for them to be together because Alex had been unable to leave his sick wife, and she, Emma, had been the result of wishing each other a passionate goodbye.

But a warm June night with love in the air and lots of nice food and wine to partake of in the company of friends was not the occasion for sad memories, and when Glenn asked Emma if she was happy, the answer was there in her eyes and the tender curve of her mouth, and as Lydia watched them she felt a rush of thankfulness in knowing that there was a happy ending for Emma's hurts of long ago.

EPILOGUE

CHRISTMAS HAD COME again and in the ancient church next to the practice the wedding march was being played as Emma walked slowly along the aisle in a dress of heavy cream brocade designed to keep out the cold, carrying a bouquet of roses of the same colour. She was holding onto the arm of her father, who was observing her with loving pride and joy as the solitaire diamond on her finger sparkled in the light of many candles.

All around them was the Yuletide smell of fresh green spruces and as Glenn stood waiting for her at the altar he sent up a silent prayer of thankfulness for the joy she had brought into his life and the lives of others, including that of his elderly best man, who had risked life and limb on their account.

Tonight he would keep the promise he had made to Emma at the side of the empty hayloft that day. There had been times over recent months when it had been a hard promise to keep, but tonight when they were alone Glenn would show her how much he loved her and always would.

And as Emma came to stand beside him, looking beautiful beyond telling, he felt Serena's presence, as he sometimes did, close by and peaceful in the ether, and contentment filled his heart as he and Emma made the vows that would last a lifetime.

They were going to honeymoon in Italy in the beautiful house where they had stayed so briefly before the phone call from Glenn's mother had brought them swiftly back home. But on this occasion they fully intended to enjoy the beauties of the coastline, now that they had all the time in the world to adore each other. And on their return to Glenminster there would be all the things that were precious in their lives waiting for them.

Such as their parents, Glenn's house, which Emma had adored ever since she'd first seen it, and their all-consuming work at the practice amongst the sick and suffering, with their love for each other their strength in all things.

* * * * *

MILLS & BOON®

MEDICAL ROMANCE™

THE ULTIMATE IN ROMANTIC MEDICAL DRAMA

A sneak peek at next month's titles...

In stores from 1st January 2016:

- **A Daddy for Baby Zoe?** – Fiona Lowe *and*
  A Love Against All Odds – Emily Forbes

- **Her Playboy's Proposal** – Kate Hardy *and*
  One Night...with Her Boss – Annie O'Neil

- **A Mother for His Adopted Son** – Lynne Marshall

- **A Kiss to Change Her Life** – Karin Baine

Available at WHSmith, Tesco, Asda, Eason, Amazon and Apple

Just can't wait?
Buy our books online a month before they hit the shops
visit www.millsandboon.co.uk

These books are also available in eBook format

7

TOB
M.R.   BY

MILLS & BOON®

Why shop at millsandboon.co.uk?

Each year, thousands of romance readers find their perfect read at millsandboon.co.uk. That's because we're passionate about bringing you the very best romantic fiction. Here are some of the advantages of shopping at www.millsandboon.co.uk:

∗ **Get new books first**—you'll be able to buy your favourite books one month before they hit the shops

∗ **Get exclusive discounts**—you'll also be able to b our specially created monthly collections, with up to 50% off the RRP

∗ **Find your favourite authors**—latest news, interviews and new releases for all your favourite authors and series on our website, plus ideas for what to try next

∗ **Join in**—once you've bought your favourite book don't forget to register with us to rate, review and join in the discussions

Visit **www.millsandboon.co.uk**
for all this and more today!